A GOOD COUNTRY

The Walking

The Age of Orphans

A Good Country

A NOVEL

Laleh Khadivi

BLOOMSBURY

NEW YORK · LONDON · OXFORD · NEW DELHI · SYDNEY

Bloomsbury USA
An imprint of Bloomsbury Publishing Plc

1385 Broadway	50 Bedford Square
New York	London
NY 10018	WC1B 3DP
USA	UK

www.bloomsbury.com

BLOOMSBURY and the Diana logo are trademarks of Bloomsbury Publishing Plc

First published 2017

Emoji art supplied by EmojiOne.com

ISBN: HB: 978-1-63286-584-7
ePub: 978-1-63286-586-1

LIBRARY OF CONGRESS CATALOGING-IN-PUBLICATION DATA

Names: Khadivi, Laleh, author.
Title: A good country : a novel / Laleh Khadivi.
Description: New York : Bloomsbury USA, 2017.
Identifiers: LCCN 2016050042 | ISBN 9781632865847 (hardback) | ISBN
9781632865861 (ebook)
Subjects: | BISAC: FICTION / Literary. | FICTION / Coming of Age. | GSAFD:
Bildungsromans.
Classification: LCC PS3611.H315 G66 2017 | DDC 813/.6—dc23 LC record available at
https://lccn.loc.gov/2016050042

2 4 6 8 10 9 7 5 3 1

Typeset by Westchester Publishing Services
Printed and bound in the U.S.A. by Berryville Graphics Inc., Berryville, Virginia

To find out more about our authors and books visit www.bloomsbury.com.
Here you will find extracts, author interviews, details of forthcoming events, and
the option to sign up for our newsletters.

Bloomsbury books may be purchased for business or promotional use.
For information on bulk purchases please contact Macmillan Corporate and
Premium Sales Department at specialmarkets@macmillan.com.

Radical—radık(ə)l

Adj.
Relating to or affecting the fundamental nature of
something; far-reaching or thorough

Chemistry
A **radical** (more precisely, a **free radical**) is an atom,
molecule, or ion that has unpaired valence electrons. With
some exceptions, these unpaired electrons make free radicals
highly chemically reactive toward other substances, or even
toward themselves

North American, colloquial
Very good, excellent, awesome or impressive

PART I

To Mexico

1

Laguna Beach, California, Fall 2011

THEY TOLD HIM it was the best, there was nothing better. After they started, at twelve and thirteen and fourteen, his friends tried to convince him to try it. *Rez, dude,* they'd say, *it's no big deal. You don't puke. You don't pass out. No one can even tell. It's like daydreaming, like that second just before you fall asleep, but for hours,* they said, for the whole of eighth grade, their eyes glazed with the shine of the newly converted, and by tenth grade they gave up and now, start of junior year, it was habit to make fun of him every time there was occasion, every time they circled up to light and puff and smoke, these friends.

If he wanted, it could have happened last night, or even two weeks ago when Johnson's parents were in L.A. at an industry party and Johnson opened his house to anyone with a six-pack or a girl or a bag of weed. At midnight Rez found them in the laundry room, empty beer bottles and half-smoked cigarettes all over the place, and he sat and drank and talked like everyone else. When it was finally rolled and passed, Rez stood up right before his turn.

I gotta piss, and walked out of the circle.

Bullshit, coughed Johnson, the smoke coming out of his mouth in big clouds.

We all know you can't hang, Rez. Never have. Never will. Those Persians keep a tight leash on their kids . . .

He felt a few laughs at his back but kept going, out of the laundry room, down the hallway, out of the house, and into the backyard, where kids rolled around on the perfect grass, swam half naked in the pool, and ran hand in hand to dark corners. He found a spot by the fence, beside the empty dog crates and gardening tools, and let go, his heart one big pump and burst, pump and burst, as the piss rushed out of him in a long furious stream.

*

He didn't know what he was afraid of. It wasn't like with the girls, a want and a want and a want until everything centered in his crotch and he moved forward without thought, without fear. No, this was different. He wanted it, to be inside the circle, to stay and smoke and laugh and feel whatever it was that was so good, but he couldn't stand the complete unknown. What if I lose it? What if I black out? What if I start crying? What if I get addicted? How much trouble will I be in if Dad finds out? All the trouble. I'll be in all the trouble.

In the dark yard he felt his father about him, a thick outline traced atop his own body. He looked around, shook himself dry, zipped up, and walked back to the house. He moved from room to room, looking, thinking, and tried to bring himself to do all that was being done by the kids in his grade and the sophomores and juniors and seniors above him, and the more he saw, the more he wanted to go home. A girl from chemistry lab caught his arm and pulled him into a doorway and then into a room of people, who saw him and yelled, *Yeah! Rez! Dare! Dare! Dare!* And he drank vodka straight from the bottle up to the count of ten and then stuck his head and hands up Sophia Lim's shirt to feel the smooth mounds and tiny buttons of nipples and wanted badly to suck but did not. When it was over and everyone clapped and yelled and Sophia turned away and tucked in her shirt, Rez walked quickly back outside and threw up in a planter of cacti. He lay down on a lawn chair, shivered, and spat the sour out of his mouth and counted the nine stars above him again and again, until Matthews showed up and said it was time.

Let's go home, man. I'm through with this.

They left without saying good-bye and found Kelly passed out in the back of the Matthewses' SUV, his hoodie backward on his head, face covered, arms crossed like a kind of corpse.

Dude. Get up. This isn't a hotel.

Matthews poked him and pulled the hoodie down and poked him again until Kelly sat up, yawned, and made a face at Rez.

Puked again? Ah, puking. How come the smartest kid in the class is always the stupidest kid at parties? If you would only smoke a little weed, you could keep your liquor down, didn't anyone ever tell you that? My dad told me all about it.

Kelly rambled on and Rez looked out the window and Matthews drove and after a time no one said anything. There was nothing to say, the night had come and gone and Rez still hadn't done it, but he knew he'd have to, soon, if he wanted things to stay as they were. If he wanted things to get better.

Last night at the beach wasn't it either.

The bonfire wouldn't catch and some guys from Santa Ana set up just down the sand and gave them shit.

Hey, faggots! Who's got the tightest pants over there?

Does your mommy know you're out so late?

They ignored the voices and kept trying their fire, and then an older voice shouted from the dark.

No way. No, man, his mommy don't know he's out here 'cause she's at home fucking my brother, her gardener, right now!

Man and *Oh, man* and *That's fucked up* and laughter surrounded them, and Johnson rolled the joint faster, and when it was lit, Matthews took his long deep puff and they passed it fast and smoked fast and again Rez shook his head no.

I'm good.

They left him alone and he worried about the fight coming and the black, gray, brown marks on his face from the guys in the dark and how would he explain that to his father, who would add to it, or take away from it, by calling him a girl or who knows what else? He didn't want his first time to be high and hurting, high and fighting and he waited for his friends to finish their smoke, but they didn't get a chance because the voices came out from the dark again.

Your mommy sure does take a long time, and with a Mexican too!

She must like it. That OC pussy needs a trim!

Rez looked at the eyes of his friends, Peter Matthews, James Johnson, and John Kelly, names of the Bible, apostles, each a right-hand man to Jesus, and he saw them now as one. Hunched over the smoky fireless fire, their shoulder blades spiking up through their thin T-shirts as they sucked at the joint and took the taunts. When it was done, everyone stood up and kicked sand over the two steaming logs that never caught, and the voices from the darkness stepped in, took the shapes of faces and bodies and walked around them, smiles shining through the murk.

It's cool. It's cool, my brother is done with your moms.

You can go home now.

Don't look so scared!

We ain't gonna waste time with you shrimps anyway.

Yeah, man, stupider than hitting a girl.

The apostles shouted all the way home. High and angry, they were a single voice bellowing through the truck. *My brother knows a guy from Huntington, a senior, skinhead . . . he would fuck them up for sure. Laughton knows how to get a crew together, football guys, they did it once when one of the Asian gangs gave them shit at South Coast,* and on and on with *dude* and *bro* and *fuck 'em* and *wetbacks* until Rez's ears were full and his heart and gut clean with fear. Matthews, who normally drove like the sixteen-year-old stoner with a learner's permit that he was, now sped like an idiot down the 1 and the wide streets of Dana Point. Rez opened the window and let the fast wind hit his face and watched the streets and houses and yards pass by, all asleep, no witness to their aimless rage.

It was going to be today. Not because someone had an open house or there was a party or a girl he wanted to impress, but because everything had come into alignment and finally he didn't care. The recklessness was in him now and it made no difference if he puked, if he said stupid shit, if he got in trouble or addicted and spent the rest of his life begging on the street corner, a shame to his family, he was over it.

The midterm grades were e-mailed that afternoon and Rez forgot. He took the bus home and skated to his door and found his father, at three thirty, on the front steps of the house, a thin piece of paper in his hands, tie loose, eyebrows pushed together. Rez felt his stomach jump and he kicked the skateboard into his hand and dropped his head and ran through the classes. Math. Chemistry. Physics. English. Spanish.

Government. Logic. History, it was history; it had to be history and the quiz on the first Iraq war the night after the bonfire. He took the quiz without studying and thought his GPA would cover it, but now his father was on the steps, which meant a B was printed on that paper and the ceremony would begin.

It started the same way it always started. His father silent and Rez silent and then the first question.

Do you like your life?

Rez knew there was only one right answer.

Yes.

You have enough to eat? Good clothes to wear? A nice school to go to?

Yes, Dad, I forgot the quiz was that day

It is not important. What is important is that you like your life. You are taken care of. Am I correct?

Rez said nothing, in the script he was to remain silent, and silence was the safest bet, the fastest route to the end. He nodded his head in agreement.

Good. Then I have done my job. And yet you have not done yours.

His father went on, his face set in anger, his mouth opening and closing around the words *ungrateful, punishment, worthless, pathetic, loser,* until Rez swallowed the sobs that came up his throat and tried to blink away tears filling his eyes. The rough sandpaper on his skateboard rubbed against his fingers and he thought of the apostles and how they would laugh if they saw him now, crying, and so he stopped and wiped his face and began to shout.

What did I do? Tell me what I did wrong! I didn't do anything wrong. I got a fucking B. That's all!

His father, surprised but not alarmed, closed his eyes and shook his head.

A disrespect. Your laziness is a disrespect to me, to your mother, to everything I have done for this family.

Rez heard the words, but this time they did not make it all the way down to his heart. He stepped outside himself and saw a boy, nearly as tall as his father, a father, a tyrant without cause, a mass of dark and aimless energy. He saw the boy in a bright light, innocent and right, and the father, misguided and dim, his only power humiliation. Rez kept shouting until his mother came to the kitchen window, until the squeaky eager yells of an eleventh grader came out, until he was shaking with the words *Fuck you* and *I hate you* and *You are an asshole*, so loudly and with such fury he could not pull back the new bold spirit fast enough, could not push himself back into the body of the boy in time to move out of the line of slaps that sprang from his father's palm onto his soft waiting face.

He skated the two miles to Matthews's house, some of it crying, some of it running. Matthews and Johnson played Xbox and said *What's up?* but didn't look at him. Rez didn't say anything and waited and finally Johnson looked up.

What the fuck, man? You look like a bitch that's just been dumped. Your face is all puffy.

Rez tried to swallow and put his hands in his pockets to keep them from shaking.

Whatever, man. Wanna go to the cove?

They stared at him for a moment and then another moment and Matthews threw his controller on the couch.

Yeah, let's do it. The cove. Today's a good day for the cove.

They picked up Kelly, and when they got to the cove, they walked around it and cleaned up the trash before saying one word. It was an old habit, a leftover from their elementary school beach-cleaning field trips. When Johnson's backpack was filled with pulped cigarette cartons, chip bags, used condoms, and spent lighters, they sat down in a circle. Cool clouds came in from the west, low and to the water, and a damp, icy breeze filled the shallow cove. Rez lifted his face to meet it, to let it press all over the hot prints in the shape of his father's fast hands.

One person pulled out a baggie and the other had the papers and the other had a Zippo and each of them had already done it a dozen times or more and Rez squinted into the cool wind and waited his turn. The joint came by lumpy and crooked and he held it between his fingers and then between his lips and all he felt was fuck. I don't give a fuck. Fuck him. He remembered not to breath too deep. He didn't want to choke and didn't want them to laugh. But it was smooth. Smoother than he could understand, and the cold came in with it and he exhaled into the crossed legs of his lap. The apostles looked at him and he nodded without a cough and they smiled one big friend smile.

Yeah, dude. Yeah.

He sat up straight, stretched his back, realigned into another person in another life, and grinned.

Yeah. Totally.

2

THE RUMORS GAVE him courage. *Dude, that chick Sophia is totally hot for you.* And *Bro, you must tap that ass right away.* Rez laughed but he also looked at her, in class or walking down the hallway, talking to her friends. He always pretended he was looking at something else, someone else, and she always stared back and smiled. He did nothing, and then one morning in chemistry his lab partner, Lila, asked if she could give Sophia Lim his phone number.

What for?

Lila stared at him through her plastic protective eyewear, her eyes big and brown and already laughing.

You know what for.

By the afternoon he had a text.

Hey Rez, this is Sophia. Wanna go to the vista after school? I've got a car.

He read the text ten times as if the sentence were Sophia herself, spread out in front of him, naked, rubbing her nipples and sucking on a red lollipop. That was how it was on the porn he watched, like that and some other ways, any way really, but always and only on the computer. In life he had seen little. A few girls with their shirts off, bikinis he took off in his mind, his mother once in the shower when he rushed to tell her he was a finalist in a statewide chess championship. The possibility of Sophia, her body naked in his hands, pushed through him with such boldness that Rez couldn't think or see or hear for the rest of the day.

Yeah. That sounds cool. I'm down.

They drove the steep and windy roads up to the vista and didn't talk. They listened to Lady Gaga. *Girl pop* the apostles called it and Rez couldn't stand it but didn't say anything because he was too busy watching her dance as she drove, little shoulder shakes when the beat got faster, and head moves as the music slowed. Her hair was long and black and soft and rolled down her back all the way to her butt. He let himself stare and he let himself wonder: Who is this girl? She was in tenth grade, they had never spoken and had none of the same friends. There was the time at Johnson's party but Rez could not remember it clearly and knew only that it involved vodka and puking, but that couldn't be enough for this invitation, for this ride. He rolled the window down and saw his reflection in the rearview mirror, an eleventh grader with buzzed light brown hair, a square jaw, and green eyes. He once heard one of Matthews's brother's girlfriends say Rez was going to be good-looking when he grew up, but she was a fat girl and most days he still felt like a kid.

They parked in the empty dirt lot between million-dollar homes. The view looked straight down the Laguna cliffs over the expensive beach shacks and Highway 1 and out to the Pacific. The ocean seemed huge from here, as far as you could see, the line of the horizon broken by a few small boats and the shape of Catalina. She turned off the car and snapped down the sun visor, checked her hair, and, satisfied, searched the compartment in her door. She handed him a delicate box of thin wood with elephants painted on it.

Can you roll?

Inside was a small plastic canister of crumbled weed, some papers, and a lighter, all organized in their own sections.

Is this how girls carry their weed?

She laughed.

Plastic baggies are for drug dealers.

He started to roll and she turned back to the mirror and opened her lips to reapply a layer of thick glossy pink lipstick, then she shook her hair out a little bit and looked at him, her whole face, the lips, the eyes, the hair, twinkling somehow.

For the first time since the rumors started Rez didn't look away. He stared at the endless black hair and white skin and the black eyes that turned up with a seductive delight. Her face, her voice, her name, everything about her was something else, different. She was not familiar like his mother and like the porn he watched but couldn't touch, and as this made him sit back, made the desire center in him, he rolled faster. When it was finished, she took the joint from his hand and the lighter from the box and wrapped her perfect lips around the paper and sucked in the flame slowly. She inhaled and laughed and coughed and smiled and her hair was everywhere and her eyes shone and Rez wanted to jump inside her.

What they did was as much as he'd ever done and it was clear she had done more. She pushed his chair back and slid down in between his legs and took him between her glossy lips and into her warm mouth and Rez felt the world end. His muscles turned to water and his mind evaporated and he was sure it was death, a kind of slow, soft death, and that was all right. He was high and every touch, every lick, opened him up and brought him forth. It had never been like this, not with the porn that jolted and pressured and drew him out in a tense awkward way, not with the few girls in closets and on floors at parties. It may never be like this again, so why live? When she stopped to look up at him with her dark eyes and her open pink mouth, he wanted to push himself in to keep the rhythm going and fuck her mouth the way he had seen it done, but she was in control and she started again and he died again and after a time he let go and came like the happy accidents of his dreams.

Finished, he had nothing to say and she smiled at him and zipped his pants and put herself in the driver's seat, where she took little sips from her water bottle and then fixed her hair and added more lip gloss. She started the car and looked at him with a mischievous smile.

How was that?

Nice. Thanks.

Good.

She drove him to the gates of his neighborhood and he wanted to hop out quick, before his mother or father might see, and she gave him the smile, coy pink lips spread across perfect teeth.

Maybe we can hang out again? I don't have class seventh period.

Yeah. Totally. I'm down.

He walked home and felt himself get hard as he thought about Sophia Lim, and her body, and that she was a bad student with bad grades and her father was known for gambling in Las Vegas every weekend and gave huge donations to the school every year and they lived in an enormous mansion in Costa Mesa, and even though she was only in tenth grade, she had her own car and it was new. She was a cheerleader. Rez remembered when it was her turn in history, she told Mrs. Heinz her grandparents came to America from Vietnam on a boat with no engine, and Mrs. Heinz said that is impossible and Sophia told her to read her history.

3

HE WAS LATE for dinner. Not just once, but all the time now. Rez opened the door and found them as they always were at this time of day, around the long teak table—mother, father—Meena and Saladin, in a room with three walls of fine art and one sliding glass door that led to a pool, the water still and steel blue to match the California dusk. Food was set, a meal Rez had eaten all his life, fried eggplant in a stew of onions and tomatoes and beef, buttered rice, fresh greens and radishes. There were the glasses of water, the same knives and forks and spoons as yesterday, the flower piece a bit more dead. None touched their food, none moved, and his father sat at the head of the table, typed into his phone, and said nothing when Rez took his seat. After a few minutes his father put the phone down, lifted and dropped his napkin, and sighed.

Someone has to pay for all this.

Then his father reached for the rice and piled on the stew and ate without talking or looking up. Without appetite Rez watched his mother take her turn and then he scooped the rice onto his plate and then the stew on top and stared at the mound and thought, I have eaten this food, this same stew, these same grains of rice, my whole life. This is the oldest food in the world, and his parents ate it and his parents' parents, and since it was a dish from Iran, maybe the first Iranians, thousands of years ago, ate it too. Rez thought about the apostles and wondered if they ate food from the beginning of time, and what was the beginning of their time? Where did the time of their families start? Ireland? Germany? France? Some mix of all those things that gave them no one old food, no long straight line, no place? Rez had heard his father boast of it. Their place, their line of men and warriors that stretched all the way back to an old village in the oldest mountains. Now Rez sat, stoned out of his mind, at the end of that line, at the teak table and listened to his family chew and sip and swallow and he thought, What does it matter? We are all animals anyway. He remembered a picture from psych class, a group of chimpanzees sitting around the table, naked, hairy, crouched over and reaching for the dishes with their long ropy arms.

Where is your appetite?

Generally his mother said nothing at dinner. Rez looked at her and she smiled. She knew. How could she know? It was a mistake to smoke so late into the afternoon. He knew it was a bad idea, but when he skipped soccer practice to meet Sophia at Johnson's pool house, he thought about the sex they would have and nothing else. When Sophia showed up and lit the joint, he was still only thinking about sex, and when he got stoned and fucked her, he wasn't thinking about anything, just feeling and being felt and doing with his hands and mouth and tongue what was good. After she left, Rez and Johnson took a swim and Johnson teased him.

I don't think I've ever seen a half-Vietnamese, half-Persian baby before. Have you?

Whatever, dude. It's casual.

Yeah, casual until her father hears about you.

Rez thought about her father and then thought about his own father and then remembered he was late for dinner. He dried and dressed quickly and let Johnson put the Visine drops in because it freaked Rez out to do it and skated home and told himself he was fine, it was wearing off and no one could tell and it was just dinner and then he could say he had a lot of homework and go to his room. He walked into the house and walked straight to the table and sat down and tried not make a big deal but he had never been stoned in his own home and this was not going to be a happy high.

His father looked at Rez and Rez watched as he took a long time to finish his bite, his glasses moving up and down on the bridge of his nose as he chewed, his beard working like a separate animal beneath them. Rez wanted to laugh and tried not to think about the chimpanzees, their jaws chewing in circles, their bony fingers and yellow teeth.

How was soccer practice today?

That was the life his father and mother thought he lived. Chess club from seven thirty to eight fifteen. School. Varsity soccer at three thirty and then home by six. A healthy well-rounded day, nothing of the distractions that led to the embarrassment of his grade in history a few months ago, nothing of friends or girls. Rez kept his grades high, and when he went to wake and bake with Matthews, Rez finished the chess sets on his phone and sent them in to the teacher in an e-mail. He went to every other soccer practice, showing the coach a forged note about extra hours in chemistry lab. The schedule was, for the first time, his own and everyone left him alone.

Soccer was fine.

And you are not hungry after that running? Are you sick?

The apostles were always talking about hunger, the way weed made them go in search of nachos and ice cream and how they would walk three miles just to eat at Jack in the Box, but Rez never felt it. He smoked and it settled him and the sensation of food, its temperature and textures and smell was too much, disgusting.

No. I ate before. I skipped lunch to study for my math midterm and then ate after school.

He was surprised at the lie, how cleanly it came from him and how much sense it made. His father nodded in approval and dropped his focus back to his plate.

Let's try to get back on schedule tomorrow. It is not good to waste your mother's food. Meena, leave a plate for him in the oven in case he gets hungry later.

He'll be hungry later.

He picked up his spoon and began to eat and wished for his father to ignore him so he could leave the table and sit in his room. The sounds of the knives and forks against the plates went on around him and the time of the dinner passed slowly and Rez did his best to eat and listen to the little talk between his mother and father but could not concentrate because his mind returned to the afternoon and how he had just fucked and smoked and his family, who had known everything about him all his life, knew nothing of him in this moment. They must be full of secrets too. He was sure of it. His powerful father and his silent, dutiful mother. He was certain they left behind empires of lies to come and sit at this dinner table every night and say nothing. Now he had joined them and he let his mouth fill with rice and his mind fill with Sophia Lim and fucking a few hours ago, three times in a pool house, her thin white body under his and over his and in front of his, and that he had put a finger in her for the first time and that felt like nothing he had ever felt before and how is it that people aren't always fucking? He tried not to look at his mother and father, who had fucked to make him, tried not to think of that, but with all the not and the don't and the looks away, the images only came at him more sharply, razors on his mind until there was nothing left to do. He took the napkin off his lap and stood up.

Thanks, Mom. But I don't feel great. I think I am going to go lie down.

He pushed the chair back from the table. His father caught his arm.

Reza, your face is flush. Meena, go take his temperature, see if we need to call the doctor.

I am ok. Just tired.

They all looked back at him and Rez looked at his reflection in the glass doors that led out to the pool, dark now, and saw an image he had not seen before, his own face, a boy, almost a man, tired, conniving.

4

Laguna Beach, Winter 2012

AT FIRST ONLY the kids with dads or uncles that followed the news-
papers and weather channels talked about it. They spoke in a secret
jargon that made it *their* news, information for the initiated: code. From
the southwest, off the Tahitian shelf, two-minute-long breaks. Double
head high! Everyone else just watched it rain and thought: rain. Rain
like every winter there was rain, gray and slightly warm and brief. Just
enough to wash down a few unsupported slopes and fill the terra-cotta
fountain in the backyard. For a few months every year the air became
water and the ocean ate up the land. The beaches were covered in sea
litter, exoskeletons, long hoses of kelp and faded plastic containers with
foreign writing. Rez's mother refused to drive the low stretches of
Highway 1 for fear the ocean would, in an instant, flood the road.

What kind of people live so close to the sea? she asked, and then
shook her head at the madness battering the shore.

Cool people, Rez muttered as the windshield wipers kept the beat
and they waited to cross the rush of sewer water that poured out in
front of them.

Last year the rain came and went and Rez didn't know anything
about a swell. He hadn't yet surfed and went to the beach like a little
kid goes to the beach, with a picnic of chips and grapes, a shovel and a
love of jumping in waves. If his little cousins came, he'd build sand
castles with them and his aunt would laugh at him. Aren't you too old
for that? He liked the water but never swam out past the break, never
in the open ocean away from whitewash, never out past where his toes
did not easily reach the sand.

This year he was different. A junior at Laguna Prep. He smoked and had
been with Sophia more times than he could count and the kids at school
were different with him. More people talked to him. Not just the apostles

or the kids in chess club, but other kids, boys who let their hair grow as long as was allowed, who wore caps as soon as they were outside, the juniors and seniors with orange-brown skin from days and days of salt and sun. They looked like kids from commercials; guys from the billboards up and down Highway 1 that showed life as if lived entirely on waves and mountainsides, with hot girls, half naked and wanting.

His father saw a group of them greet Rez through the windshield of the car at carpool one morning. Peace signs and nods and their hair still wet from surfing before school.

Those boys.

His father shook his head.

They will wake up twenty years from now, part-time jobs, divorced, living in shitty apartments, alcoholics, or worse. But now, hey, now life is good. What a waste.

Rez said nothing to his father, but when the guys looked Rez in the eye in the halls and said *What's up?* he said *S'up?* back and pretended it was nothing. He watched them in the courtyard at lunch and during class, where they seemed bored out of their minds, silly with energy that kept them tapping their feet and twitching their pens and laughing at nothing, in some antic state waiting, waiting, waiting for the bell to ring so they could explode onto wheels or water and just be. He saw them in the parking lot too, gathered around their old trucks, hardcore and Beastie Boys playing out just so loud as to keep them from getting a demerit, their blazers tossed onto the ground, their striped school neckties wrapped around their heads like skinny bandannas, shouting back and forth about the swell and what spot they were going to, some girl or two or three, sitting on the hoods or bumper, laughing. He saw them and listened to them and this year he knew that it wasn't enough to smoke or have sex, but to be like that, to be easy and always happy, he had to surf too and so one afternoon he found Matthews and tried out the new tongue.

Let's go to Old Man's. The swell is right.

Matthews didn't say what Rez thought he was going to say, which was *Fool, you don't even know how.* Or *what are you going to do out there? Swim?* No, Matthews looked at him, smiled.

Dope. Killer swell. My brother told me about it. Let's roll.

In an hour they had Kelly and Johnson and without Rez's asking someone lent him a spring wet suit and someone else a longboard and they didn't take him to Old Man's but to a shallow inlet by the Dana Point harbor, a sewage-filled learners' spot none of them had come to since they were four or five. They gave no instructions, just let him paddle, push up, balance, and try to ride. He fell every time but the apostles did not laugh. They waited for him to paddle back to them and one would say *Wait a few extra seconds* or *Paddle harder* or *Push up faster* and Rez would nod and they'd all just sit there and stare at the sea and wait for the next *set*, which was a word Rez didn't know that morning, but understood before he fell asleep that night.

Now he knew all the words. *Swell. Face. Tube. Sucked. Wall. Ripped. Grom. Wash. Turtle.* And this year when the rains came, he was as excited as the rest of them. Girls. Books. Movies. Video games. Nothing came close to the feeling before doing it, the lead in the pit of your stomach and the butterflies in your chest and then the feeling of a wave, the wave that had rolled over thousands of miles of ocean to push you fast fast fast toward land, so fast his hair nearly dried once. And then there was the feeling afterward, the salt caked onto his skin; the tired, blessed state. Hunger and exhaustion. His body understood what was right, fast, dangerous, and safe and his boards got shorter and his friends took him to beaches he'd never heard of, beaches without parking lots, beaches you couldn't even see from the road. He started to care about conditions and the weather because a storm meant a swell and a swell meant epic surf and epic surf meant a hero could grow from your skin.

5

GONNA BE EPIC. So epic. El Niño strikes again.

They were taking rips at Kelly's house, just the two of them passing the bong back and forth, packing it full of herb and passing it back and forth again. The smoke filled the glass tube in a massive way, and when they exhaled, a proper cloud lingered in the air for longer than anyone would have thought. They sat under a yellow-and-black-striped awning and watched it rain into the pool. Kelly lived with his mom and dad and sisters in a huge ranch house in Laguna Niguel. There were horses in a stable and an actual grove of orange trees. The family used to own most of the county, at least that is what Matthews said, and then *they went military.* His dad was a colonel at Pendleton and had been to Afghanistan and Iraq. His brother was at MIT, studying engineering, and his sisters looked like Barbie. Rez liked to walk around the immaculate house and pause at the layers of framed photographs on every polished surface: trips to Washington, handshakes with the first Bush, handshakes with the second Bush, their dad skydiving, Paul standing in a river, an enormous fish hooked on his finger, John on a snowboard at the top of a white mountain. Throw pillows were on all the couches, many of them arranged to highlight the colors of the American flag.

Yeah. My dad says last time it got this big he was in high school, my age. He's been doing curls in the garage every night just to get ready.

Rez let Kelly talk and then he let the silence fall between them, there was no rush. He'd learned when to let a moment go, to wait and let himself fill with certainty and then talk as if he didn't care if anyone heard. It was a new kind of confidence, this waiting, and he felt it more now, a thousand times more than he'd felt it in tenth grade and a million times more than he'd felt it his whole life before when he was just waiting and thinking and quiet.

Baja, man. That is where we should be. The swell is going to be epic. Kelly stared at him.

What do you know about Baja? You've only really surfed San O's and the Point. Your dad doesn't even know what a surfboard is. Rez, please.

Now he was himself, Rez, and he surfed and fucked and smoked almost as he liked. He no longer cowered before teachers, parents, the world, and when the courage came to him, he didn't tamp it down but let it go, all the way sometimes, and took all the consequences for what they were: inconsequential. He did like Matthews told him, took care of his business, kept Visine in his bag, and looked his father in the face and lied. He lied whenever he needed to, and when it worked, he relaxed and lied again and one bravery led to another and when Johnson told him to say he was studying at his house, Rez did it and they both went to Palm Springs for a rave and took ecstasy and were back in their own beds, still tripping, by six the next morning. He found courage in his success and the next time he told his mom he was staying at Matthews's house to help him with his math homework, and when Rez went directly to the cove to smoke and wakeboard and prank call Alyssa Mathiesson, he didn't even worry about it. Withdraw money he'd won in the debate championship and buy his first eighth instead? Fuck it. Hide the plastic baggie in his sock drawer where his mom could easily find it when she put away his laundry? Fuck it. Tell his dad there were curves on the science quiz, no one scored above an 82, so his 78 was considered an A when it was the same C it had always been? Fuck it. He'd make it up at the end of the semester. The lies came easy, and when he remembered, he tried to be careful, but most of the time he thought fuck it and opened his mouth, closed his mouth, and waited for the moment to pass.

Whatever we get here, it's gonna be twice that down south.

Rez said it like it was his talk, from the center of himself, not from the magazines and movies he pored over every night when he was supposed to be studying. It would be great. He knew it. Because of the Pacific shelf. Because of the curve of the land eastward and in. The waves would be higher by at least a foot and the rides would be longer by a minute. Rez didn't say any of this to Kelly, but Rez knew it and kept quiet like someone who knows more, knows so much he doesn't have to say.

Kelly stared out over the pool and Rez watched the idea occur to him.

Yeah. Baja would be sweet. I mean, anyone who stays here this weekend is a chump. We'd have to get a car. And a few more boards. And get out of school.

Don't stress, man. I've got it all figured out.

Kelly laughed at Rez and took the bong back into his lap.

Oh, do you? Mr. Strictest Parents in America? How are you going to figure it all out?

I got it.

I bet. Kelly lit the darkly packed ash and inhaled whatever was left.

I bet you do, he repeated, exhaled.

Baja. Man, sweet. I should have thought of it.

But you didn't, Rez told himself. I did and now we are going and it will be my trip and the stories that come will be because of me. He took the bong from Kelly.

Yeah, bro, you would have thought of it eventually. It's so obvious.

By Friday they had a truck. Double cab, air-conditioning, a few inches above factory, a little tree air freshener dangling from the rearview mirror. Freddy, one of Matthews's older brothers, a senior who'd dropped surfing to join the varsity football team, charged them twenty dollars a day. For the driver's license with the picture of a red-haired, wide-shouldered, freckled jock that looked just like Peter Matthews but was named Fredrick Matthews, Rez agreed to take his SAT test for him. At first Freddy didn't believe him, didn't think it was possible, but Rez insisted, told him about the math whiz Arash who'd taken the test for Kelly's older brother and no one ever found out and now Paul was a sophomore at MIT. They wrote up an informal contract on the back of Rez's biology study sheet and the license was theirs. For the few days before the trip they practiced calling Peter Freddy but then realized they all called him Matthews anyway and so it didn't matter.

They stocked the truck as they saw fit. Eight boards, five wet suits, two tents, a cooler full of beer and cold cuts and vodka ice cubes Kelly's sister had made them and no other food. No one brought a toothbrush and no one brought a pillow or soap. Their phones were full of music and a half pound of grass sat in the glove compartment next to a cake of board wax and gas station sunglasses. Rez thought to bring sunblock because he could hear his mother's voice in his head—*You are turning into a Pakistani*—but he liked the new dark of his skin. More important his light brown hair was turning gold and something in his heart jumped every time he saw himself in the mirror.

They left with the calm hearts of good liars. Rez forged a flyer on school stationery about a mandatory, last-minute field trip to Pyramid Lake. He went to the office of Mrs. Bonau and asked if she could find Mr. Francis's yearbook picture for a retirement card the class was making, and when she left her desk to look, Rez took what he wanted of the stationery and a few envelopes and a stamp of the principal's signature he thought might be useful later, if only for a good trade. The heart of prestigious Laguna Prep, all of it at his disposal. The courage was all of him, all through him, and before she came in he gathered himself on the right side of her office and pretended to stare out the window, staring instead at his reflection in the glass of the tall windowpanes, the orange skin and copper hair, the dumb visage of a bored lion.

He chose chemistry because it was his best subject and he wrote out the information in the most succinct and forward manner possible.

Unscheduled Field Trip Opportunity for Select Advanced Students.

A three-day trip to Pyramid Lake to study the effects of unprecedented rainfall on the phytoplankton and pH levels of the lake.

Extra credit awarded to those students who turn in a photo essay on the trip, complete with tables of measurements and synopsis of ecological conditions and hazards.

Johnson cracked up when he saw it.

Dude. I have a D in chem. My parents are not going to believe some shit about *select students.*

So Rez wrote a separate flyer for each apostle, according to his needs. Johnson got one from the English teacher and Kelly got one from

Coach Sterns about a special orienteering trip for eleventh graders who had excelled in survivalist skills. Matthews didn't need one because his parents had six sons and never noticed if he was around or not. Rez sometimes thought What if I had five brothers? What if I was part of some huge American clan? at Matthews's house, as Rez ate food their cook Blanca made or slept in the pool house the housekeeper kept clean, or laid out on the lawn cut by Amado, the silent old gardener with arms covered in faded tattoos of big-breasted woman and fighting cocks. Six sons and rich. No parents. No sisters. No back home that is not here.

Everyone went for it. Rez's mother stayed up late Thursday washing his sleeping bag and sewing the hole in the raincoat he hadn't used since eighth grade. He pretended he needed his father's signature and took the letter to him after dinner on the night before they left. His father read the letter and let out a laugh.

The pH of a lake, as affected by rain? What is this?

It's a field trip, Dad. For the advanced chem students.

Yes, but you and I both know that lake is polluted with runoff. The pH will never be accurate. Here we are spending all this money for the best private school in Orange County and this is the smartest field trip they can come up with?

Rez stood beside the recliner, mesmerized. His father spoke playfully, a light and gentle teasing. Since the last fight there had been the usual seriousness, nothing better, nothing more, and here he was now, joking with Rez as if he too knew the permission-slip joke, the lie of the whole thing. Rez felt the blood go cold in his body and waited for the other side of his father to make himself known, but his father only took the pen and paper and scribbled his name on the line.

Yes, yes. Go. There will be teachers, by law there have to be, eight to one I think, and it will be miserable and wet but you might have a chance to sit next to a girl around a campfire . . . I know why your eyes are dancing. Not for pH, I can promise you that!

Rez stood beside his father and smiled. His father smiled back.

Don't think I don't know . . . I was a young man once too.

Rez took the paper and walked away. A young man. A girl by a fire.

*

They reached San Diego by noon with half a tank of gas and less than twenty miles to the border. They stopped at two In-N-Out drive-throughs and got so full on fries and milk shakes and double cheese-burgers Animal Style they had to smoke again just to stay high. They decided not to stop after Ensenada until they got to the most perfect Mexican beach.

Until the Mexican Pacific licks our toes! Rez shouted like a moron, and this made everyone laugh so hard they didn't notice they were stuck, sweating in bumper-to-bumper border traffic, waiting to be waved across. The high wore off during their wait and they sat quietly and listened to Nas's *Illmatic—Then writing in my book of rhymes / All the words past the margin*—and mouthed the stories about drugs and women and guns and pride and watched the people in the cars next to them, stock-still, heads erect, silent and glassed off. At the first sign announcing the border checkpoint Matthews suggested they hide the weed and they passed the bag around and spoke in serious and knowing tones.

Too big for the glove compartment.

For sure. Under the backseat?

Spare-wheel spot?

Naw, they always look there.

Rez finally opened the toolbox at his feet. Inside Freddy had orga-nized the top shelf with paper clips and scissors and small pincers to hold roaches too tiny to smoke with your fingers. Underneath, in the storage area, rolling papers, a small bong, lighters, a few empty baggies, and small shreds. All of it useless in car repair.

Dude. Perfect.

Rez put the weed with the bong and tucked the whole thing under his seat. At the border they sat up straight and kept responsible, distracted faces as they drove past an empty kiosk with a wooden arm that lifted and lowered automatically; like that, they were in Mexico.

6

Highway 1 continued down and they recognized it and followed the signs. Matthews drove slow down the small, blasted streets of Tijuana. No one said anything about it but they heard Freddy's voice: *Don't even fucking think of stopping in TJ. Don't do it. My truck will get jacked and the cops will arrest you and then ass-fuck you in a Mexican jail. I don't care about your ass. Bring this truck back exactly as I gave it to you.* So they drove on, past the taco vendors and bars that would let them in without IDs and small dark doorways guarded by women, young and old, in spandex skirts and no one said a thing about stopping

Five minutes out of America and it's like another planet.

Matthews talked to himself. He drove with uncharacteristic tenderness, as if the road were lined with babies, and it made Rez nervous. This was not the Mexican surf trip he'd planned, the city felt like some sort of trap, and he wanted Matthews to drive faster, to get out of town and back to the beach, where everything would look like the magazine pictures of perfect beaches with perfect surf. Kelly pulled his Game Boy out of his bag.

A new planet for sure. A shittier planet.

Kelly pressed buttons, flicked his fingers madly, and small gunshot noises came out of the device. None of them had been to Mexico before and as a rule it would be Kelly to hate it first, to call it names and pretend it was a stupid waste of time. Rez wanted to check his phone and see how long until they were out of the city, at the beaches, surfing, but the battery had died and all they could do was crawl south through the unending town and watch the beggars and old ladies and young fathers move about their afternoon.

Rez looked out the window. It was hard to see at first, the plastic of his sunglasses covered in fingerprints, and the high he'd been working on since Dana Point had blown up in his head like a balloon, but he tried to keep focus as Tijuana slid past him like an ancient circus. Planets. It wasn't another planet at all, it was this planet, the same planet as San Diego and Laguna Beach and Los Angeles, just more fucked-up. Hydrochloric acid, he thought. Not another planet, just a city sprinkled in hydrochloric acid. In middle school he'd done a report on it in chemistry, drawn to the total anarchy of its composition and the way nothing withstood it, not bone or rock or lead, and now here was a place where everything seemed in some state of decomposition or decay. Up around them on the hillsides tiny shacks clustered together, their paint peeling off and colorful chunks of concrete crumbling into the streets. The sidewalks were chipped and the roads full of potholes. Rez watched a group of girls in school uniforms and white shoes walk into the dark mouth of an old church and he wondered how they stayed so clean. They passed stall after stall of tourist crap, each with a thousand skull statues in a thousand colors, a thousand skeletons drinking a thousand bottles of Corona from their bony hands. The skeletons freaked him out. The way everything looked poor and dirty freaked him out. Nothing at home was so dirty or so poor. Even their maid, Ysenia, lived in a nice apartment compared to this. She had a balcony with flowers that smelled like bananas, and when Rez's mother gave him the check to drop off, he'd always wait a few seconds outside her door just to breathe in the jasmine. Then he'd press the bell and a girl, a few years younger than he was, would answer, take the check, and close the door without a word or a smile.

At an intersection Rez watched a man piss between two parked cars and thought about saying something so they could all laugh together but let it go, his stomach turning at the sight of someone's dick in public. *America is a good place,* he heard his father's voice say. *A good good place.* The shadow was in the car, the long shape of his father sat between him and Johnson, taking up the space with a cool resolve. *We cannot complain. Look at this mess.* His father raised his hand into the air and circled it around. *They don't even have a war here and still they can't keep it clean like we keep our cities and children and grown men clean.*

28

Who was thinking these thoughts? Rez looked at Johnson staring out the window, his bony shoulders turned away. Was it the weed? The car was quiet and Rez looked at the boys around them and considered they might simply be miniature versions of their fathers, nothing more. Johnson turned.

What?

Nothing.

Rez sat up and tried not to get nauseous from the drive and the sweat and the thoughts. He didn't want to come undone in this place that was coming undone around him. He leaned forward and punched Matthews in the shoulder.

Dude. Whose grandma are you? Do you want to get wet today? Drive faster!

Matthews said nothing, simply lifted a single finger off the steering wheel and pointed in front of them where a man pushed himself down the middle lane of the highway in a wheelchair. Kelly laughed.

Everyone but Kelly stared out the window as Matthews drove carefully around him. The man was skinny. Rez counted seven veins popping out from the man's neck. His head was covered in long white hair but his face was soft and brown and had no certain age to it. He wore sunglasses and a Chicago Bulls jersey and faced forward as his arms pumped up and down to move the chair down the road, two long denim pant legs dragging behind like streamers.

Totally pathetic.

Kelly scoffed and Rez sat back and closed his eyes like he was also bored by Mexico and pretended to sleep when really what he wanted was to stop seeing so he would stop thinking so he could stop the sound of his dad's voice and the nausea, just for a little while. Johnson grunted and laughed.

Yeah. That dude should get a fucking room already.

The meanness of the words shocked Rez. Johnson was not nice like Matthews but he wasn't an ass like Kelly and Rez opened his eyes to see Kelly's wide white palm in the air.

High five to that.

*

The first beach outside Tijuana was a dump. The sand covered in trash and the tiny breaks onshore gray and churning, and Rez felt his heart drop. He convinced them not to stop until K55, the first famous spot, and no one objected and they drove by the ocean for a long time and said nothing. Men and women and children walked together or alone, few in bathing suits, most with enormous plastic cases that looked like luggage or laundry. No one swam. No one lay out. It was a long fifty-five kilometers after an already-long drive and even though James Johnson kept pulling himself up from the seat every half hour to show how much ass sweat he was sitting in, they kept going, each of them waiting for the same sign—a beautiful beach—before they could stop.

A few hours and the sun dropped on their right and the cities turned to small villages that turned to road stops with taco stands, gas stations, and stores that sold garden pots and ceramic birds in cheery colors. The beaches emptied of people and garbage and started to look a little more like California beaches, a little more like the beaches in the magazines Rez had studied before they left. At the sight of the familiar landscape Kelly turned the AC off and Johnson rolled down the windows and Matthews started to drive fast again so when they heard the siren and saw the Nissan SUV, they thought it was for speeding and started yelling. Matthews told everyone to shut up; his brother had given him tips on how to handle this.

Mexican tax time. It's cool. I got it.

The police were exactly like the police from home. Rez tried to find something different about him, but it was all there, the aviators, the uniform, the forearms, the hair, all just like an American cop, maybe a few shades darker. Matthews's voice came steady and willing like it was when he bullshitted in class or talked to a girl he liked.

Yes, officer. Can I help you?

The policeman cocked his head.

Perdón?

Matthews tried to keep his cool but there were no more words between them for so long that everyone got nervous. The policeman took off his glasses.

Otra vez por favor.

We didn't do anything. I was just driving . . . Matthews gestured to the car full of them and their eight surfboards and block of weed and wallets full of money.

Sí. Por supesto.

The policeman pointed to the rolling papers on the dashboard. Matthews shook his head.

Wait. Please wait. Here.

He reached into the back pocket of his shorts and opened the wallet with the crisp bills he'd taken from the ATM this morning. He offered three of his dozen twenties.

The cop stared at the money and then into the car and for a moment Rez could see them as the cop did—four rich kids in a nice truck, young, clueless—and when the cop gave a little smile, Rez felt ashamed. The cop spoke now, this time in near-perfect English.

You were speeding. Fifteen over the limit. Your car smells of *hierba* and here I don't need a warrant to search. Rich kids, boards, suits, nice trucks, they sometimes have trouble on this side of the border. You should be careful. For your convenience, a more substantial payment, and the ticket will be overlooked.

Matthews took another three twenties from the fold and the cop placed the bills in his breast pocket and backed from the car until his hand was on the front of the hood.

Vaya con Dios.

He smacked the hood and Kelly cursed under his breath and Johnson joined him and Rez said nothing, having heard it all before. He kept his mind on the waves and checked the rearview mirror to get a look at Matthews's face and saw he was not pissed at all. His eyes were full of relief. It had always been kindness with Matthews, even in third grade, Matthews was just nice. Nothing else. Rez had watched the boys and girls change, turn onto one of many sides, shift depending on the light and the time and the need, but Matthews was always and only good, a single surface all the way around. Rez relaxed and looked out the window and tried not to hear Kelly talk about wetbacks and illegals and fucking Mexicans and how California should start a war and take Baja, which he was going to call basura from now on.

Basura, you better watch out!

Johnson laughed.

Dude. How did you remember the word for "trash"? That's so fresh.

And that's how it came back, with a laugh, and then they were talking again and everyone knew it was fine because they were rich kids with money to pay off cops and no Mexican prison and no calls home and no damage to Freddy's truck. Now they could just surf and go home and talk about pH levels in Pyramid Lake with their parents and their epic barrels with their friends. Rez felt his gut loosen from all the nerves, and when they turned a curve on the highway, he was the first to see it, the beach, miles long, pristine, at the bottom of a line of short white cliffs. Low in the sky now, the sun reflected off the cliffs so they looked like a kind of pink alabaster or marble or tusk and it didn't matter because it was as he imagined it and they stopped and got out of the truck and stared way out into the sea as the sets came in long and even and glassy and arced, like the grooves in an old record, one after another after another, in just the right rhythm.

They surfed under a soft dusk, the half-moon rising in the east. The water was warmer than they were used to and no one wore a suit. Then they all swam to Matthews, who took a plastic baggie wrapped around a plastic baggie wrapped around a plastic baggie from the key pocket of his shorts, and sat on their boards far from shore and waited for their hands to dry so they could use the lighter and smoke a joint. Then they spread out again, each taking his own slice of sea, and the water turned the same navy as the sky and when Rez paddled out far from the breaks to take a rest, the water grew still and he saw little flecks of stars in the ocean, their shimmer mixed with the easy rolls and laps of the sea. Sandwiched, he thought, folded in, a galaxy above, a galaxy below. This abandon was new to him, new to know his smallness in the scope of everything around.

When they came back to shore, the moon hung on the opposite end of the sky and their skin puckered from the salt. Cool air moved quickly across the sand and Matthews and Johnson gathered driftwood while Rez and Kelly set up the one small tent, not because they were going to sleep in it but to have something to do, a task to keep the feeling of the ocean inside them until there was a fire to take over. Rez had never slept outside, did not know the pull of stars on dreams, had never woken up with a face covered in dew. He did not mention this to Kelly, who took yearly hunting trips with his dad to a logging forest just outside Yosemite. *There is nothing like shooting a deer,* Kelly once bragged. *You own everything after that shot, the whole world is yours.*

Kelly told endless stories about hunting and guns and fishing and airplanes his father landed on secret lakes and everyone pretended to ignore him, but Rez listened, unbelieving that Kelly's father trusted a sixteen-year-old with a six-inch blade or that he knew how to bleed animals dry by hanging them from trees. My older brother Paul taught me how to do it. And my dad taught him. It's not that big of a deal, Kelly explained when everyone called bullshit. Tonight Kelly set up camp like an expert. With little of Rez's help Kelly put together the tent and pulled out the cooler, arranged the tarp and a few headlamps so that they had a little shelter and a little light. It was as if he'd spent a lifetime living out the back of a truck. Rez tried to help but ended up sitting in the sand and looking around at the nothing that surrounded them, the ocean's even breaks, the sand and water alight under the half-moon, the dark desert that braced against them from the east, and wondered, What have I spent a whole life doing?

They ate the little food they had left over from the In-N-Out in San Diego and drank all the beers. No one talked about hunger or thirst, their exhaustion was so great. They threw their wallets into the glove compartment, locked it, locked the cab of the truck, and took their sleeping bags and towels to the sand and fell off, one after another, silently, slowly, easy with the earth and with the water too, their shoulders sore, their skin tingling from a wind that blew sand across sand.

*

33

Rez dreamed of swimming, in the open way of an octopus, in constant extension, without confines of air or the stiffness of bones, everything in reach.

The sun woke them and they took their crusty faces and hair and boards directly into a water that welcomed them and made them new again. Rez rode a dozen waves before stopping to see the place by the first real light of day. An empty beach. Behind it a desert of scrub and brush. Every few minutes a car along the highway, no sound, no faces. No power lines. No cities. No signs of life except for their bodies and whatever lived in the dark sea in which they swam. He thought of home, the view from the ocean toward the shore, all roads and parking lots and groomed parks and fast food all the way down the coast. He'd never been to a beach this raw, not even Old Man's in San Onofre, which was far from the highway but right up against the two boobs of a nuclear reactor that hadn't stopped working in forty-five years. He wondered if all the beaches he knew, all the beaches back home, had once been desert too, now dressed up deserts that were made pretty with extra water and gardeners and too many people. Rez circled his feet in the water to turn himself around and paddled back out.

By midday they were in the truck again, shouting over one another about that tube and that wipeout and that ride and no one needed to be better than another because each had had their own glory. They ate at a taco stand on the side of the highway. The woman who served them was young, and pretty, with a little baby nearby so no one looked at her twice, though they did look once. Rez wondered what it would be like, with a mother, a young beautiful mother. All the girls he fantasized about were from school or TV or porn and they all had the same bodies and so he could not imagine it, the small belly, the full chest, the way her legs touched in the middle and then curved far out and tapered at the ankle but the more he thought about it and the longer he watched her chop at the meat with the side of a spatula, the harder he got. He took two Jarritos from the cooler and went to sit down. They were the only customers and hunger focused them. They ate more than normal and after a while the corners of their mouths and palms were stained red from the chili oil of the carne asada. Kelly looked around and pointed.

Dude. You guys look like melting clowns.

It was funny enough and they laughed because no one cared, no one felt the small self anymore, the one that told them, *I am Kelly and no one else* and *I am Matthews and not Rez* and *I am Rez alone* and on and on, and different by father and mother and sisters and brothers, and instead they sat, exhausted and full, with the one self they shared now on this adventure in and out and in and out of the sea.

After lunch they drove on. Salsipuedes. Shipwrecks. Punta Baja. Isla Todos Santos. Leave If You Can. Drop Point. Rez's Spanish was better than his Farsi and he rolled the words around his mouth and mastered them. The names had a dark thrill to them and he let their mystery call out as he sat in the backseat and listened to Tupac and felt the dry air blow across his naked chest and neck, certain now how he would spend the rest of his life, and then he fell asleep.

When he woke up, they were parked under a grove of palms, the fronds clapping insanely in the wind. Matthews had the driver's seat tilted back as far as he could without hitting Johnson, who had his head against the window and was snoring. Rez unfolded himself from the compacted position he'd slept in and felt pools of sweat in the creases of his body and a spicy unease in his gut. Outside, beyond layers of low dunes, a beach, busier than the one yesterday, with people laid out in pairs and trios, and an ocean, blue and empty except for an enormous rusted ship hull split in two where surfers jutted out fast and to the right.

Apostles.

He tried once and the bodies in the car did not stir. He opened the door and stepped out. Behind him Johnson fell to the side, took up the space Rez left behind, burped and farted and curled into a little ball. Rez slid his borrowed board out from under the others and found a half chunk of wax, covered his board with it, and turned to the beach.

He walked past a group of women and girls having a picnic on a rug of woven plastic threads. Their food did not look appealing and even though he stared not one of the women looked up to notice him. Five or six boys kicked a soccer ball. An old woman, fully dressed, napped on her side, a small dog curled into her chest. When the water hit his toes, he turned his attention to the sea and the rusted monster rising from it. Surfers paddled in just at the edge of the ship's eroded iron ribs and waited for the sets only to ride out quickly, careful to avoid the jagged metal posts. He's seen guys do it at the Venice pier and once in Santa Monica, but he'd never tried. *Fuck it,* he whispered to himself, and his soul lifted and he ran in until the water was hip high and then he started to swim.

The apostles joined him one by one. The swell was perfect and the water was busy. They kept their distance from each other but it was hard to keep space with the other surfers. No one smoked that day, and when Rez caught sight of one of them, their faces folded in with concentration or blank with relief once they had navigated the iron jaws without a scratch, he felt their joy and knew they would return home heroes all.

The last wave of a set rolled and Rez paddled to it, his rhythm matched by the strokes of the surfer next to him, a surfer his age, maybe a few years older, skinny and strong. Rez wanted to swim some space between them and maybe even give him one of the looks surfers in Laguna give that says *Back off* or *This one's mine* or *Go ahead, all yours,* but he let it go. What difference did it make? To the ocean they were all the same, so why not be the same? In any case the wave was coming and they only had a few seconds to turn around and paddle forward and jump up and in those quick seconds Rez hopped up and balanced. He looked over his shoulder to see the guy get barreled, his hands up above his head as if keeping the tube open with the length of his body. When the wave shot them out, they locked eyes, nodded, and swam back to the ship without a word.

*

No one wanted to leave Shipwrecks but a fog came in and one by one they went and sat on the shore, hungry and spent. They rinsed their boards in the whitewash, loaded Matthews's truck, and drove as far south as they needed to find a store with food and water and beer. The food was mostly packaged and the beer was only so cold but a small grill sizzled in the back and the old man who ran the place said Sí sí sí when Rez asked him if he made tacos.

Por supuesto. Tenemos lengua y cabeza. Ricos los dos.

Rez told the apostles.

Tongue and brains. He says they are good.

Kelly doubled over and pretended to vomit.

Come on, man, that's rude.

Matthews hit Rez on the back a few times.

I'll take five of each. I am so hungry I'd eat goat nuts if that was all he had.

Rez gave him a fist bump and they ordered fifteen tacos while Kelly and Johnson ate tostadas and pepitos and something that looked like Mexican Twinkies. They drank beer and sat there for more than an hour and the old man came in and out to give more food and take away empty bags and plates.

No hay cominda en el norte? he joked, and Rez smiled but he didn't translate and no one asked. The bill came to six dollars and they spent four more on beer and a kind of Gatorade drink and then looked out at the night and the dark highway and Rez asked the old man, Hay una playa, para camping? Cerca de aqui?

The old man gave directions to a pullout five minutes down the road.

No hay nadie. Limpia. Seguro.

They drove the short distance and parked in a flat sandy spot where cars had parked before them and Matthews pulled out a six-pack and his sleeping bag and, drunk and tired, they all did the same and stumbled to the sand, where they found a stone circle with usable wood still in it, some new, some only partially black, and Kelly worked to stack and light and relight until there was a fire. Rez threw down his sleeping bag and wanted to say, *This is the shit. This is the best. I am never going back.* But knew he would sound like a pussy and so just lay down and listened to Kelly tell stories about him and his brother Paul in Lake Tahoe last summer and normally one apostle or another would tell him to shut up but they were asleep and Rez heard the stories in fragments that mixed with his exhaustion and he fell asleep thinking about bears, severed legs, ant piles, long hikes in pathless woods, triggers, steady hands, older brothers, and marked men.

Rez dreamed of a girl from his chess club, Maryam. In the dream she worked at a grocery store and no matter how nicely he asked, she wouldn't give him his change. She laughed and said, *No. Sorry, no change for you.* And then went on punching numbers into her toy register. Behind him a small woman had a basket full of breasts and bras, and when the sun woke him with its early light, Rez shook off the dream that left in him equal parts lust, frustration, and disgust.

The waves at this beach, even and glassy, were the best waves he had ever seen. Rides two or three minutes long. He sat still for as long as it took to clear his head of the beer and the dream, drank what was left of the Gatorade, and when there was no reason to wait any longer, ran to the truck to get a board and paddle out and wash off the sand and sweat and fly through water again.

The first truck he came to looked just like Matthews's truck, but it had long white key marks dragged along the sides and there were no boards on top and the driver's side window had been broken. Sucks for them, Rez thought, and ran up the beach to look for their truck. He jogged a minute and then two and then thought the walk last night was not this long, and there were no other cars parked along the roads and only one pullout. He turned around.

Fuck!

Smashed glass covered the driver's seat and he saw their wallets strewn about, empty of licenses and money and credit cards. In his wallet he found a library card and a Laguna Beach trolley pass.

Fuck.

The boards were gone, all eight, including the two he'd borrowed from Matthews. The cooler, the weed in the toolbox, their phones, and the pine-tree air freshener, all gone. Rez stopped himself from crying. Why did he want to cry? It wasn't his fault. It was his fault. It wasn't. But it was. The trip was his idea and so this was his fault and even if it wasn't, it would be, they would all remember it as his fault. He pressed the button for the radio to turn on. Nothing. Worse and worse. He didn't walk back to the apostles. He sat instead up against the wheel well and waited.

They got a jump from a delivery guy, his truck covered with pictures of the packaged food they'd bought at the store the night before. When he was done, Rez said, Gracias, and the guy waited for money, a tip, something, and Rez looked back at the truck with broken window and scratches and his pissed-off friends, who walked and kicked the tires and bit their fingernails, and finally the guy said something under his breath and left. Matthews, who accidentally fell asleep with the keys in his board shorts, broke the rest of the driver's-side window with a rock, cleaned the glass off the seat, got in, started the truck, and they all followed. He turned the truck north and gunned the engine and said the same thing he'd been saying for the last two hours.

Three hours to the border. Half a tank of gas. No money. No driver's licenses. We are so fucked.

They flew down the highway and Rez, tired of talking, tired of convincing them he would pay for the boards, pay for a new paint job, pay back the money they'd lost, confess to their parents, said nothing. He just sat there and looked out the window at the perfect waves lapping the perfect empty beaches.

They were mad the moment they saw it and they stayed mad on the drive, erupting, one by one, until the ire was spent. Kelly bitched that his short board was a present from his dad, for his birthday, hand carved by a pro, and there was no way Rez was going to be able to afford another one. Johnson said his credit card had a fifteen-thousand-dollar limit and if it was maxed out, his father was going to shit a brick and how was Rez going to fix that? Matthews, driving Freddy's scratched and shattered truck, said the least, and that made Rez feel the worst, and the last hour was silence and Rez rolled the window down to watch the desert stream by and wait for the graffiti and garbage of Tijuana.

They sat through Sunday-night border traffic in silence. One hour passed, then another, and finally a third and their car—even in the US RESIDENTS lane—had moved less than a quarter of a mile. They knew they had no identification; no cell phones and no paperwork to show the car belonged to them. When the arguments hit a panicked pitch, Matthews broke his silence to explain his brothers went to TJ for the weekend all the time and always came back without showing anything.

Dude. Look at us. Do any of us look like we are sneaking into the country?

Kelly laughed from the front seat.

Rez does look a little non-gringo.

Everyone turned and looked at Rez, his tan skin and salt-bleached hair.

Kelly turned around and put on a militant face.

If they call you out, you stay behind. Understand? You can call your old-school dad to come and get you. You are not our problem anymore.

Matthews shook his head.

No, dude. Chill. We went in together, we leave together. Shit is fucked but it's not that fucked.

Dusk in Tijuana and the world outside their car, a show of the shitty life, passed by. Women and children and more children and a few men and a girl of ten or eleven, holding a tiny baby, moved slowly through the lines of cars. Rez thought about his father, how his father never wanted to go to Mexico, never wanted to go anywhere. And maybe he was right for that. The shadow that had left Rez alone these last two days was close again, walking leisurely beside the car, lecturing like a teacher on a stage. *America is a good country.* The shadow looked over the chaos of the border and put his hand on the hood. *A good country. We should be grateful. A fair place where even an immigrant like me, no papers, no schooling, can succeed. These poor people.* And he walked off into the beggars and broken streets, a dark stain in the form of his father, and before Rez could shake the sight of him, they were at the checkpoint and Matthews leaned out the window as if he had just rolled it down.

The border patrol looked like a cop, his uniform green instead of khaki or black, and his face reminded Rez of the PE teacher they had in ninth grade with the thick mustache and almost-long hair.

The patrol looked at Matthews and then in the car at each of their faces and the mess of water bottles and towels.

Good surf?

Yes, sir, Matthews said after the right amount of time. The swell was pretty incredible.

That's what I hear. I've been trying to get in as much as possible at the point over in Ensenada. Where are your boards?

We borrowed some from some buddies we met down there. Didn't want to risk it.

Smart move, son.

Kelly couldn't help himself and leaned over Matthews, and Kelly's voice rushed with ease and confidence and relaxation to talk to the patrol, to someone who was like him, familiar, safe.

My uncle surfs that point. He says it's great even when it's just hip high.

The patrol smiled.

We are indeed blessed. Welcome home, boys. Enjoy those hot showers.

The metal arm of the checkpoint rose up and the truck was through. When they were a few miles across the border, Kelly made Matthews pull off at a gas station and *stop the fucking car* so Kelly could get out and kiss the ground.

Like the pope, Johnson said. Like the pope when he gets off a plane.

Then they were in the stream again, on Highway 5 at night, the fast traffic and bright roads and smooth overpasses to take you from the clean shopping malls and their spotless parking lots to the enormous

41

grocery stores and back home to the clean toilets and sterile kitchens, the network of invisible sewers gushing under everything and the fair laws over them all, good police who don't fuck with you for no reason and the taxes to pay for some Mexican mother to send her six kids to day care or to help the shitty countries out when an earthquake or hurricane tears up their shitty cities, and laws to make sure that every man can carry a gun but that gun cannot be used against another man in an act of crime, and the honor in that, the honor in sending your kids to schools that make them pledge allegiance so that they can know where they are and who they are with, and when it is time, they can know what they must defend against jackasses from places with no law but fears and from the stupid old shit they believe that hasn't changed in a thousand years when they used to kill each other for fun. They had long passed San Diego and were driving north along the black stretch of scrub desert before Rez realized the talk was not in his head, unspooling in a senseless mass, but coming from Kelly's mouth. John sat in the front and said all of this in the slow, calm voice of a man giving a talk to his friend, like a man, grown and cool and knowing, like the man he turned into every night at the campfire. Rez closed his eyes on the dark America that passed outside and whistled in through his cracked window and tried to feel safe enough to fall asleep.

7

THE GAS RAN out in San Clemente. They coasted down an exit ramp and into an Exxon station, where they pushed the car to a pump and Kelly turned to Rez and smiled.

Close but no cigar. Time to call Daddy.

Rez went to the pay phone and stared at it for a minute. He picked up the heavy receiver and pressed zero and a voice asked what he wanted. He did his best to explain that he wanted to call a number, but couldn't pay.

The voice, a woman, informed him, That is a collect call. I will put you through.

The phone rang three and then four times and Rez waited and heard his mother answer and wanted to hang up. She said yes and then yes and then he heard his father's voice.

Where are you?

In San Clemente. At the Exxon off Pico.

What? The lake is north, why are you so far south . . . ?

Dad can you come pick us up?

Who? Where are the chaperones?

—

Reza?

Yes. Please just come get me.

The line went dead and Rez walked back to the truck but didn't get in. He leaned up against the bumper and waited and thought. There was no precedent. Never had he committed such disobedience. There was the unknown of his father's reaction, the unknown of his punishment, the unknown of how to pay the money back, fix the truck, buy the boards, one hollow wrapped around another hollow around another and he tried not to panic and concentrated instead on the attitude that had helped him these last months as he came home stoned, with the smell of Sophia's cunt on his fingers, or lied about studying with Matthews or going to soccer practice and going to the cove instead and getting high. Rez took a deep breath and leaned forward: *Fuck it.* He exhaled and inhaled and said it again. Again and again he cultivated the thought and it stopped his knees and hands from shaking, kept him upright and dry eyed. Rez watched the lights of cars stream south to San Diego or north to Los Angeles, and he thought about his father and who punished his father? Another father, his grandfather, an opium addict, military man, too distracted to put the full focus of love or hate on his twelve children, and who punished him? Another man Rez would never know, and on and on back to the first father and the first son and the first disobedience and defiance, and has a boy ever survived untouched? What is the worse he can do? He can't kill me. Anything short of that, fine. But he can't kill me. So fuck it.

The luxury sedan pulled into the station and drove up beside Rez. The apostles hopped out and Kelly whistled.

Nice to see you, Mr. Courdee. You sure did take your time.

The window rolled down and Rez's father, the long face, the glasses, and the mustache, the beard, made no response.

Get in the car, Reza.

No one moved and finally Rez found voice enough to explain they all needed rides. Or money for gas.

Why is that your problem?

His father, logical as ever. Rez looked at his flip-flops and thought, It will be boarding school, military academy. That is what it will be.

But, Dad, our phones and wallets and they don't . . .

Get in the car. They can call their own parents collect. They still have their fingers, don't they?

Rez walked around and opened the passenger door and got in. He heard the sounds behind him, the *No way; no fucking way* and the *You have to be kidding me* and worse than that faded as his father rolled the window up.

*

44

They drove in the opposite direction of their house. His father turned away from the highway that would have taken Rez to his mother, to his bed, to sleep, and turned instead east down Avenida Pico, where they drove for minutes and then an hour, and then longer, past strip malls lined with gyms and pet-grooming stores and frozen-yogurt shops. At the speed limit they drove away from the endless empty parking lots and gated entrances to neighborhoods with names like Vista Mar and Sunset Villas and Golden Valley, their fountains gaudy with colored lights and Italianate concrete god heads that spouted dirty water from their mouths. The rich ones had a guardhouse with a guard and a flickering television, but as they drove, the guardhouses gave way to simple code boxes and then cheap wooden signs that read DESERT FLOWER, ARROYO HEIGHTS. The stretches of desert were longer and longer now, and the golf courses disappeared and then there was only a single gas station and nothing else for a long time. Rez thought, He can't kill me. He won't. What father kills his own son? They drove on, the streetlamps fewer and fewer, the stars above them more and then many.

In the dark nowhere his father slowed the car and turned right off the road onto the bumpy shoulder and then onto a dirt road. The headlights showed rocks, a few thorny plants, and crushed cans of beer. His father seemed to have a sense of the nowhere and drove easily until they reached an iron cattle gate that said NO TRESPASSING and turned the car off. With the lights of the dash gone, darkness was all around and Rez tried to concentrate on the skin of his hands and knees until his eyes adjusted and all the time he thought, He can't kill me. My mother. The police. He cannot. He won't. It will be bad, the worst, but he can't go all the way. He won't go all the way.

Get out.

His father opened the door and steeped out and Rez did the same. And I can't kill him. No. My mother. The police. Prison. If I had to . . . ? He is taller, stronger. His hands heavier than mine. Bigger. Rez walked around to the front of the car where his father leaned up against the warm hood and stared out into the empty desert night. Whatever mountain the two had been scaling all these years, that hard rock of suspicious and fear and nerves, they now summited and Rez stood beside his father, faced the car, and tried to focus his eyes enough to catch sight of the road. When he finally saw it, or what he thought was it, he looked at his father, the profile of him in close-up now, an old man, but not completely old, not old in flesh or form, only in relation to Rez. Rez saw his shoulders broad and lean, his mustache and buzzed hair mostly black, his long straight torso thin from the collarbone to the belt. He was a well-made man, and even though his head hung down as if the rocks and scrub held some information, Rez saw now that he was not old, no, but tired, too tired, and a part of Rez stepped down from the summit and gave way. His father spoke.

Is it something you enjoy?

What?

Lying to your father.

No.

And tell me this: Are you afraid of me?

—

Then why did you lie? Whose idea was it? The trip.

Mine.

And the theft, boards, the damage to the car . . .

I said I'd pay for it.

His father lifted his head.

So you have taken your life into your own hands. Tried to trick me into thinking of you as my dutiful, honorable son, while you try to live in your own way. By your own rules.

I thought if I asked you wouldn't let me . . .

Were there drugs?

Yes.

The truth came up from his mouth before he had a chance to catch it, to keep it and think it over and calculate the damage of it. It came out of Rez so quickly he had no moment to prepare for his father's reaction, the head dropping again, and then the tears shook up and out from his convulsing chest and dripped down off his squeezed face onto the dry, dusty ground.

I, a good man, good citizen, honest husband, and responsible father have such filth for a son? How is that possible?

Rez took a step away from the car. He heard an escalation in the question, a change of tone from pitiful to angry, and knew it from the times before. He took a few more steps back and stopped when he thought he was far enough, when he realized there was nowhere to go. His father looked at him directly.

You must apologize.

I am sorry.

No. You must recognize yourself. Admit to me who you have become. Say, I am an idiot. A filthy idiot who keeps the company of fools.

—

Say it and then it will be done. Say what you are and then I can let you back into the car, the house, the family, because you have named yourself and you will walk with that name for as long as I live beside you.

—

I am a filthy idiot. Say it and let's be done.

—

Reza, my patience is only so long.

No.

And it came in a rush. From stillness to motion in less than a second. His father charged him and before he could move out of the way Rez felt the rocks of the desert digging into his back, into his side, and then into his face as his father's hand pressed down the back of his head as if to drown him in the dirt. The bone behind his eyebrow began to sting and then the bridge of his nose burned too. His father pushed his face into the floor and grunted once for each time he smacked Rez in the back of the head. Tears came and they were not from the pain of the body, which was sharp and unusual and made in part of his father's weight forced onto him, but some older pain, a pain he'd carried since he was four or five, the first pain he could remember and the words that followed then, that first time, followed now, resurrected, the same words in their same ageless plea.

Baba, why are you hurting me? Baba! Why are you hurting me?

8

THE FEVER LASTED five days.

He stayed in his room and sweat and slept and sweat again. His mother brought him watermelon and bowls of herb soup. Rez touched the bruises on his back and they felt small but deep and his whole head throbbed every time he smiled or winced or began to cry. Weary of expression, silent and locked away in his room, he stared at the ceiling, watched television, and avoided the mirror in the bathroom whenever he had to piss or shit. His mother came and went. If he was watching reruns of *Seinfeld* or *The Simpsons*, she would sit on the chair beside his bed and neither of them would laugh or say anything beyond *Are you hungry?* and *No thanks* and *Yes* and *Maybe later.*

His phone died and his laptop battery drained and he made no efforts to connect to anything or anyone beyond the walls of his room. At night when he was too hot to sleep, he stared at those same walls, one and then the other, and saw pro surfers glide down faces of water so high he almost didn't believe they existed. Kelly Slater. Laird Hamilton. Fiji and the North Shore. Tahiti. Injury and glory. Freedom without end. An ocean home. Some part of him believed it, lived in the dream of such possibility, and another part of him saw the photos the same way he saw images of Pluto or the rings of Saturn, awesome but beyond his reach. Beside those hung posters torn from European soccer magazines, players from his favorite teams. Barcelona and Manchester United, teams he adored in middle school when he and his father would shape a whole Sunday around watching the games during European prime time and American dawn. The players, soaked in sweat and in the moment either before or after a goal, moved with composure and full strength. In Rez's time playing soccer he'd felt that once, maybe twice, and usually tried his best at the far distant defensive positions the coaches put him in.

A few Japanimation sketches he'd made of characters from the graphic novels that obsessed him as a boy and a photo of him next to the HOLLYWOOD sign, not smiling. In the empty spaces between his mother had put up the many plaques and ribbons and certificates for chess matches won, math competitions won, science fairs won. The walls talked.

Without sleep Rez looked again and again at the room around him and saw himself as the walls showed him: once a boy, Reza Courdee, with a family, a life of school and games, hobbies and achievements; and now, not yet a man, with dreams of worlds far from this room, this house, and the people who made him. Inside him now the boy began to diminish and he felt emerge the Rez of the apostles and the ocean and the search for pleasure at all cost, the liar and the desperate soul. Or at least that's what he'd thought, these last months until a few days ago when the boy cried and begged into the desert night, *Please please please stop. Please get off me. I was stupid. I am sorry.*

On Saturday morning the fever broke and he sat up in bed and drank orange juice and played backgammon with his mother, who, in her relief at his wellness, joyfully beat him every time. When they heard the footsteps come down the hall, he looked up at his mother's face and she met his gaze but did not move. His father stood on the other side of the door, not knocking, not opening, just shouting.

Reza, come. Let's go for a walk. The morning is a nice one.

The voice was normal and regular as if announcing *Lunch is ready* or *I found my sunglasses.* The footsteps went back down the hall and Rez's mother nodded to him as if to say, *Go, go on, nothing bad will happen.* He stared at her for a second longer and then put on his shorts and a dirty T-shirt and went out to wait at the end of the driveway where he squinted at a sun he hadn't seen in days.

They walked around the neighborhood of manicured yards with bonsai gardens and boulders hauled in from faraway wild rivers now placed decoratively here and there. His father stood straight and walked quickly, keeping himself a step or two in front of Rez. They approached a woman with two small dogs on two thin rhinestone leashes. She wore cataract glasses and sensible shoes and opened her mouth slightly in a smile and perhaps a greeting, but by the time they passed she reconsidered and looked down at the pavement without even so much as a nod. Rez wondered what they must look like, he and his father, on this morning walk.

They climbed the quiet streets, higher and higher, to the cul-de-sac where the neighborhood ended and the scrub of the hillside began, and there his father stopped and wiped his brow with a kerchief he pulled from his pocket. He was not winded but the day was hot and it was the heat, not the pace, that made Rez feel an uneasiness slip in his gut, the hazy ends of the fever as it crept back into his skin and behind his eyes. Gathered, his father looked off to the horizon and began to speak in Farsi.

The sound of the language had always aggravated Rez and he waited to feel the slight gag in his own throat at the guttural noises and the weird sounds. But today there was nothing. His body had no reaction but for the slightest twinge of pleasure in understanding the words, and the sudden intimacy the language caused between them.

Ok.

His father started up the trail that led to the ridge and Rez followed, the two of them in a line, past the artichoke cacti and sagebrush and the absence of house or man and after a few minutes Rez relaxed and the fever let go a bit and he felt the goodness of movement and breath and his body. Rez lifted and dropped his legs and his father did the same and then the neighborhood was far behind and some sort of uninhabitable dryness spread out in front of them and his father walked into it with direction and purpose. In Farsi his father spoke to the empty land before them.

You are passing through a rough time. That is normal for your age.

The hill tilted and his father slowed to catch his breath and Rez turned off the desire to jog up the hill and get to the top and kept himself quietly behind, in his father's wake.

I was a boy once, and my father was strict. Much more strict than I am and all I wanted was to get away.

They reached a vista that showed the curve of the beach up against the land and Rez saw where the waves came in strong and high and he let himself imagine the cool water on his hot skin and the wind of surfing, the fantastic wind of it that reached them all the way up on this high hill. His father went on.

I wanted to leave Iran, move to America, become my own person. I cannot tell you how impossible that was. I had no money. No plane ticket. No passport even. Just thinking about it was like dreaming. Sometimes, this is how it is for men.

Rez looked at his father and wondered how many selves he carried within him. There was the self that stood on the arid trail and looked toward the Pacific, and another self left behind a boyhood in a rocky place where he had mountain dogs and loved his rifle and wanted nothing more than what was. There must be one more, the one between, the one who left it and made a journey without return, without looking back. Rez thought of his mother, and her selves and the way they all came to the teak dinner table and said nothing of their halves and quarters and ate the food and stared at the still water in the blue pool. He looked back down at the coast. The waves would be fantastic today, he could tell by the breeze.

I am not a perfect man. I should not have hit you. That was not right. Not in a good family. I apologize.

His voice was soft with an unfamiliar tenderness and Rez took a step away from his father and faced the ocean and the breeze that moved through his short hair and tickled his sore face. He waited for the mistrust to fill him but nothing came, and Rez let the wind blow onto and through him.

Those boys, the ones you think are your friends, will always think of you as an outsider, the foreign kid. If you go with them, try to be as they are, I will not be able to help you in that life.

His father looked to the horizon and Rez waited and watched to see what other new tone he would set, what else the old man knew that Rez did not. But his father was silent and the two stood side by side as a pair of turkey vultures spiraled up a thermal far above them and the ocean twinkled, gold across the surface of its blue. For a moment nothing felt wrong.

In this life, I can help you. That is what I am supposed to do. Help my son become a man. I will promise to respect you. To keep my temper calm. And in return you promise honesty. That is all I ask.

Fifty-six years old and still, when his father asked for something, his face took on the pleading look of a three-year-old. Fifty-six. If Rez made it to fifty-six and told himself the story of this day, he would say that he was tired, his body was tired from sickness and his head from confusion, but on this day his father changed. Rez could not say what exactly changed, or why he wanted so badly to trust it, or why he wasn't full of suspicion that a fist would fly at his face again. Maybe at fifty-six years old he would understand these unknowns, but on that morning he knew only that he was tired, that the wind was warm and the ocean blue and ruffled, that the earth was under his feet and the sky above, and that he stood beside his father as a man with another man, maybe a father, maybe a friend, maybe even a stranger, on a walk across a dry land. The sensation invigorated him and he breathed in the windy air again and again, as if it were food, and nodded and the two men took up their walking, moving up into the hills until another direction was necessary.

9

HE MOVED BACK to the front row, open notebook, ready pen. The teachers noticed but said nothing. In the hallways Rez kept his head down and didn't answer the *Whassup*s or *Hey, bro*s that came his way. He spent lunches in a window seat of the library study tower and tried to read and tried to eat but just looked out the window, down and over the quad, where clumps of students talked and laughed, pushed or draped arms around each other. He watched Sophia walk the brick paths from class to class, her shiny black hair sliding from side to side, ear tilted into her phone, plaid skirt rolled up at the waistband, her legs thin and pale, always alone. In chemistry lab Lila told Rez, without his asking, that Sophia had a new boyfriend.

A basketball player from Anaheim High. Varsity. He's got his own apartment behind his parents' house.

That's cool.

She told me she still really wants to be friends with you.

That's cool.

No one called. No one invited him over. He went to school, soccer practice, home for the quiet meal with his mother and father, the hour of television, the two hours of homework, the long shower and the long sleep that ended just after dawn when he woke to do it all again. The drone and habit of this life calmed him and after a few weeks gossip about the trip and the theft died down and when the spring storms finally ended, he thought he had a chance at normal, at forgetting the mess he'd made. The stolen credit cards were maxed out and then reimbursed. The boards were replaced by Matthews's dad's insurance company, and the car got a new paint job and window replacement courtesy of Rez's father, who offered it to the Matthews family. Rez listened to his dad on the phone with Mr. Matthews.

Let us be grateful they all came home safe.

His father repeated it again and then shook his head slowly.

Yes. Yes. Not at all. Sons at this age, well . . . we've all been there.

And after the rains had long dried up and the end of the school year was a few months away and all everyone talked about was prom and graduation and summer, Kelly still wouldn't let it go. He told anyone who would listen that Rez Courdee was a poser who didn't know shit. He said Rez weaseled his way into going on the trip and then made them camp on an empty beach even though they knew it was dangerous. Kelly wanted a public feud, and every time they passed in the hall, Rez felt a knock at his shoulder and heard, *What's up, faker?* If Rez raised his hand in class, Kelly started laughing or sighing, loud enough and long enough that the teachers asked him to leave the room and he'd say, loud enough for everyone to hear, *I'd be skeptical of what Mr. Courdee might say. He's been known to tell a few lies.* And just like that the class and the teacher would stare at Rez as Rez's hand slid down back onto the desk and he forget what exactly he was going to say. In the locker room after soccer Kelly followed Rez pinching his nose and shaking his head and shouting, *Has anyone ever noticed how Persians smell? They have this stinky sort of stink to them . . .* Rez pretended not to hear and quickly covered his body with clothes and tried to think of other things—equations, historic dates in the Nez Perce war, his SAT prep book—to keep himself from hearing Kelly and keep himself from crying or fighting or something worse.

For a while Kelly had a small crew, Johnson and a few other preppie guys with dads from old OC families who did not mix with the new OC families like Rez's. They gave him shit for a month or two and Rez kept a low profile and after a while most people stopped caring. Everyone knew Kelly could be a dick and Rez had no friends now anyway, so what was the point?

Matthews, with the shittiest deal, stayed close. After all it was his brother's truck that was scratched and his brother's license that was stolen and he had to tell Freddy and so suffer the punishments assigned through some internal system of brother justice. For a while Matthews came to school with long-sleeve shirts and buttoned his collars all the way up and Rez knew underneath the clothes were bruises from punches and pushes but Matthews never mentioned it. When the other apostles weren't around, Matthews asked Rez out to the car to smoke and they'd sit together in the haze and get retro and listen to Pink Floyd or Red Hot Chili Peppers and talk about USC football or the Angels or anything that wasn't surfing or Mexico or otherwise laced with shame.

10

THE YEAR ENDED. Term papers, assemblies, awards, signatures on the inside covers of the yearbook. *Smellyalateralligator. Have a great summer. Seniors rule. Keep it stoked.* Rez didn't take his out of his backpack, and when someone asked him to sign theirs, he'd write his initials and a smiley face and nothing more. In his photo, taken last fall, he had just smoked with the apostles in Kelly's car, and there he was, a black-and-white head and shoulders amid a sea of black-and-white heads and shoulders, a goofy fuck-it-all smile and wild ocean-stiff hair. On a dare from Kelly he wore his tie crooked and tried to cross his eyes. The photographer wouldn't have it and asked him to straighten up. He looked at the photo and tried to recognize himself and saw only a moment, an expression, a collection of feelings and ways, now passed and far from reach.

On the last day of eleventh grade Rez and a handful of other students sat on the stage of the auditorium and waited as the headmaster called out the names of the best and most promising and honorable and other words that made parents smile and clap and pull out their cameras. Rez wore a new pair of shoes and a pressed shirt and let the boredom settle over him. He stared out at the audience, the first ten or twelve rows full of parents, some old and some not old. There were parents who were happy and parents who appeared otherwise. Rez found the face of Joseph Peterson's dad, Old Peterson they called him, tan and fit and well into his sixties, a known stoner who'd inherited money from old OC land holdings and lived in a house that took up an entire ridgetop above Laguna. He flew a little airplane to L.A. every time he wanted to, surfed Mavericks, had courtside tickets for the Lakers, and didn't go to work. His son, Joey, a straight C student and mediocre jock, had taken a photograph in art class that won a prize and now he sat two rows behind Rez. Old Peterson. He held the left hand of a small Asian woman who looked fifteen years old, his third wife, a woman from China who spoke no English and wore short shorts all the time and covered her mouth when she smiled. She was not smiling now, and her face looked ashy and sullen as it stared into a phone. Beside her, Old Peterson, a man big enough, blond enough, and tan and pleased enough to seem from another species altogether, smiled directly at Rez and winked. Rez sat up straight and shifted his gaze and found his own mother and father, a few rows back, their faces small and somber, empty of elation or surprise. Then he heard his name.

Reza Courdee.

He stood, smoothed out his pants, and walked to receive the certificate and shake the headmaster's hand and take congratulations for proving that he knew more about AP chemistry than any other junior or senior in the state.

A promising senior year lies ahead for that young man.

The headmaster's hand was warm and plump and Rez nodded and walked back to his seat. Next to him another eleventh grader, Arash Dobani, recipient of the presidential honor for academic achievement, the highest prize handed out all year, smiled and flipped his long inky hair back from his eyes.

Nice work, brother, another certificate for the wall. Make Moms proud.

Arash put out his fist and Rez bumped it and Rez smiled at the words and thought about his walls at home and the posters and the prizes and wondered how Arash knew.

Arash leaned to Rez's ear and whispered, You blaze?

Rez looked at Arash, who looked ahead at the parents and teachers in front of them. He too wore a starched oxford shirt and clean shoes. His hair was as long as allowed and his skin was tan and smooth and even over the square bones of his face. He had rolled up his certificate just like Rez had and they sat onstage, homologues of a kind. Rez looked over the parents in the audience, catching the gaze of his mother, who smiled and dabbed at her eyes. His father, who stared at the headmaster with a dropped and flat brow, and then Old Peterson, now looking out the window with the same broad grin.

Yeah. Sometimes.

Sweet. Let's celebrate.

The assembly went on and Rez said no more and then the event was over and everyone stood and clapped and smiled and students walked offstage and Arash stopped Rez.

Let me give you my digits. A few of us are meeting up later. Give a shout when you're done with the family stuff.

Yeah. Cool.

That was the first of it. The seniors threw their huge graduation blow-outs and Rez didn't get invited to any of the parties he'd gone to last year, not Matthews's or Kelly's or any of the volleyball girls', but ended up elsewhere, at parties with grandparents and babies and uncles who spoke no English and smoked cigarette after cigarette on lawn chairs out by the pool. The tables were covered in presents and fat envelopes that stayed sealed and Rez stood in family pictures next to people he'd just met who draped an arm around his shoulder, around his waist. DJs played music from all over the world and he danced with round old aunts who sweated through their silk blouses and smiled up at him coyly. The parties were catered and the families were delirious with pride and even though Rez had only just met these sons and daughters through Arash, in the last two weeks, he was taken in time after time, and he was kissed. At one house, Mila, a friend of Arash's whose older sister was graduating and going to Harvard, he and a few other kids snuck out to a car and got drunk on a handle of vodka they passed around and around until it was empty. They went back to the party and talked to parents and laughed and danced with little cousins and Rez grabbed Elissa Vasquez by the hand and they walked around looking for a place to make out and ended up in a neat small room with a huge silk rug and a framed portrait of Mecca on the wall, just like the photo his mother kept, in miniature, in her coupon-and-bill drawer. He closed the door and they kept going until they found a guest bedroom and he and Elissa did everything he and Sophia had done and it was different and it was just as good.

PART II

To a Brother

11

Laguna Beach, Summer 2012

THAT SUMMER HE was with Arash and his crew, Yuri, Omid, Cyrus, every day. They were guys Rez knew from class or sports or around but had never spoken to, and except for the different names and darker hair and that they preferred chlorinated pools to the ocean, hanging out with them was a lot like last summer with the apostles. Hip-hop all the time, long stoned mornings, fast-food lunches, naps, long stoned afternoons at someone's country club or backyard, evenings at the movies, weekend trips to Vegas, all the same boast and dare and lust talk. No one had jobs and they sat around and smoked the same weed, joint after bong after vape until nothing mattered and everything was all good. Rez stood beside the body of himself as one world of high school male flesh eclipsed another and the revolution of days, nights, wet and dry, traffic and flow, stayed exactly the same.

Except Arash. Arash was different. Before that summer Rez knew nerds and surfers, preppies and jocks. He'd seen goths and gang kids at the In-N-Out trying to get away from the Christian born-agains they'd hung out with last summer at the mall. This was high school; you started out as one thing and ended as something else. They all started out as boys together in the ninth grade and now they were all trying to turn into something like men, and Rez watched as every single kind, regardless of how tough or cool, stumbled before the leap, grew sour, slipped back into babies and cried for their mothers only to swear them off two minutes later. He saw it and knew he did the same and wasn't proud of it but this was the way it was, becoming was a shitty business. And then he met Arash and saw someone not at all in the process of becoming, but who already and completely just was.

The first few weeks everywhere Arash went, Rez went. He had more freedom now. Ever since he'd won the prize his dad didn't press him about studying and tests, and his mom, glad he wasn't sad anymore, let him come and go with his new friends. And it was easy to do. Arash kept the parties going, the pipes packed, and the friends in circulation, and when Rez walked in, no one stressed and no one gave him shit for being the new kid in the group. Girls were always around and everyone watched TV or swam and talked about college or the Kardashians or some smart gossip and Arash got everyone high and bought takeout and gave rides to whoever needed a ride. He never dipped into a mood, never left anyone out, never switched off the generosity, never talked smack. The one time Yuri tried to cut down people who hung out with Kelly, called them *OC neo-Nazis*, Rez watched and waited to see what Arash would do, but all he said was *Come on, man, why you gotta talk like that? There's no need . . .* And then he'd move the conversation away from the dark place and take the sulking friend for a ride and they'd come back happy and high. He lived in an open house, no questions asked, and always leaned down to kiss both his parents regardless of whether he was coming or going. He loved all parents, all families, and the first time he picked Rez up at his house he came with a large, many-bloomed orchid and a small smile on his smooth tan face.

For the lady of the house.

Rez and his mother both came to the door and she let out a little gasp. Rez rolled his eyes.

That is not from Trader Joe's.

No, Mrs. Courdee. Our family friend has an orchid greenhouse. Rez told me you liked plants.

I like plants? I said that, Reza?

Rez stood behind his mother and shrugged. His mother stared at the tiny faces of the flowers.

It is true. I do like plants. I didn't realize my child noticed. Please come in.

Rez elbowed Arash.

Dude, you could have honked from the curb.

Arash smiled and soon they all leaned up against the marble countertops and drank orange juice while Arash answered her questions about Syria and his family houses in Damascus and Aleppo as Rez's mom listened and nodded and then told them things about her home in Isfahan and the garden with the blue fountain in the back filled with koi and other details Rez had never heard. All Rez wanted was to leave, to get out of the house. He hadn't smoked all day, hadn't done anything all day, was bored and fidgety and ready to split and go to the show. When he heard the sound of the garage door opening, he cleared his throat.

A, it's almost four, there will be traffic . . .

Please, would you stay for a minute to meet Sal? Reza's father would like to meet this new friend Rez has told us so little about.

Meena did not even look at Rez and kept her smile on their guest as she rinsed green grapes in a colander. When Rez's father walked into the room, Arash stepped toward him, offered a hand and a full name. Rez's father, caught off guard, took the hand and went through the introductions as if Arash were a colleague from the lab. After a long look and a few grapes he started his questions and Arash answered them with a calm politeness that Rez wanted to call out as ass kissing yet could not. Syrian. Born here. Parents, doctor, housewife. Yes, they'd like to meet you too. Two brothers. Both older. One a surgeon. One the president of a tech company, lives in Newport. Stanford. They've contacted me so I am hoping for early admission. Physics. I think, but I might change my mind. My parents say I am at a good age for changing my mind. Rez watched to see what his father made of this perfect son who was not his. His father popped grape after grape.

I have noticed a change in Reza these last months, you must be the source. Nice to see him making some smart decisions about the company he keeps. It hasn't always been that way . . .

Arash. I think it's time. The show . . .

Arash put his empty glass down and nodded respectfully at the parents.

Right. It is getting late.

His father looked at them.

Show? What show?

We are going to the Hollywood Bowl. My parents gave me tickets as an end-of-the-year gift.

Very nice.

Arash did not mention the show was by a famous rapper who had served time in prison and had rebooted his career by pairing with a classical violinist from China.

Go. Go. You boys should go. Traffic will be terrible regardless, but the earlier the better. It is good. Good to relax a little before this next year. Things will be challenging for you as seniors. Much to be accomplished.

Ok, Dad.

Arash thanked Meena for the orange juice and walked to the front door like he'd been to Rez's house a thousand times already. Rez followed him and mumbled his good-byes as his parents smiled and walked with them to Arash's BMW coupe. The engine started and Rez waved and his parents waved and Rez felt like a dork and Arash drove under the speed limit until they were around the corner and up the street, all the way to the vista, where Arash parked and pulled out the bong and passed it to Rez like he did every time Rez got in the car.

Ass kisser.

Come on now, bro. No need to hate. What can I say? I like parents, old-school, old-world parents. So real. Just think of all they've seen in their lives. They were born in another world and now they can watch it on Google maps. So much change for a single soul to see. That has got to take some balls. Respect, man. Gotta respect.

Rez choked on the smoke he held in his lungs, and laughter and smoke exploded all over the car and Arash started to laugh and then they were high and driving and gone.

The afternoon was hot and all around them on Highway 1 cars stopped and drove and stopped and drove. They kept the windows down and drove through Corona del Mar and Newport and up to Huntington and Seal Beach and past the refineries and loading docks in Long Beach. They listened to the Roots and then to MGMT and smoked a skinny joint while they checked out the skinny women jogging by the beach and the women driving SUVs and the women stopping to let their dogs pee on the palm trees planted into the sidewalks. At a stoplight a cop car pulled up beside them and Rez sat stock-still and stopped breathing, the joint smoking in his lap. Arash kept moving his shoulders to the music and pushed his sunglasses up the bridge of his nose as they slid down. He half sang the words to the song and then the light turned green and they drove on and Rez exhaled and then inhaled and Arash gave him a friendly punch on the shoulder.

Relax, man. You have got to relax. How much herb is it gonna take?

At Artesia and PCH they turned right and drove away from the coast. Within two blocks the fancy facades of the high-rent strip malls turned grimy with liquor stores next to OTBs next to doughnut shops with scratched-up windows, all of it circled by parking lots and empty buildings with faces and figures in bright graffiti on their sides. At a stoplight Rez watched a woman push a stroller full of groceries as she held an umbrella over her head to keep the sun off. Beside her a man held the handlebars of a bike that was loaded, bag upon bag, with glass and plastic bottles. He wore dark sunglasses, no shirt, and a long black cape and walked with a sense of purpose for another world.

Arash turned up the music and they cruised, intersection to inter-section, down the streets of Compton, and Rez wiped the sweat from his palms and told himself to sit back and relax. Arash kept singing.

This show is going to be so dope.

Totally.

By the time they turned off Artesia onto a side street the western horizon was behind them and every object cast a long shadow. They drove down the streets of a neighborhood where each house had the same square yellow lawn and each lawn had its own collection of thirsty shrubs and plants. A few houses had Astroturf and a few lawns were overrun by toys and press benches and weights, and a handful had elaborate rock and cacti gardens. They stopped in front of a house that looked just like the rest and Arash got out. He walked toward the door and turned around.

This is the stop I was talking about.

I'm gonna stay in the car.

That's rude, bro. My friend lives here. Come say hello. We'll be quick. You'll like him.

Rez remembered Arash was picking up a half pound from a friend to have at the show. *To sell?* Rez asked. *No. To share,* Arash responded.

Now they were here, all Rez thought about were the movies he'd seen in middle school—*Murder Was the Case, Boyz n the Hood*—films with guns and drug deals and random stupid deaths. He remembered the lyrics of songs about the never-ending war between the Bloods and the Crips and thought about all the spray-painted murals they passed driving in—*RIP RIP RIP, Our Dear Father. Our dear brother. Our dear son*—and he felt the fool in himself, a kid from OC who loved hip-hop, the beats and the hard lyrics and the anger it let pulse through him, anger he felt but did not have the lyrics or the life for. He felt the fear of a kid who had only ever fronted, who acted tough in a soft world but was scared everywhere else.

Dude. You coming or what?

Rez stepped out of the car and got shoulder to shoulder with Arash.

Man, you don't even need this weed. You buy from Yuri's guy and that's from the clinic. Why are we even here?

Are you whining? Relax. We gotta let the dollar circulate, it's the only way.

Arash pressed the beige circle next to the door. A soft dirge played on the other side of the wall.

Arash said that line a lot, talked about money and how it needed to circulate and if it stayed in one place too long it would go stale and curse its owner. That is how he explained it when Rez asked him why he always gave out weed and offered to pay for food. *It all comes back. In Islam, generosity is a big deal. You can't be Muslim without it.* Rez listened for noises in the silent house and thought about all the free weed Arash would pass out to strangers they would meet tonight and how those strangers would turn into friends for a half hour or so and all of it would be so chill, the edge puffed off. Part of him got it and part of him stayed confused and he slouched a little and tried to stand casual but found no way to be normal in the time between doorbell and door answered.

The door opened and an old man in gray sweats with salt-and-pepper hair and a small prayer cap filled the entire doorframe. Arash stepped to him and they embraced in a big silent hug and when they pulled apart the man put his fist out and Arash bumped it.

All good?

Alhamdulillah. All good, Yusef. And you?

No complaints.

The enormous old man looked at Rez and Arash spoke without hurry.

This is my friend Rez. We go to school together.

Salaam alaikum.

Yusef offered no hand, no fist, and kept a downward gaze on Rez's face.

Rez. Short for something? Reza maybe?

Yes.

Hm. It's your name, you can do what you want with it I guess.

He led them into the kitchen and poured out three glasses of orange juice and for the second time that day Rez stood awkwardly with the bright happy liquid in his glass and waited for the moment to pass as Arash played the part of gracious guest. He answered Yusef's questions about school and the mosque and his family and asked his own questions about the same things and they followed Yusef to the living room, where he filled up all the corners of a recliner that did not recline and Rez and Arash sat on the edge of the couch opposite. Arash told him about graduation, about the prize, and Yusef nodded and Rez looked around at the walls of the room, covered in framed photographs of men and women and children. Face after face after face. Soldiers in uniforms. Women holding round babies. A large group, all ages, in matching T-shirts gathered around a beatific old woman in a wheelchair. Rez's eyes stopped on a series of school photos, the same boy, handsome and smiling and large like Yusef. At seventh or eighth grade the photos stopped and Rez looked away and tried to seem interested in the conversation but could not focus because a sinking feeling started in him and didn't stop. Yusef nodded at what Arash said and Arash nodded at what Yusef said and this went on and on.

Well, you heard about Malcolm's new job, data work, or some such. Says he can do it right from his bedroom. I think he got hired because of that program you all did a few summers ago, that computer program down in Irvine where you met. That did change him. Changed his prospects.

He showed a lot of talent for it. More than most of the other kids there.

Yes. Well.

Yusef grew silent and tapped the empty orange juice glass on his knee.

Yes. Well . . . he said you'd be here about now. I'll take you to him.

Arash stood slowly and Rez stood too quickly and they followed the old man down a carpeted hallway with more framed photos, these older and faded, their subjects wearing dated hairstyles and clothes Rez had seen in movies and reruns. They stood before a door with a poster of Tupac on it and Yusef knocked with one knuckle.

Mal? Arash is here.

A voice from inside said, Cool, and Yusef opened the door and walked away down the dim hallway. Arash went in first. The room was small, crammed with a single bed, a desk, turntables, and a laundry hamper. In front of the desk a broad-shouldered man, a few years older than them, sat in an electric wheelchair. The same handsome smiling face as the boy in the photos on the wall, long past eighth grade, shirtless and broad through the chest, a tattoo of a lion spanning from nipple to nipple. Rez tried not to stare and took the few steps he could into the room, bumped the fist that was offered, and took a seat beside Arash on the neatly made bed and tried to untie the knots in his gut.

The door, man.

Malcolm gestured to Rez with a tilt of his chin and Rez stood and closed it and at the sound of its shutting Malcolm wheeled around and let out a loud bright welcome.

What! Is! Up? Arash! Been a long time.

Same old same old. All good. What's new with you?

Same as same. Got into this Anonymous shit online and tricky stuff, change the world from my wheelchair while paying the bills with data entry. Hustle here, hustle there.

Sneeeeaky.

Indeed. And you? What is in the works for nerd boy?

Same nerd stuff. Science, college, the search for a nice girl . . .

Malcolm pressed a single key on the keyboard and music came on, deep bass and the sounds of a young woman's moans.

I hear that.

Malcolm smiled at his pun and Arash made fun of him for the stupid joke and they talked about school and computers and programming and Rez watched Arash, who was, as ever, himself. The same Arash from his kitchen at home, with the crew, with the girls, with their teachers, in the mirror. The only self he had. Across from him, in his wheelchair, Rez saw that Malcolm was a number of different people, all of them flitting around the room, depending on the topic, careful not to land anywhere. Rez focused on Malcolm's face, the hands of the conversation, the posters in the room, anything to keep him from staring at the empty pant legs that dangled from the edge of Malcolm's chair. Rez tried so hard to do something else that he got nervous and nearly started talking. One of Malcolm's many selves noticed and he turned his attention on Rez.

What's your story?

Rez sat forward on the bed.

Nothing. Same as Arash. Laguna Prep. Waiting to graduate and get out, far out.

Malcolm put his hands in the pockets of his pants and sat back, and for a moment they looked at each other, each set of eyes a vector to the next set, Malcolm looking at Rez, Rez looking at Arash for the next words, Arash looking at Malcolm and then breaking the daze.

It's cool, man, he's cool. Good people.

Malcolm took his hand out of his pocket.

A friend of yours is . . .

He let the words fall and turned on his chair and rolled across the thick carpet to the closet, where a dozen or so T-shirts hung, all a shade of navy, all ironed, and the floor was covered in stacks of neatly folded pants. He reached back behind the shirts and Rez felt his insides electrify with fear. He moved himself closer to the edge of the bed, to a window he could punch out if need be as Malcolm rustled in the closet with one hand. He pulled out an object the size and shape of a brick wrapped in black plastic. He rotated the chair and tossed the package at Arash with the other hand. Arash caught it with one hand.

The goods are good. Hindu Cush. Purple Haze. The usual.

I expect nothing less. Should we roll one?

Malcolm shook his head. Nah, man. Not with Yusef home. These are new days.

Got it.

Arash put the brick into his backpack and handed Malcolm a roll of cash and Rez let his veins open with relief and now for some reason he wanted to relax and smoke in this room and pretend he was never scared or playing out blood scenarios in his head, but he also wanted to get out, as fast as possible, before whatever happened to Malcolm could happen to him, as if tragedy were contagious.

In the car Arash tucked the bag under his seat and rolled his window down.

Not much stink for so much weed.

Arash started the car.

Be nice.

Rez didn't say anything.

I buy it as a favor. I like to help him out. These little buys go a long way and I get to pass out free bud. Win-win.

Outside the car the neighborhood switched back to strip malls and gas stations and the lights of Artesia popped on against the orange lines of sunset at the far end of the sky. A blue Malibu pulled up beside them, sparkle in the paint, chrome all over, after-market tires, the two front windows open. The man in the driver's seat looked at them and then leaned over the woman who sat passenger.

You lost?

No. We're good. Thanks.

Arash answered easily while Rez tried to push himself into the leather of the seat but the leather wouldn't give and he tried to look ahead and not think of guns or robbing or drive-bys or his stupid shitty fear and the shitty racism of his father behind him pushing through. At the sound of a woman's voice he craned his head to look over at the car.

She was beautiful, her face one curved feature atop another, all of it full and promising something Rez had not wanted until just that moment. She smiled at him. Behind her the man smiled as well.

You do look lost.

The man leaned over closer to them.

I hope you're not lost. 'Cause . . .

The light changed and neither car moved. Behind them a truck honked twice and Rez jumped in his seat, all his bones shook at once. The woman in the Malibu laughed at him and the man beside her straightened up behind the wheel and gunned the engine. The Malibu fired past them and the woman's pink hair swirled out the open window like cotton candy.

Arash moved at the speed limit and looked over at Rez.

Dude, Rez. You ok? Your face is white. Don't tell me you're a racist Persian because that is dumber than dumb.

No, it's just, you know, Compton and all that stuff about gangs and . . .

Arash shook his head, his face pressed down in frustration.

Rez, we are all in gangs, man. Think about it.

They parked far from the Bowl and took long bong rips before locking the car and walking the mile or so down the residential streets of West Hollywood. Night had come and the sky was an illuminated blue, bright from the day just passed and all the lights turning on and turning up. Not one star looked down on them, at least one that Rez could see. Their seats were dead middle and perfect and the sky turned pink and then salmon and then turquoise and Rez got high and sipped a beer and found himself close to a girl who moved gently to music that was not gentle. He moved closer and she didn't back away and he moved up to her until an arm touched, a thigh touched as if by accident and Rez felt the warm night and the hard music and her close flesh and was amazed how a single moment could push all things together like this.

They danced for most of the show, closer by accident and then closer on purpose. When the show was over, the girl said her name was Mylaa and she and her friends were going to an after-party and did Rez and his friend want to come? Rez and Arash, both close to six feet but still too skinny to be mistaken for any older than high schoolers, said yes and tried to play it cool at the house on a hill above Silver Lake, where they sat at the edge of the pool and smoked joints and gave away joints and talked to girls who said they were actresses and said *What's up?* to guys in loafers—all of it under the purple night sky.

The apostles would have died for this.

The apostles are just not as lucky as we are. At least not tonight.

A DJ showed up and the party got crowded and Rez found the girl and danced and then took her back to smoke with Arash, who had a crowd around him and talked and listened like he belonged. More people came and went and Arash handed out nuggets of the weed they'd just bought. Rez heard him say something about hospitality and stood there and stared at his friend. This boy unknown to him two months ago, just another kid in the hall, another kid like him, funny name, dark skin, smart and willing, and now here they were in hills above Los Angeles, at the edge of a pool where actresses jumped in and pulled themselves out slowly and Rez saw the unknown boy was replaced by a person and something greater than a person as well.

The party thinned out and a little light came through the eastern part of the sky. The girls had disappeared long ago but Rez didn't mind. They found two deck chairs and some fruit and Arash told him the story of Malcolm.

I met him at a coding conference for high schoolers. He could walk then. He was a computer geek who lived in the hood. And then he was a bystander.

Rez didn't say anything.

First I bought weed from him because I didn't have anywhere else to get it. Then I started to score from him because I knew it helped him out. He's a nice guy. Why shouldn't we be friends? Love thy brother. It is in all the old books.

Yeah. Love thy brother.

Rez said the words and looked at Arash and wondered if he loved him. He sat with the question for a moment and waited to feel an answer. Arash was a good guy. He made Rez feel good, better about himself, about the life around him, about the world he knew and the world he didn't know. Rez liked to be with him, to watch him move from place to place in a single mood, with a single perspective. Maybe not love exactly but he felt something for Arash, something bright, open, possible.

The music had long stopped and the still water of the pool made the quiet dawn even more so.

Time to go.

Let's do it.

They walked around the quiet house and looked for someone to thank but found only sleeping people, in tangles and alone, passed out on couches and beds and floors. Arash put a few nuggets of weed in the key bowl and they walked the hilly streets down back to the car. Rez leaned the passenger seat back and Arash tuned the radio to the BBC. Rez pressed his eyes closed in mock agony.

Dude . . . really . . . what are you? Someone's dad?

It helps me stay awake. You want me to stay awake, don't you?

Rez leaned his head against his shoulder and let the noise of the voices go in and out of his ears . . . *and today, further attacks by a group known as the Islamic State or ISIS or ISIL. Forty-seven killed in Aleppo after serious fighting with Assad-backed militants. In a YouTube video the group has announced their intentions to take over Syria and Iraq in pieces as part of a larger effort to establish a fundamentalist Islamic state in the region. Their trucks, full with devoted jihadis, pulled into Aleppo as the first front, followed by weapons and explosive specialists . . .*

12

SUMMER PASSED FAST and then it was August and they were almost seniors. They filled the last days as best they could, pool parties and backyard BBQs and other activities without consequence. Rez learned to relax in front of mothers and fathers, to listen sincerely to the broken English of old aunts as they talked about *back home* this and *now we are here* that. He said sincere *hello*s and *good-bye*s and *thank you*s and could do it while stoned. He watched Arash spot people for hotel rooms on their trip to Palm Springs and pay for rounds of golf at the country club in Huntington, where they were the only dark-haired people on the green besides the gardeners. His generosity came and came and came. Paying for a cab home for Omid if he got too trashed. Ordering pizzas when everyone was high and desperate. He listened as Arash told his mother everything—skirt around the drugs and girls, but only just—and Ms. Dobani always winked and smiled knowingly at her son before kissing his head and saying, *As long as your grades are good, go, have fun. We didn't move here for you to spend your days in a box.*

Rez tried it. He stopped sleeping in and woke up early to meet his mother in the kitchen and talk to her as she made breakfast. He forced himself over the fear and told her what club he went to the previous night and the fake ID he used and the half-naked girls dancing on platforms. She stayed quiet but stayed open and he went on and talked about Arash and how none of them had girlfriends yet and he didn't have one but wanted to and after a few weeks she began to tell her own stories of afternoons smoking apple tobacco in the cafés in the north of Tehran and long evenings driving in cars with her sisters and boys from their high school class. Rez could barely believe she'd ever been a teenager. Within the month they were talking, back and forth, story to story, every morning as she set out the breakfast and his father joined them and they ate together in one long silence.

By the time school started he was nearly a completely different Rez. The only thing that came back to him from the old life was the waves. He thought about surfing every time he drove on Highway 1, every time he stared at the flat cool vista of the sea from a far hilltop, from the balconies of parties held at houses built into cliffs along the coast. When it got really bad, he texted Matthews and they figured out where the swell was best and went out in the water and waited for waves and smoked and talked and rode.

After one easy session at Thalia Street, he dug around in his bag for something to put on his head and saw the hat he'd borrowed from Arash the night before and slipped it over his sand-crusted hair and waited. It had the words SAND NIGGER arced across the top of it. Matthews stared at him.

Really?

Sure. Why not?

First the white boys and now immigrants? I had no idea you were such a social butterfly.

It's sand niggers for me. All day long.

In tenth grade someone had spray-painted the words on Arash's car. Rumor was it was Jeddidah Paxton, whose uncle was just back from two tours in Iraq with PTSD. Bright orange spray paint and big soft capital letters. *SAND NIGGER.* The school couldn't find anyone to punish so they held an assembly about discrimination, which made no difference because Arash, smart about everything, ordered a series of flat-brimmed baseball caps with an image of a camel on the front, and SAND NIGGER written above it in the same font as the Camel cigarettes, except this camel boldly smoked something else. For a while the hats were a hot commodity and everyone in the school, regardless of where they came from, wanted one.

Matthews's face stayed blank and Rez looked back and challenged his stare.

What?

Nothing.

13

Spring 2013

THE BOMBS WENT off before noon on a Monday and by lunchtime parents swarmed the campus with quick steps and tight eyes. Everyone was confused. There had been explosions before, bombings, public massacres—the Paris subway. Madrid subway. London subway, a kindergarten in Connecticut, a military base in Houston—but they had never canceled school. Except for the first time, in first grade, when the planes crashed the Towers and Rez helped his dad stick American-flag bumper stickers on all their cars.

Rez and Arash went to the student parking lot and sat in the low leather seats of Arash's car and tried to come up with ways to spend their afternoon. Their parents checked in with them and they said everything was fine and that they were going be at the other's house, *studying*, when they knew they were going to just fuck off, play video games at Neema's pool house or go hang out with the girls at the mall. They considered going to Malick's to work out on his fancy exercise equipment or drive up the coast in Omid's new Land Cruiser, just to be in the car on Highway 1, going slow, seeing, being seen. If they had the time, they would drive all the way up to Huntington to hang out with Arash's older cousin Abbas, who made it a point of reminding them Dennis Rodman was his next-door neighbor.

Arash pulled his bag of weed out from under his seat, packed a pipe, and passed it to Rez.

In-N-Out?

Nah.

Hassan's house?

Nope. He's probably still in class. Unless UCI is closed too.

I don't know, man, where do you want to go?

Rez looked up at the clear sky, saw a little wind blow through the palms and oaks, and thought of waves.

How about the cove? I could bring a few boards, call Matthews.
Teach you . . .

Arash inhaled and exhaled and said nothing. Rez had mentioned
the cove once or twice before and this was always Arash's reaction.
Today, as Rez said it and thought about it and knew the apostles were
probably already there—no one wasted a half day like this when there
was surf—it came to him why Arash never agreed, never wanted to go
and check out the waves. Turf. Turf gave Rez the strange fear in his gut
as they drove around Compton, made Matthews say *Be careful*, kept
the Mexicans hanging out with the Mexicans and the Vietnamese with
the Vietnamese and the Indian kids with the other Indian kids. It was
like that in all the grades at all the schools, all over the malls and probably in the brick colleges and glass offices and cookie-cutter homes. All
on their own turf. With their own clans. Just like in some stupid fifties
movie. Turf. Where some people can go and others cannot. Why was
that? What for? Rez understood it in the water, in the way the surfers
raced new guys off the waves so they could have the best for themselves, to secure your own spot, and the chance at glory. It meant something, Rez knew, but he was getting stoned now and Drake was coming
into Rez's head heavy with bass and suggestions of hookups and put-
downs, and he could not think any further, so he let go the tangle of
thoughts and stared out the window as parents of middle schoolers and
freshmen walked across the lacrosse field, arms around the tiny shoulders and enormous backpacks and it all looked so weird to him, cars
and parents and kids leaving at this time of day, the sun directly overhead, no shadows for anyone.

A hand smacked the window of the car and Rez and Arash jolted.
Knuckles rapped the glass. Peter Matthews stood outside, his face red,
tap tap tap. Rez rolled the window down.

Dude, what's your—

It was Boston, the bombing. Kelly's brother was running it, and
now he is at the hospital and the police called his mother to say his legs
are fucked-up and he might die. The news says it looks like a terrorist
attack. Al Qaeda or Taliban or something, they don't know yet and Kelly
is freaking out and shouting about fucking up the first sand nigger he

can find . . . He said you, Rez, you and Arash better watch out, that's what he said . . . A lot of people might be dead, the news said it was bad, like really bad, like body parts in the street bad . . . Kelly keeps saying his brother wouldn't even be in fucking Boston if Arash hadn't taken the test that got him into MIT and all cheaters should go to hell and . . . and . . .

Ok. Ok. Ok. Dude. Ok.

You should go. Get off campus . . .

Ok. Chill out. We're going.

Matthews was still talking, his face puffy with excited eyes, as Rez rolled up his window. In less than a minute they were off campus and up the coast to Newport. They didn't listen to music or talk until Arash finally pulled into an empty movie-theater parking lot because his hands and knees were shaking too much to drive. They looked out separate windows.

This is not good. Not good at all.

Rez sat quietly. His friend's fear was new to him and he felt himself grow nervous—about what, he could not say.

14

THE BROTHERS LEFT bombs, pressure cookers rigged with nails and screws, on the sidewalk along the race route. Brothers from Chechnya. Their parents arrived in Boston when the younger one was only a few years old. *A bad time to move children already traumatized by war,* the expert psychologist explained to the news anchor. *It is common to find radicalization among adolescents and young adults who experience traumatic dislocations in childhood, some abrupt move across continents or cultures that takes the child from a known environment, often multigenerational and multinurturing to an unknown environment where they must rely solely on the nuclear family, with both mother and father suffering their own transitional difficulties . . .*

Three days after the bombing they were tired of going to the pool, to the mall, to the library but they didn't want to go back to school. Arash called Javad who said *cool* and gave them the key code and told his brother to relax, said he remembered Paul and was sad to hear it. He told them not to worry, the anti-Muslim thing would die out. No one knew where Javad lived and they should chill and make some food or go swimming in the roof pool.

Did you tell him about the test? That you took the SAT for Paul?

He knows.

Arash parked seven blocks away from the house and he and Rez walked down one street after another until they were on the thin street that paralleled the beach and Arash punched in the code and a light flashed green and then they were in a big room with black marble floors and the three glass walls that separated them from the sea.

They left their smokes back in the car and out of boredom Rez searched the fridge for a beer and the freezer for some vodka. Arash shook his head.

He doesn't drink. He's practicing.

The flatscreen went on and on and Rez, exhausted by the roll of images, turned away and looked around at the apartment. It was unbelievably clean. All in good taste—the modern furniture, the marble floors, the framed black-and-white photos of L.A. street scenes: taco trucks, dried-up concrete riverbeds, graffiti. Nothing with a human face in it. Rez tried to remember something about Javad, Arash's oldest brother, twenty-eight, a success by anyone's measurements. Stanford graduate. Invented something to do with SIM cards. Sold his first company at twenty-three for an amount unfathomable to all parents, immigrant and white alike. The last time Rez saw him was when he spoke at their homecoming assembly in tenth grade. He was tall, like Arash, with the same narrow Syrian face and the same symmetrical features that made them look like the icons Rez had learned about in school. Javad's hair and eyes were lighter, brown and green, like Arash's mom's, and he wore the relaxed clothes of a man who didn't have to wear suits. At the assembly he had talked about generosity. About his work with orphanages in Afghanistan and Syria and how at the end of the day money could only do so much, at the end of the day you had to give your heart as well. Rez remembered now: vintage Nikes with nice pants and a chill shirt. Dressed up but not ass kisser. He reminded Rez of Kelly Slater, the pro surfer Rez saw once, signing boards at a competition in Huntington, who had the same calm attractiveness, an attitude of belonging wherever he stood.

So they watched TV for one and then two hours and the never-ending news spun accusations and suspicions and eyewitness accounts around and around. At one point Rez heard a noise like a small cough and looked at Arash and saw that he had started to cry.

Man, it feels like I fucking did it. Like I fucking left those bombs. Like whatever happened to Kelly's brother *is* my fault.

These things happen. You didn't do anything wrong.

Then why do I feel like this?

Rez had nothing in his head, nothing in his mouth. He sat quietly beside his sobbing friend. What could he offer? What could he offer Arash to make him stop hating himself?

Come on, A, let's go for a swim.

I'm good.

80

Wanna go back to the car and have a smoke?

Sure.

They walked the seven blocks to the car and smoked with the windows down and smelled the salty air and listened to the waves and then went back and punched in the key code a second time and this time they kept the television off and Rez's phone started ringing with text messages from Kelly telling him *Watch the fuck out* and *Justice will be served* and *Sand niggers will be forced to go home. Start packing . . .* and then a row of emojis: A knife with blood dripping. A pistol. A rifle. A smiley face with a camouflage helmet. Then there were the rumors, texts from Elissa and Sophia and Matthews with news and ideas and questions. *I heard he's dead. Oh my god. They are having a candlelight vigil at the church on Pico tonight. People are saying someone was after Kelly and that is why the bomb was there then . . . What is going on? What if he is dead?!? OMG OMG.*

Who's texting you?

Arash looked at Rez, his smooth long face all eyes, the eyes all worry.

No one, just my mom.

Next to the sliding glass door was a small table with a wooden back-gammon board and they played as the tide came in and the sun dropped and the apartment filled with that gold light you only get at the beach. Rez caught the dice, threw the dice, made his moves, and looked around the house warm with light and design and intention and thought about how he wanted to be, after high school, after college, when his life was his own. Once all he wanted was to play soccer, drafted by a team in the Champions League, live the celebrity-athlete life. Then all he wanted was to surf, to be left alone on one beautiful beach after another, without attachment to family or future, the waves his only challenge. But no matter how he reached for that self, it did not reach back and he grew tired of craving that which did not crave him. Now he sat in this house and saw another kind of life for himself, one in which he would not have to forgo his parents' dreams for him, or forgo the sea. He imag-ined himself made of one part who he was and one part whom he wanted to be. He lost another game of backgammon to Arash and kept his thoughts to himself. The front door opened and Javad walked in. He threw his keys in a bowl, came to stand beside them, and put his hand on his brother's shoulder. For a moment they all looked out the window at the ocean, and Javad shook his head in what seemed like appreciation.

Beautiful sunset. Another day passed. Khodarashokr. Praise be to Allah.

15

EVENTS. EVENTS IN response to other events. Think about it. Nothing since the big bang has happened without a reason. And even the big bang might have come from something, because of something. One thing makes another thing, and then that thing makes the next thing. Look at these kids. These two brothers, still kids. They don't know themselves yet. They are acting in response, in reaction, passionate reaction to something that set them off, made them commit to violence. They would not be here if the United States had not invaded Iraq in 2003. The United States would not have had the fertile ground for the lie it told about Iraq, weapons of mass destruction, Saddam Hussein, etc., etc., if not for Osama bin Laden and 9/11. Osama bin Laden would not have been able to recruit those men to learn how to fly planes and then crash them into buildings if not for propaganda about the persecution of the global Muslims, Afghanistan after the Russian invasion, Chechnya in the nineties, Bosnian genocides, or any instance of Islam under attack by the West, one culture trying to extinguish another. History is always a story of cause and effect. Those kids—

Javad pointed to the flatscreen that lit up the otherwise dark house where their lives were shown in photos of the brothers as children, in elementary school, on high school field trips, their faces sometimes caught off guard by the camera, sometimes silly and sometimes sad, attractive, dark eyed.

—are just dominoes, knocked down by all the dominoes before them, and today, they have knocked down the dominoes after them whether it is another inspired bomber, another fanatical anti-Islam party in Europe, some war or death, who knows? Only time will tell us.

Javad sat back on the couch and thumbed at his string of beads and Rez sat beside him, a half-eaten piece of pizza on his lap. Rez had never heard anyone talk like that. Javad spoke as if he understood all of time and all of history and all of the facts and the way they connected and made a web that caught everything. That night Rez watched him as he walked about his well-designed house, parsed the events on the screen, ordered pizza for Rez and Japanese takeout for himself, watered his orchids, entertained the friends who stopped by—nicely dressed men in their early thirties who took off their shoes and embraced their host with an Alhamdullilah—all the while calming Arash with brotherly pats on the back and encouragements to *relax, relax.* The night went on and the house grew quiet and eventually Arash took a sleeping pill and went to the upstairs bedroom. Javad left the television on and turned off all the other lights and they sat with the flickering light and Rez wished he could see the ocean behind the television but there was only darkness and glass.

Why did he take those tests for Paul Kelly?

I dunno. Money maybe.

Arash has money. As much as he wants. Our parents give us generous allowances.

I dunno then. Maybe he wanted . . .

Kelly to like him?

Javad finished the answer and Rez nodded and tried to listen for the sound of the ocean outside, waited for it to enter his ears and calm him with its soothing crash and hush, but he couldn't concentrate enough. Javad made him nervous and Rez had to consider him, this brother, all-knowing, only ten years older than they were, but complete somehow, finished and whole and wise.

What's the brother's name, the one who's trying to kick his ass?

John.

Is he for real?

Rez thought about Kelly and his hunting trips, the guns and the deer hung upside down to drain its blood. The knife he took to Mexico. The family photos and the father in the military uniform.

I dunno. He's probably really angry now. Their family is really tight.

Javad leaned back on the leather couch and put his socked feet up on the coffee table.

Our family is really tight too.

They heard a noise from upstairs. A groan and then a cough and what Rez thought was a small sob. Then it was quiet again. Javad looked at Rez in the half light.

Why aren't you scared?

I didn't do anything. And John Kelly is a dick anyway. Has been for a long time. Maybe I am used to it.

Javad looked at Rez. Rez let him.

What is your family name? Your last name?

Courdee.

You Kurdish?

Nope. American. Born here.

Yes, but your father or maybe your mother, they immigrated.

A long time ago. Before I was born. So I could be born here.

Javad turned off the television and used an app on his phone to turn on the lights. They came on dimly, just enough to shake the edges off the dark.

We are all from somewhere. Like I said before. Events. These next few years are going to be interesting for our part of the world. In many ways I wish I could go back to be there and see the changes, be a part of this big history that is happening. Eighty years ago the Europeans came in and drew all the borders, now the tribes are redrawing them. Interesting times . . . it would be nice to see it for myself, tell my sons one day, *I was there. I saw the reclaiming with my own two eyes . . .*

Upstairs Arash's phone rang and rang. There were some muffled words and then Rez heard Arash's flip-flops slap down the stairs.

Dude, let's go. My mom wants me to come home.

Rez stood up from the couch and walked to the door, where he waited for Javad and Arash to say good-bye first with an embrace and then kisses on both cheeks. Javad came toward Rez and opened both arms. Rez took a step back and put out his hand.

Thanks.

Not a problem. You are welcome anytime. Watch out for my brother.

Will do.

*

On the drive home Arash put on an old Tupac album and they listened to him talk about dying for causes, loving his mama, failures and bitter success. Highway 1 was empty. On either side of them the shops and houses and parks were dark and even the palm trees and bougainvillea bushes had turned off their color and held still in the night.

Your brother's weird.

Why do you say that?

He's just serious, you know. Like really serious and smart.

The music played and they stopped at a light near the beach volleyball courts. A bearded man with wild white hair sat on a bench beside a neat stack of blankets and bags. He held a big-chested dog on a leash and together they looked out at the sea.

He's practicing. He got serious about it in college.

That's crazy.

What's crazy about it?

When Rez got home, the kitchen lights were on but the house was quiet. He saw the television flash and his father, leaned back in the recliner, asleep. Rez went in and turned off the images of the bombing, the faces of victims, the scroll of the death count and stock market openings in Frankfurt and London, and the room went silent. His father did not stir and Rez stared at the sleeping man. Sal Courdee. Head scientist for the Merck labs. MBA from UCLA in pharmaceutical patents. Homeowner. Husband. Father. Juror. Fan of comedies. Rez kept looking. If he stared long enough, could he see Saladin Courdee, fourth of twelve children from a small village in the mountains of Iran? The man who fled a massacre, or so Rez's mother told him once, who came from a line of Kurdish fighters but wanted to be a movie star. Rez looked and saw only an old man, handsome still, but tired, gravity pulling down the flesh on his face. *I am an American. Whatever happened before was before. A long time ago. Those things don't matter now.* His father's face, soft with sleep, said none of those things now but Rez heard their echoes in the silence of the room. He looked a moment longer and searched for himself in the face, for the fathers before and maybe even the sons and grandsons to come and found only a singular old man. Rez shook his head to break the trance and then exhaustion flooded in, the night behind him now, part dream, part delirium, and he walked to his bedroom and let go into a wide blank sleep.

The next morning his mother drove him to school and they listened to the news and she cried. Three dead—an eight-year-old boy among them—and 264 injured, many single and double amputees. Rez waited impatiently at the stoplights and intersections and counted the corners until they were at the school, where he hopped quickly out of the car to get away from the sounds of her, of the news, of this new reality that gripped them all.

Be careful, Reza joon.

Bye.

Students were everywhere, waiting for the assembly to begin. Rez walked down halls that now felt like tunnels of stares and whispers. He kept his gaze fixed on his shoes until he got to the auditorium and looked for Arash but only found Omid and Yuri at the top of the bleachers. They sat staring at their phones until the headmaster stood up and the students and teachers and staff got quiet and announced that Paul Kelly had just undergone a double leg amputation and was in critical to stable condition, but alive. The auditorium erupted with claps and cheers and Rez saw a lot of the senior girls cry and hug, and some of the teachers do the same. Inside his chest, his breath coiled tightly and he coughed to get air, to open up the pressure that began to wrap around his lungs and heart. The headmaster went on. He spoke now with a gravitas that no one, not the teachers or students, thought him capable of and the audience sat rapt as he carefully dispelled one rumor after another and explained that the chances of Paul's survival were very good and that the family requested privacy during this period and that John Kelly appreciated the calls and messages and hoped to be back at school soon.

It is your friendship that he is coming back to, the headmaster went on. The warm open arms of this school and this community of classmates. Please let us take these next few days to practice and prepare our best selves so to welcome John and his family back from these trying times.

The headmaster went on and on to explain classes were canceled for the day and students and faculty were to break up into small groups to focus on grief management and healing. Students were required to attend workshops on culture and conflict and engage in a variety of discussions aimed at *bringing together our diverse student body in under-standing and compassion.*

Yeah, right, Yuri muttered under his breath. It's gonna get real now.

The headmaster continued in his sincere and hopeful tone.

We must not let these events fracture or divide our community.

Events. That was the word Javad used last night, Rez remembered, Javad's voice calm, the glass house with the ocean just outside. *Events come from the events before them.* Rez thought about the event of the assembly, the event of a man without legs, the event of no John Kelly, the event of no Arash, and wondered what events followed those.

Two days later Arash came back to school, his easy smile gone, dark bags under his eyes. Kelly stayed gone but his crew, Johnson and the rest, did their best to represent, slamming lockers when Rez and Arash walked down the hallway. The crew would wait for the bang to catch everybody's attention and then pretend to cough or sneeze and shout *towelhead, asshole,* or *terrorist* under their breath. Rez and Arash said nothing, did nothing, kept to themselves and their crew, away from games and parties and girls. The girls were the worst for Rez; girls he had known and liked since sixth grade barely made eye contact now, and when they did, their faces were masks of anger or terror. He tried to do as he had done before, keep things normal, sit at the front of class, answer the questions only when no one else could, get high at lunch in Arash's car, and wait for it to pass. There were moments, with Arash, when things got all right, and the two of them talked about music or classes or teachers or weed like nothing happened. One time Rez got to the car late and saw a girl in the passenger seat, where he usually sat, laughing with Arash. He looked through the windshield to make sure

Arash was actually laughing and he was, the big white smile gleaming through the glare.

What's up?

Not much.

Arash passed the joint to the backseat to Rez.

Fatima is making me remember the Eid party when we put tooth-paste on the toilet seat and sat outside the bathroom and listened to people freak out. Not nice . . .

But fuuuun. Come on, we were only eight.

Fatima sang the word and then laughed.

Rez knew who she was, but didn't actually know her. He had seen her a million times; she was the same grade and smart and at the edges of Arash's parties, always alone, always on her phone until the party got big and loud and people got lit and then she'd step in and dance and hang with the rest of them. Rez recognized her as hot, her face a pale white circle in the center of an orbit of black curls, the body beneath it petite, bony and fleshy in all the right places, and yet he'd never given it more thought or flirted with her because she was otherwise so cold. Now here she was, sexy and talky and not afraid, rolling the next joint and thinking out loud in that way some people did when they were stoned, her thoughts slicing at him like blades.

This must be really weird for you, Rez. It is Rez, right, not Reza? I remember in middle school it was Reza and then you changed it. Anyway. This must be such a strange time for you. Weren't you, like, close to these guys? Friends with all of them? You and Kelly used to hang out, surf, do all that American-white-boy shit. Didn't you even go to Mexico once? I remember hearing something about a car getting jacked, or something . . . I am guessing you and Peter, James, and John don't chill anymore. Sometimes you just have to pick a side . . .

Rez looked out the window. It was April and the spring rains and swells had come and gone, filling the breaks with surfers and turning the valley and the hillsides green again.

. . . It doesn't seem like you really know, but Arash says you are cool, then you are cool, right, habibi?

She stuck her head in between the two front seats and Rez smelled the scent of her shampoo, something musky and deep, and the smoke on her breath fresh and grassy, and however much he had turned off to her, stopped listening, tried to ignore her presence in the car and the truth in her questions, his whole body turned on at her closeness. He stared out the window and tried not to see or smell or want her.

On the other hand, Arash thinks everyone's cool. That is why we love him.

She slid back into the seat and Rez heard the sound of a compact opening, then closing, and things being tossed into a purse and a door opening.

See you guys tomorrow, same time, same place.

The door closed and they watched her walk across the parking lot, pulled-up knee socks, blazer, plaid skirt, long thin legs coming out from underneath—her curly black hair bouncing on her shoulders and down her back with a life all its own—Rez felt himself warm, and he shifted in his seat, and looked past her to the dozens of girls in the same blazers and plaid skirts, and the warmth went away. Arash remained still, silent, unmoved.

Dude, A, how long have you had to listen to her?

Our families have been friends since we were babies. There are picture of us naked in bathtubs together. That kind of thing.

Oh, Rez teased, *that* kind of thing.

Arash did not smile. He opened his door and stepped out and Rez did the same and they entered into the stream of students heading out of smoke-filled cars, music-filled cars, food- and makeup-filled cars, gossip- and sex- or almost-sex-filled cars, walking through the parking lot to the sterile halls. A few spaces away Matthews and Johnson tumbled out of Matthews's truck, coughing and laughing, and slung their backpacks over their shoulders. Matthews saw Rez and nodded and Rez nodded back and the afternoon went on, sleepy classrooms, loud bells, notes, and daydreams.

The first day John Kelly came to class Arash left after second period with a note from the school nurse about a migraine. Rez watched as teachers and students and coaches and even Enrique, the high school janitor, came up to offer John their hands and hugs and sad eyes. Brittany Foster, a girl who missed her entire junior year to model in Europe, walked the halls holding Kelly by the hand, playing with his hair, leaning against him whenever he stood still. Normally this amount of personal physical contact got you a demerit, but no one said anything. Rez passed him in the halls a few times that week and Kelly paid him no attention, made no effort to catch his eye or say a bad thing in his direction. That afternoon Rez texted Arash and said things were cool and the school was chill and if he wanted to come tomorrow, Rez thought it was a good idea. Arash came back and there were a few more teachers keeping their eyes on the hallways between class and a quieter atmosphere in the locker room after gym, but otherwise it was just another day.

And for the next week the days went like days. Class, break, lunch, parking lot, Fatima talking and talking, class, break, study hall, soccer practice, home, dinner, sleep. By Friday Arash relaxed. No one had spray-painted his car. No one had slashed his tires. Kelly hadn't said anything to him and no one had said anything to Kelly. At some point Arash and Kelly even sat near each other in physics lab and Arash leaned over and said he was sorry about what had happened and if there was anything he could do and Rez braced himself for the cold brush, the punch, something, but nothing came and Kelly muttered, *It's cool,* but didn't take his eyes off the board. During Friday's eighth-period study hall Arash and Fatima checked their phones for parties or clubs to go to and Rez sat beside them in the shade of the founder's grove and loved that he had friends, that it was Friday and he was a senior with summer in front of him with nothing on top of it or below it. Just summer and smoking and swimming until it was time to sit in a classroom in Berkeley and learn and learn and learn until he was deemed smart and grown, and what could be better than that?

My friend's sister is throwing a party in Hollywood. Rich kids from Mumbai.

Could be fun.

O'Neil's is always good on a Friday.

91

I am not hanging out with old white fishermen.

And on and on, nothing of consequence, nothing at stake, just a night ahead, to do with as they wished. Rez plucked pieces of grass out of the lawn, and when the loud voice of the school secretary shouted through the PA and over the quad, he flinched, it was so aggressive, so unexpected.

Could Arash Dobani please come to the main office. Arash to the main office.

Arash looked up from his phone and his face went pale. He stood up from the grass and pushed out the creases in his khakis. From across the lawn Kelly and Johnson started to laugh quietly to themselves. Rez stood up beside Arash.

I'll walk with you.

Fatima stood.

Me too.

As they passed the apostles, Johnson called over loud and taunting, That's right. A Rash. Could we get *A Rash* in the office please? Rez, could you tell your friend a rash the principal needs to see him.

Rez turned in their direction and felt himself solidify, with a hard body and a hard mind and hard eyes. If there was going to be a fight, he felt himself brace to give and to take, a kind of fuck it—physical, of the body and will—he had not experienced before. A sudden necessity to right something with force of flesh. Arash held his forearm.

Dude. Leave it.

Before the period was over Arash had been expelled. The charges— cheating, use of false identification, and forging a state-mandated test—were leveled with evidence from the Kelly family. They showed Arash the closed-circuit camera footage of him going in, showing the Paul Kelly ID, and sitting to take his SAT exam. Arash was in ninth grade, Paul in eleventh, and the test monitor had barely looked at the driver's license that Arash presented before turning on the computer in front of Arash and saying, *Good luck, Paul.* Arash was told to empty his locker and made to stand, with the school guard, as they searched the contents. They escorted him to his car and forced him to sit in the passenger seat until the car was off campus property, and only then did the guard give him the key. Rez and Fatima watched from the parking lot as the car made a right turn onto PCH, no blinker, moving at far below the speed limit.

That is so fucked-up.

Rez saw his friend drive away and two thoughts punched each other in his brain. *But they are right, but they are wrong. They are wrong. This is wrong. But cheating is wrong. Arash is not wrong.* Until they exhausted themselves and turned into a long-repeating question. *What is wrong? What is wrong here?*

Beside him Fatima kept spitting out short, angry sentences, her voice getting weaker and weaker with each one.

This is so fucked-up. His life is fucked now. His parents are going to freak out. He doesn't deserve this. Paul *asked* him to do it. *Paid* him.

Fatima's face was tense, pulled at the edges, on the verge of cracking open.

You know those guys. Can you please tell me what the hell is going on?

Her wide black eyes were glossy and the smooth surface of her cheeks turned pink and then red. Rez had no words for her, nothing for the kids who shuffled past them and whispered *Oh, shit* and *Where'd he go?*, nothing for his parents later that night as they sat in shock around the dinner table unable to untangle the wrong from the right. Rez shook his head back and forth at Fatima and turned away from her and walked to the edge of the campus and then down PCH to the bus stop to be alone and think about events and the way they led to other events and the events that followed after those.

16

FATIMA LIVED IN an eight-bedroom mansion on the high cliffs above Dana Point. Her father dealt some sort of commodity from an office in Irvine. Every morning at dawn a driver picked him up in a limousine with tinted windows, and after midnight the same car and driver brought him back. Between those hours the house hummed like a train station. Fatima, the youngest of three sisters, one in university in Paris, the other in Damascus, was the last child left. The mother's family filled the house. When Rez and Fatima arrived at the door, her grandmother greeted them with a gold-and-alabaster grin and cupped their faces and waited for a kiss. Rez didn't do it at first, unsure whether he was supposed to touch the old woman in her copious black robes, but then Fatima tilted her chin at him and he kissed the thin skin of the old lady's cheek and just like that she called him habibi and moved aside to let him in. Beyond the grandmother was an enormous living room with floor-to-ceiling windows that looked over the cliffs and the ocean. The television spread out like a tapestry across a wall and was only and always on one of two stations, the Home Shopping Network or Al Jazeera. If it was on HSN, then the room was full of women, aunts and cousins, who sat with tea and telephones and ordered whatever struck their fancy. If it was the latter, the room was full of men with tea and telephones who texted people not in the room, not in the country, and spoke little to one another. The men and women came and went separately, peacefully, taking turns with the room and leaving the children and the old people to themselves. Fatima's mother stayed in the kitchen all day and looked over the work of the two Salvadorean cooks while she talked on the phone. Ellie is what everyone called her but Rez called her Mrs. Hassani and she never hung up the phone when he walked in, just nodded at them and then looked back at the cooks and the ledgers in front of her, everything, the talk, the type, in Arabic. She wore colorful silk headscarves, Hermès or Gucci, pulled back just enough to show her golden hair. Rez wondered why she bothered. She took Fatima's kisses on one cheek and then another and winked at Rez, and when it was time, it was her voice that called *Ok!* in a thick accent that brought everyone together in the dining room to eat and smoke and speak to one another in a language Rez didn't understand. He watched Fatima smile and laugh and listened to her speak in Arabic. She turned to him.

This is how we live. Clan-style.

And made sure to remind everyone who asked that, yes, this was her chemistry tutor and if she planned to pass the AP exam and skip her first year of science in college then she needed to study. *Ok, ok, you know best, habibi,* they all said, and Rez looked back at them and tried to seem honorable, tried to sit and eat like he was intelligent.

They never even opened their books. She had an A- in chemistry, out of laziness more than anything, and after the first awkward session when they spent most of their time on her bed, watching TV, talking about Arash, arguing about this and that, accidentally brushing body parts against each other until the electrical currents in the room fused mouth to mouth and crotch to crotch, and chemistry was never even discussed. They fucked and then went to the balcony attached to her room and smoked and looked over the ocean and the small green-yellow sliver of Laguna Niguel canyon, where coyotes could be seen if the moon was full enough. After the first time they didn't watch television and stayed off the Web and seemed content to press themselves together with a heat born of their deception and then to peel apart and fall asleep or do some other homework or play games on their phones. She always drove him home before eight and his parents left him alone to ride the high and he'd sleep and dream about waves, or mountains from landscapes he had yet to see.

The next day Rez would meet her at lunch, in the parking lot, and go to classes, where they sat together and answered no questions and refused to socialize with anyone who thought what happened to Arash was fair or just. Their silent protest caught no one's attention but it made for loud sessions of sex in the back of her Lexus SUV. Rez thought about her, her thin body, the black hairs against the pale skin of her arms and thighs, her crazy hair, and wanted her all day long, but kept it to himself until they were naked and together again to fight it all out by fucking with a quiet vengeance.

They tried to visit Arash every afternoon but only made it three or four times a week once he moved up the coast to live at his brother's house on the beach. They'd show up with bags of burgers and half-melted milk shakes and Arash opened the door with his hair messed up and his eyes zoned out from too much sleep or too much TV. The TV was always on. Al Jazeera. BBC. CNN. Anything as long as it was news. If the room didn't have a TV, then the radio was on, tuned to an all-hours news station. The end-of-the-world tone in all the voices of the hourly broadcast annoyed Rez and he waited for the ten or twenty minutes it took for Arash to get distracted by the food or Fatima and then Rez would mute the TV and turn down the radio and Arash always caught him and said, *Hey, man, I was listening to that.*

If the food and the company cheered Arash up enough, Rez could convince him to go to the beach and the three of them threw towels over their shoulders and walked the ten steps off Javad's porch and onto the sand, where they dropped their towels and went into the water. In the water everything was good again. Rez floated and swam around Fatima, who walked in hip-deep water and dragged her fingers behind her. He kept sight of her long back and the way her wet black curls snaked down it. If she turned around and caught him staring, he grew shy and tried to look away before she smiled, the white of her teeth glinting bright like the light off the water. Arash came and went, floated and kicked and splashed and dared Rez to race him in the butterfly or backstroke, strokes neither of them knew how to do, and the circus of their bodies flailing around the shallows broke the tension every time.

They dried out on the warm sand and Rez dug in his feet and watched the seagulls and rolled a jay. Groups of girls, in their twenties or younger, in high school and middle school, walked by in bikinis and every time Arash averted his eyes. Rez watched him to make sure and each time was the same. This is not what Arash had done at pool parties or on rooftops in Vegas last summer, he gazed as long as the rest of them at an ass, at tits, a waist and hips. Rez offered him a hit and Arash shook his head back and forth.

Nah, man. I am taking a break.

Really? This is the Cush you were always so excited about, Omid got some from his brother. I can get you—

No thanks. I'm good.

Fatima held it between her fingers and took a long pull as if it were a cigarette. After a few minutes it always made her pee and Rez waited to watch her stand and shake the sand off her thighs and ass and walk back to the house, her hips swaying side to side from the uneven footsteps in the sand. Her hair, almost dry now, flew up and over her head in the wind, black coils raging all around her, and Rez kept a hard and steady gaze until Arash said something.

Looks like you two are hanging pretty hard these days.

Arash smiled, slightly, more than he had in weeks.

Yeah. She's cool. It's easy.

I'm glad. I should have guessed she was your speed.

Rez thought about that. Speed? She smoked, she was smart, she had a fast tongue that didn't let anyone get away with anything. Still, the word didn't sit well with him and he stared at the ocean where a few sets of waves crashed in front of them.

Fatima and I are going out tonight. That chick Emma is going to be there. The French exchange student, the one you sat beside in physics. Wanna come with?

Arash picked up fistfuls of sand, held them up, and let it drain through his closed fingers. His profile was as it always was for Rez: straight lines, perfect alignment, no contradiction, no clash.

Thanks. I am going to stay in. Javad is coming home early. It is Friday.

Ok. But there is nothing a little pussy won't—

In an instant Rez felt stupid saying it, it sounded like an old man's word, a word from old rap songs, and before he could finish his tease, Arash interrupted him.

Everything is not about sex. It's not good to think like that. These are our sisters. We have to respect them.

Arash kept his eyes on the horizon in front of them and Rez saw the profile align and set.

And women have to respect themselves too.

The words were sour. The expression was sour. All of it was not Arash, was not normal. Rez held his hands up and moved his torso back.

Wait a minute. What? I am sorry about what happened, but you need to figure out a way to chill out, if it's not girls or herb, then something . . .

Rez watched Fatima's lanky figure walk toward them from the house. Rez nearly got hard just watching her, the long white body in the one-piece with cutouts along the sides and back, the red lips that she never painted and the big black eyes. The turn-on made him feel bad for Arash but Rez was still pissed at him too, for being so sour, for being so serious, for not being nice-guy Arash. Rez stood up and grabbed his towel and flip-flops.

Come on, Fatima, we've got to go. I forgot I had soccer drills this afternoon.

What are you talking about? It's Friday . . .

I forgot. Special spring practice.

Fatima looked at Rez and he looked away from her, one glance and she'd know something was up. She probably knew anyway. She bent down and looked at Arash.

You ok, habibi?

Yeah. I'm good.

Her face warmed and opened toward Arash and she threw a cotton dress over her swimsuit and grabbed her bag and towel off the sand. As they were walking up the steps back to the car, she said nothing and he said nothing until the engine started and the windows were down.

What crawled up your ass and died?

Dude, Arash is going a little kooksters. You should have heard what he said when you were in the bathroom. And what is it with the news, and Syria and all that shit? Do you think his brother is brainwashing him? Is he going to start doing the prayer push-ups now?

She drove and said nothing, did nothing to break open the tension with an answer, one of the soft chatty explanations she had when she told him things that had never crossed his mind.

You've never been back, have you?

Back where?

To where your parents are from.

Oh, come on . . .

Wait, I forgot. That's right. You are *American.* Just a regular American.

She pushed the engine harder and the car sped up.

Please. Give me a break. You are kidding yourself if you really believe that. You can only be American if you turn into one. Which means a new name, a new nose, new skin, new tongue, new everything. Otherwise you are an immigrant, or the child of an immigrant, and this is not your home.

Now the car was going so fast down Highway 1 that the traffic next to them seemed asleep or drowsy as they passed, the drivers staring ahead into the dimness of their sunglasses, necks craned forward. Rez looked out at the streets and the ocean beyond them, a view he had been looking at all his life. He had spent every one of his days on this strip of land next to the sea; it was beautiful and it was home and he hated Fatima for her question, for thinking anything but what he knew was true. They passed the Jack in the Box in Laguna where he and Matthews sat in the drive-through at six A.M. waiting for it to open so they could have something in their stomachs before they surfed. The lady who took their order was always in a good mood. Always greeted them with Buenos dias, guapos.

Give me a break. You, Arash, all your shit. Whatever. You'll never be American because you can't stop being something else. Next thing I know you'll come back from freshman year all covered up like your mom.

And then it was out of his mouth and he couldn't take it back. The words smashed around the car like a trapped bird and Fatima drove even faster. She stared at the road and kept both hands on the wheel and Rez wished she would at least turn to him and see that he was sorry.

She stopped in front of his house and he got out without looking at her or touching her neck or saying good-bye. Later that night he got a text.

What you said about my mom was rude. Check yourself.

Rez wrote out an apology, probably the longest text he'd ever written, then erased it and turned off his phone. He felt bad and went to the living room and watched television with his dad, an old movie, black-and-white, with corny jokes and corny acting.

I used to watch this movie when I was a boy. I must have seen every screening at the tiny theater in our town. I couldn't even imagine it—the men and woman, talking together, going to dinner in fancy restaurants. Everyone with a car. Unbelievable to me as a boy . . .

His father trailed off and Rez didn't hear anything. He thought about Fatima and felt shitty that he had said something so rude. He wasn't a rude person. Even when he hung out with the apostles and they wanted him to be rude and it was cool to be a dick and make fun of other kids, Rez couldn't do it. And now he had, and he'd meant it in the moment and didn't want to mean it ever again. There was no reason to be that way. He wanted to be a better person. A right person. A person in line with the good and the true. A person whose heart would never let him say a hard word about a mother or a friend.

At dinner he watched his mother set down the plates, pick up the plates, wash the plates, in the same gestures she had done all his life. They ate in silence and he thought about Arash's house and Fatima's house and how noisy they were with guests and talk and laughing. It was never like that at his house. Rez's father did not like to entertain and Rez's mother was not allowed to have her own friends. When the family sat together at the table, they did not talk beyond the necessities of the day.

At the end of dinner Rez followed his mother to the kitchen and stood as she cleaned. He wanted to help, her small frame thinner and thinner every year, the lines of exhaustion, once temporary, now permanent, across her face, but he just stood there, and said, Thanks for dinner, and went to his room. He wrote out a simple text to Fatima: *I am sorry. It wasn't right. What I said about your mom.* After fifteen minutes he got a text back: *It's ok.* He put his phone away and thought of Fatima, her face and the swirls of hair, the puffy lips and wide eyes with their gaze that pulled him to her regardless of where they were, or when. He jacked off and then fell asleep, his whole body soft, expansive, open to whatever came next.

17

THEY PADDLED OUT until it was calm and straddled their boards. No one was in the water, it was the middle of the afternoon on a Wednesday, and the seniors, less than a quarter away from graduation, got half days on Wednesdays because all the acceptances had come in and no one could concentrate anyway. Rez usually went up to see Arash, but Fatima was having her wisdom teeth removed and he didn't want to be alone so he texted Matthews: *Surfy?* Matthews texted back: *You suck. Long boards at old mans?* They spent twenty minutes in Matthews's garage looking through his dad's boards and then twenty minutes in the parking lot at the beach, listening to Queen and getting high. By the time they made the water they realized there was absolutely zero swell, but they didn't care. It was a warm day for spring and their suits fit snug and the sunlight twinkled on top of the water like diamonds.

Maybe we'll see a dolphin.

Maybe you'll turn into a princess.

Rez was so happy to be kidding again, to be joking and laughing and shooting the shit. Matthews paddled his feet around and around until he was rotating in slow circles and Rez whispered, Faster, faster.

The horizon did not change. Nothing came in and they goofed off and caught some whitewash and then paddled back and fucked around some more.

UC Berkeley, not bad. Not as good as USC.

Ah, yes, but my dad isn't on the alumni board. Ahchoo! Nepotism! Rez teased his friend, who laughed. You see, when you get a full ride you don't need someone to chaperone you in.

Matthews shook the water from his hair until he looked like a porcupine.

True that. It's all bullshit in the end. Four years of partying before the real school starts. And it's good you are going up north. I can drive up, hang out in the Bay, surf Mavericks, meet some nerdy girls.

Totally. Where is Kelly going?

Air Force Academy.

No shit.

Shit.

Rez kicked his feet in the water and wished for a wave but every-thing around was flat. Matthews lay down on his stomach and tilted his head toward Rez.

Is Arash ok?

Yeah. He's ok.

Not going to Stanford?

They withdrew their acceptance. It's standard if someone is accused of cheating.

So what's he gonna do?

Don't know. He listens to the news a lot. And he doesn't puff anymore. And he's going to the mosque with his brother, says it chills him out.

That's weird.

Show some respect, dude. You wouldn't say that if he were going to church.

Maybe I would.

Maybe you would. Everything is weird for a dweeb.

Rez splashed at Matthews with the flat of his hand and Matthews feigned a clumsy fall off his board into the water in a jokey display.

They ate at a taqueria in San Clemente and ordered everything a twenty would pay for, including beer, because the lady behind the counter never carded, even if they did look like unwashed children who had just crawled out of the sea. Rez loved this feeling more than all other feelings, the sand in his hair, the salt still on his skin, the great wash of waves still in his ears. Only the feeling after sex was just as good.

What's up with you and Fatty?

Don't call her that.

She let everyone call her that in middle school. She was so skinny, it was a joke.

Careful, hombre.

All right, all right. Fa. Ti. Ma. You guys serious?

Just hanging.

I always liked her. She was in my ninth-grade English class. Didn't let anyone get away with anything. And then her hair.

Yeah. There is the hair.

Like Beyoncé.

Yup. Like Beyoncé. It's fun.

Everything is all fun from here on out. Senior summer, buddy.

Rez looked at his friend Matthews, who chewed and then downed his beer in clumsy gulps and sighed the sigh of a glad dog, and Rez could not help but love him in that moment. His love was open and flat like the sea had been that day and he thought how strange that their lives should be like this, happy and chill and of such little consequence. Senior summer and all the ease that stretched out beyond it and how could someone take to it like Peter, without a worry, and someone could be like Arash, a ball of nerves, quiet and angry and torn? How is that? Rez lifted his beer to his mouth and drank the two thirds that was left and felt a sudden wild satisfaction, gold and effervescent.

18

THE ROOM SMELLED like shoes. Shoes and feet and men. Rez breathed through his mouth and then after a while he'd forget and breathe normal and in a second the stench filled his whole face and head and he thought he was going to puke. Arash didn't seem to notice, and if he did, it wasn't a thing. It was part of the whole thing, this dank man smell. Rez slipped off his flip-flops and pushed them up against the wall with the other shoes. Did the woman's side smell as bad? His mother's feet didn't smell, and Fatima's feet, the painted toenails with little gemstones, could not smell, it was impossible. And with just the memory of them they were in his mouth, like yesterday, round and slippery and clean, her legs stretched up to his face. He stared at the pile of shoes, inhaled a few times through his mouth, and went and stood beside Arash in line.

The line was long and slow and Rez looked around to keep himself entertained, to keep himself quiet, to keep from saying anything mean or pissy or rude. True, he didn't want to be here, but also true that he was here and knew it was no big deal, just a few hours and then done. Whatev. Ahead of them men bowed and stooped to wash their hands and forearms and elbows. Rez saw them lift the water to the back of their necks, across their faces and temples, into and out of their mouths with forceful spits. They cupped the water and breathed it into their noses and then blew, one nostril and then the other, quick and violent.

Arash stood close. Rez felt Arash's eyes on him.

You know you don't have to do all that.

Yeah. No. It's cool. I was just checking it out.

You only have to wash your hands. Three times. And your face. You took a shower this morning, right?

Yes indeedy.

He had done all Arash asked. Taken a shower. Kept off the smoke for the morning. Didn't fuck. Didn't have Bloody Marys with Fatima when she picked him up for brunch. He wore khaki pants and a button-down shirt. Skipped a whole Friday at school. He could wash his hands three times if it meant that the thing would be closer to over and they could go to the beach, light a joint, and chill. Arash seemed pleased.

And your intentions, you got them straight?

I do.

Rez lied to his friend. It was not a word in his everyday life. *Intentions.* And the last time he heard it was in a yoga class Sophia dragged him to in eleventh grade. The yoga teacher said it once—*Now before we start, let us all take a moment to set an intention for your practice*—and Rez was so stoned and the room so hot that the teacher transformed from yoga instructor into an isolated voice that butterflied its way around the room, into his ears, and down his throat, void of all literal meaning. At the end of that class she asked them all to hum a long hum—*Now remember your intentions*—and he still had no idea what she was talking about but opened his mouth anyway and let out the same note that vibrated with all of the other notes in the room.

Arash slapped Rez's shoulder a few times with his palm.

Awesome, man. That's awesome. I knew you could do this.

Rez wanted to remind Arash what awesome was. Awesome was what they did on this day last year when they rented out Sloop, the whole restaurant, in Newport and danced until three in the morning and sang "Happy Birthday" every time they smoked a joint or did a line. *That* was awesome. This was just weird. Rez held his friend by the arm and gave him a friendly squeeze. The worse he felt, the better he lied.

Good, man. I am glad you're happy. It's your birthday, you should be happy.

Rez couldn't figure out why he couldn't just let it go. This is what Arash wanted. When Fatima asked him what they could do for his birthday this year, Arash shook his head no to every suggestion. No to the weekend at Joshua Tree with a night in Palm Springs. No to the barhopping in the Dana Point harbor. No to all of it, Arash dropping his head lower and lower with each suggestion.

So what do you want?

My birthday is Friday. I go to mosque on Fridays. I want you guys to come with.

They agreed as if it were nothing, and Fatima borrowed a silk scarf from her mother and they followed his rules, and now, in the preparation room that led to the prayer room, Rez was antsy, his every thought annoyed. But he kept it together and stood beside his friend as they shuffled forward toward the sinks and Arash received the hugs and kisses of men, young and old, who came up to him and said the same words over and over, their faces solemn with happiness.

As-salaam alaikum.

Wa-alaikum salaam.

Today is a great day, brother.

Yes, brother. A great day.

Rez wanted to make a joke about the hugging and kissing, but left it. *Be good,* he heard Fatima remind him as they'd split up into different washrooms and shoe rooms. *This is an experience with someone's beliefs.* One joke was not going to hurt anyone.

Hey, A, how do all these dudes know it's your birthday? Was there some sort of mosque e-mail?

Arash did not laugh. He looked ahead at the sinks and the washing men.

Everyone always greets each other that way. And today there is a guest imam. He is leading the prayer. We are lucky to have him here.

Then it was their turn and Rez watched Arash and copied him and did almost all the same washing that he did except for the nose part and then they dried their hands on clean damp towels and walked toward the entrance to the prayer room, a large doorway closed off by a thick burgundy curtain. Rez took a deep inhale through his mouth and sighed.

May the force be with you.

Arash stopped.

Are you nervous about something?

No. Why?

Because people make stupid jokes when they are nervous.

No, I am good. I was just . . . sorry, man. I am good.

It's ok to be nervous your first time. Just get your intentions straight and everything will be fine.

Rez nodded. This time Arash put his hand on Rez's arm and Rez saw the look of Arash's whole face, a new face, a different face from the one he had in eleventh grade, the one that sat next to Rez in the assembly and asked him if he blazed. This face now belonged to a young man going in a direction, toward a thing, not yet arrived but determined. Rez tapped his temple.

Intentions. I got 'em right here.

Arash put his hand over his heart in response. His eyes glassed.

It means a lot to me that you came today.

Of course. A birthday is a birthday. It's your day, bro.

Arash patted his heart again and they walked into the room, their bare feet silent on the end-to-end rugs. Rugs everywhere, Rez had never been anyplace with more complicated carpet. Maybe Vegas. The farther they got into the room, the more Rez stared at the carpets and remembered that guy, his father's old friend, the rug seller who lived in Ventura, the widower with the house full of plants. Rugs everywhere. In the kitchen. In the hallway. On the patio and in the bathroom. Rez would sit down in a corner and stare at the patterns and the colors and listen to his father and the rug seller speak in Farsi. They were nice afternoons, no women, just the three of them sitting and talking and drinking tea, the rug seller letting Rez take four or five sugar cubes from the tea tray and then sneaking him a few more. The scent of the tea, the afternoon sun across the rugs in bands of gold, his father's relaxed and happy moods. The memories came back to Rez with such vividness he thought he was stoned. Following Arash, Rez heard his father's voice on their car rides home from the rug seller's house. *He took me in, in the beginning. My life here in America is because of him. My success. You. Your life and success. A good man.*

Arash pointed to a far back wall where a few old men, too old to sit up without support, leaned back against the wall, moved strings of beads through their fingers, crossed and uncrossed their skinny legs.

You can sit there. You don't have to do anything but listen.

I can do that.

Rez waited for Arash to add one of his wisecracks like don't fall asleep or don't fart or something stupid just to keep it lively but Arash just turned around and walked into a gathering of men, a back among backs.

*

The room, enormous, spread out under a single cascading chandelier hung from the center of the ceiling. Rez was glad it was a big room, full of people he didn't know, all facing away from him. He could sit here for an hour and stare at these guys. He could do that. There were all kinds of guys, blond golfy guys, black guys, really black guys, Asian guys, lots of brown Middle Eastern–looking guys like Arash, whom Rez could no longer find in the crowd. They lined up in rows and sat cross-legged or on their calves and kept their eyes closed and their palms up, everything so ordered and quiet Rez was afraid they'd hear his nerves, the jingle of change in his pockets, his quick and cynical heartbeat.

Far ahead, at the front of the room, a little stand with a narrow staircase led to a podium under a miniature minaret. The structure was not unlike the gazebo in Johnson's yard, the same one Rez and Sophia used to make out in after swimming, splinters in their backs, a view of the birds' nests in the beams when she was on top of him. He thought of her, the straight black hair spilling all over him, her ass in his hands, and Rez looked up at the chandelier and down at the lines of men and knew these thoughts were wrong for this room and he took a few breaths and tried to give himself to the experience, to give the experience a chance. He looked around. Everyone here seemed so easy with it. The man next to him offered his hand.

As-salaam alaikum.

Wa-alaikum salaam.

When the words came out of Rez's mouth, they felt dried-up, like fall leaves, and he croaked them again, held the man's soft old hand in his hand and his soft old eyes on his eyes and let himself join for a moment and then unjoin and then he was relaxed, a bit at first, and then a lot, and sat back against the wall and slowly let loose all his tight doubt.

A man in a white turban and pale robes floated the ten steps up to the podium. All rose to their feet and a wind of moving bodies went through the room and Rez felt it, knew it as intention, and he sensed it move through his skin. Intention filled the room, singular; encompassing; certain; silently impassioned, and Rez stood too.

For one hour all reality of the room—Arash, the brightness of eleven o'clock in May, the glistening crystals of the chandelier, the snakes and gardens woven into the rugs beneath his feet—dissolved and Rez, in bits and pieces, did too. He slowed his heart, and he craned his neck to hear the man who had not started to talk, and it became clear that these were not entirely his choices, that the air in the room changed and he, Rez, no longer controlled what he felt, thought, believed. The skeptical skin shed itself and he stood and sat and listened and breathed and let himself be one among the many.

The imam spoke with a soft voice. His gestures were gentle, and his face, from what Rez could see, kept the expression of a man about to tell a joke, joyful at the coming joy. Rez let the feeling of the room push him forward to hear, and when his mind wandered, the speaker quickly brought it back with a single word.

Brother.

It was the start of most sentences and the end of many. *Brothers, here we are in the beautiful mosque of Anaheim, California. You must be proud of your brothers who have come together to build this . . . with your brothers, for your brothers.* The imam said it again and again. Rez looked around at the men. Are these my brothers? They all kept a presence, open and receiving; a quiet devotion. Rez tried to hold himself back, to observe and not join, but the atmosphere of the room refused to let him sink into heavy, dull emotions, and so he listened and so he let himself hear.

Today I have come to ask you, What is a Muslim in the world?

The room kept still.

It is a man, or woman, who moves with Allah as their guide. Do not let yourself be distracted by the circus around you. The devil has devised many enjoyable and dark temptations, and heaven will slip from your grasp.

The old men beside Rez sat still but did not fall asleep.

Who creates this desire? What drives a man to villainous acts? To jealousy or anger or mean deeds?

The speaker waited.

A distance from God. And how do we come closer to God? To resist the temptations of the devil and become better Muslims? Through service. Service and duty. I have seen so much suffering and death across this Muslim world, over every continent, on every stage of battle and peace, and the only thing that I have seen again and again is an ache for union. A need to reach out across oceans and help our brothers most in need. For if they are sacrificed, if they go to their deaths against the armies that seek to destroy Islam, then who will we commune with, how will Islam keep its rightful place among the men of earth? You must strive to join your brothers.

The speaker paused and the room and positions changed, prayer beads clinked through fingers, backs stretched. The speaker waited and continued but Rez could not follow the words. His thoughts stayed on brothers, how he had always wanted one. A brother to kick it with, a person to be loyal to, without thought or guess. Once he wanted the apostles, but they were not brothers, except maybe for Matthews, and now Arash, who brought him here today, to show him what a brotherhood could be. Arash, who kept to the goodness of his heart; the worse things got, the more Arash kept faith. Arash his brother since the beginning, since that day at the assembly, since that *Nice work, brother.* Rez sighed and a big want carved a hollow in his gut and he stopped his thoughts and turned his face toward the speaker and the soft voice chronicling a harsh message.

It is the age-old call for the union with all belief so Muslims may be victorious in this world. So your children can grow and live without fear. Your lives are beautiful now and for this we must thank Allah. And when Allah comes to ask you for your service, you must be ready. This is the exchange of love, the exchange that is devotion.

Rez was sure that if he had a brother, older or younger, it didn't matter, he would defend him. Yes. He would. That is the meaning of *brother.* The connection between you makes it so. He looked around the room; all the men had stopped their breaths. Their chests stood flat as boards and their eyes focused and somewhere above them their hearts floated, full of the electricity of new passions. He saw the backs of necks, pillars of blood life, lined up all the way to the front of the room and he saw Arash's neck, skinny and tan, and the part of Rez that had just joined this room rushed to the front of his mind. *Yeah, dude. I'd save your neck. I'd do that. Totally.*

The speaker led them in another set of prayers and the men stood and bowed and muttered and held their elbows and opened up their palms. Rez wished he knew the prayers, could join in with words, drop and lift his body in sync. His voice was dry and small when he repeated the *Allah be with you* and he felt instantly fragile and undone as if some solid thing in him had evaporated and his body had not realigned itself around the new vacancy just yet.

They met on the sidewalk outside, the midday sun bright and their eyes squinting at the Anaheim streets around them. Fatima was pale now, paler than Rez had ever seen her, and she talked with Arash about the feeling of it, using the word *feeling* over and over. She held her scarf, and her hair was damp and flattened from the cover. *That felt so good. So right. I felt my whole body relax listening to him.* Rez watched her talk and it seemed frantic, a little nervous, different from her normal sure self. Rez said only single words: *Awesome. Super. Relaxing.* And stared at the cars and their drivers as they stopped and went at the light on Milva. Men in trucks. Men in Humvees. Men in cheap cars. All alone. On the phone. Smoking. Listening to music. Men in a brotherless world.

They kept talking, Fatima asking questions and Arash answering, and Rez felt nauseated from the emotions, the new chemistry roiling through him vaporous and cold. The sun felt good, the traffic sounded familiar, and he craved the beach and a joint and a moment to forget and return to the knowing solid form he was this morning as he tried to convince Fatima to put the scarf on and take all the rest of her clothes off. *Please. Just for a minute. Arash will never know! Nudity wasn't a rule!* He felt eyes on him and saw Arash and Fatima staring, saying his name again and again.

Dude, you ok?

Yeah. Just hungry is all. That was so cool. Thanks, man!

Rez smiled like a loon.

Anyone up for lunch? Smoke? Beach?

His friends stared back at him and Rez felt his teeth start to chatter. He lunged forward and hugged Arash, the thin body slumped in its skin.

What do you say, birthday boy? In-N-Out? Newport? A puff?

Arash shook out of the embrace and stepped back from him.

No thanks, man. Another time.

Arash turned around and walked away, and Rez knew Arash was upset but didn't care. Rez's whole body was freezing and his mind jumpy and his teeth chattered in the cage of his mouth. He might care later, when he could get himself together a little bit, but right now he need to leave, warm himself with Fatima or smoke or the beach. They walked to her car and she wouldn't fuck him near the mosque or in the parking lot of the burger stand or behind the rocks at the beach. And eventually Rez let it go and they sat in the sand, a new silence between them, and stared out ahead at the horizon, the dead flat line of the ocean that gave no hint of the life forces beneath.

19

. . . EVERY TURNING BROUGHT the lights of the town more and more completely into view, spreading a great luminous vapor about the dim houses. Emma knelt on the cushions, and her eyes wandered over the dazzling light. She sobbed, called on Leon, sent him tender words and kisses lost in the wind. There was a poor vagabond wretch who wandered the hillside with his stick . . . a mass of rags covered his shoulders . . . in the place of eyelids empty and bloody orbits. The flesh hung in red shreds, and there flowed from it liquids that congealed into green scale down to the nose . . . to speak to you he threw his head back with an idiotic laugh . . . he sang . . . Maids in the warmth of a summer day, dream of love and love always . . .

Rez fell asleep and the words came to him in shorter and shorter bits. For long stretches the world of the classroom turned black and his mind, gone elsewhere, saw all Emma Bovary saw, the cobblestones, the lush brocade of her dress, the horses and the steam of their breaths. His consciousness gave up, and up and up until he shook himself awake at the sight of the blind man and the bloody orbs of his eyes. No one in the class noticed he had fallen asleep. No one cared. Twenty-four days before graduation, AP English, it surprised Rez anyone was awake at all.

Mr. Josephs front-perched on his desk, one leg on the floor, book at crotch level, and listened as Meegan, the girl reading the passage out loud, went on and on, in love with the sound of her voice, with the wanting of the woman in the story. Only Fatima, in the seat next to Rez, seemed totally awake, awake and angry. He watched her for a few seconds. Her knees pulsed up and down and she shook her head in the angry way girls did right before they were about to get into a fight. Rez thought to tap her shoulder and say *What's up?* but he was too drowsy to get the words together and it didn't matter much, she was pissy now most of the time anyway.

She raised her hand and Mr. Josephs put a finger up in the air to signal one minute or hold on or you know where the bathroom is and wait and Rez wondered if he should follow her when she left and then they could make out in the empty girls' room like they had twice this week when classes were in session and no one was in the halls. Since their visit to the mosque she was insatiable. Her desire to be fucked like a hunger he'd never known in a girl before. Everything up until then had been good and fun and exciting, and when it was awesome, it had been awesome, but he'd always lose himself in his own experience, glad the girl was there but also glad that he was there too, doing it. Now it was different. Now he woke completely awake to Fatima, to her body and its appetite and to the ways in which he could feed it. For the first time in his life he'd gone down, a thing he'd avoided because the talk was always that it turned you into a pussy, that it tasted like shit, but that is not the way it felt to him. He got between her legs, took his time, tried to avoid it but couldn't help but let his mouth go to all the dark places and lock into her, her pleasure deep, infinite in a way that was totally unlike anything he'd ever experienced. The giving just kept going and the taste stayed with him for hours afterward, Rez passing on the smokes and the drinks at the party they were at, to keep that new intoxication at the front of his tongue. Meegan finished reading and Mr. Josephs, blond crew cut, blond eyebrows and eyelashes, looked at Fatima.

Yes, Fatima?

Why is this book still important? I mean why are we still reading it?

Excuse me?

Emma Bovary is a selfish woman who only cares about pretty clothes and having affairs. She makes women seem vain and shallow. Not all women are like that. I mean, this woman has not one moment of generosity. Not one second when it isn't about her. It kind of sucks, to have to read this *Real Housewives of Rural France* stuff . . .

I like her.

Meegan, her book still in front of her, held up a hand of immaculate navy-painted fingernails and spoke, and the whole class looked up from their doodles and cell phones and daydreams about summer, college, smoking, and fucking.

I think she's a strong woman. Just because she wants more than what Charles, who is pretty pathetic, can give her doesn't mean she's a bad person. I mean, women have been told to grin and bear it since the beginning of time, and here is Emma, finally, who wants something more beautiful, more passionate, than her stupid muddy life. I like her for it. I think she is a great main character.

That brings us to a good question, Mr. Josephs began, about who exactly is the main character in this book. One the one hand Emma transforms, but so too does Charles—

Emma Bovary leaves her two children to go sleep with some guy who gives her nothing. She has absolutely no honor. Not as a mother and not as a woman.

Fatima was not shouting but her normal even-toned voice, the one she used every time she spoke in class, the one that always had the right answer but didn't brag, was gone now. She sounded older. A slight but desperate edge ended each word and Rez thought she might cry. Meegan raised her own voice to match.

Just because she wants more than she has doesn't make her a bad person. She's a dreamer. And I think she's brave.

The class turned their heads, all chins pointed at Fatima. Girl fight. Rez wished it were with another girl so that he could enjoy it instead of worrying about Fatima, who had become so quiet with her mind these last few weeks and so loud with her body. All the time they spent together had to do with sex and he missed their talks about their parents, or being together in the Bay next year, or even the fight between Drake and Jay Z. But he let it go. Girls were weird, he knew this from his mother and the few friends he had in middle school who were girls, and if they sank a little, it was best to be nice to them and leave it alone. He didn't want to fuck up the sex. Across the room Meegan sat, her face pink now in the center of a million blond curls. Meegan the prom queen. Meegan who dated Johnson for a while in ninth grade but wouldn't give it up and Johnson dropped her and she said whatever. Meegan who was going to Princeton next year because that is where her mom went and her dad went and they said she could bring her horse.

Fatima laughed.

There is a difference between being a slut and being brave.

The room made some small shocked noises. Mr. Josephs put down the book he was holding and crossed his arms but said nothing. Rez watched Fatima's smile get bigger and bigger across her face, almost reaching out into her hair. How could she say this? She had put him in her mouth just yesterday. She liked sex. Was this about sex? What was this honor she was talking about? He was not her first. Wait, was he her first? She had been with other guys. He tried to remember who but didn't get the chance because Meegan, of the debate team, of the SUPPORT HILLARY 2008 sticker, already had her own smile on.

I forgot, Fatima. Your culture believes women are most honorable when they are invisible. That makes a lot of sense, doesn't it?

The shocked noises again, this time louder and this time Mr. Josephs spoke up.

Ok. Now we have brought up some worthwhile issues here. Let's try to talk about them through the lens of Flaubert's work—

Wait. Wait. Let me just point out that in your *culture*, Meegan, a woman can't say anything until she shows her tits and legs. Unless she's something to stare at, a woman has no voice here. That's real honorable . . . Fuck this.

Fatima stood and grabbed her bag and walked out of the room with a strong, straight back. The class erupted with *Oh, shit*s and *It's on*s. Rez grabbed his bag and stood up and then sat back down and then stood up again and followed her out. Behind him the class erupted and Mr. Josephs's voice tried to reach through it, tried to reach above and over it and tap it down, but there were shouts and the sound of girls' voices, three or four saying, *It's going to be ok, Meegan. It's all right. Fatima is weird, she's always been weird. She doesn't know what she was talking about . . .*

20

IT ONLY TOOK less than one minute to get out of the classroom. He spent a few seconds watching Meegan and then a few seconds to tell his arms and legs, *Get up, get up, go, go find her. Backpack.* By then she was gone. The waxed linoleum floors of the hallways shone under the orange afternoon light and Rez walked past empty lockers and closed classroom doors to the exit that took him to the parking lot, where he could find her, jump in her car, make her feel better. Maybe she'd be crying and they'd fool around a little bit because she looked hot when she cried and then she'd start the engine and let him put his hands between her thighs. The parking lot spread out around him, completely still. Her car not there. Now committed to this exit, Rez started to walk and thought about the bus and the few dollars in his pocket and why not, it was sixth period and this was a good reason to skip the rest of the day. He got on the one bus that went up and down Highway 1, paid his fare, and sat as far away from the other three passengers as possible. It was only two or three miles to her house and he looked out the window at the small waves and enjoyed the view from the big windows.

He got off at the gates of her neighborhood, said *What's up?* to the guard that watched the monitors, and walked up the steep streets that took him to Fatima's house. The gates to the driveway were closed and he looked in and didn't see her car, or many of the cars normally lined up in front of the two-story mahogany doors, and then pulled out his phone.

Where are you?

Javad's.

And the sickness started in his gut. He put the phone in his pocket and walked down the hill back to the bus stop to ride up to Newport. The wait was longer this time and he watched the cars blow by him and the light turn from orange to a dirty color without a name that led to dusk. A car full of old women all turned their heads and stared at him. Another car, a gardener's beat-up truck, slowed at the sight of him and then stopped and the passenger, a young man just a few years older than Rez, rolled down the window.

A donde vas?

Rez shook his head.

No. Thanks. I'm good. Todo bien. Gracias.

Bueno.

She wasn't crying when she opened the door but her face seemed washed clean, no eyelash stuff or shadow, just the white skin and dark eyes and pink lips. She looked up at him and her eyes said come in, but her body, so alive to him these last weeks, stood back and stayed cold.

Whatsup?

Nothing. I wanted to be with Arash.

That's cool with me.

From behind her Rez heard the low sound of the new Kanye record and then the louder sound of something on the TV, someone with a British accent speaking in flat, evenly paced sentences. Then he heard Javad.

Rez? Come in. Come in. Close the door behind you.

She moved out of the way and Rez took a step toward her and waited for her to meet him and reach up and wrap her arms around his neck so that he'd know everything was all right, but she turned and walked into the living room, where she sat on the couch next to Arash, who watched TV without saying *Hey* or *Whatsup*.

It was not the regular TV. Not a channel from cable. The resolution was strange and the words at a lag and he saw a computer hooked up to the TV screen, a website image small and then large. An imam in a turban, the same imam who'd spoken at the mosque on Arash's birthday, stood in a different little gazebo and spoke passionately. Arash finally looked up at Rez, a thin smile on his face.

Glad you came. Fatima told us what happened. Pretty crazy stuff.

Yeah.

So much for diversity of opinion at Laguna Preparatory Academy. I guess.

Rez turned his face to the television and tried to block out the imam's words and listen to the thin threads of Kanye coming from Javad's bedroom. Another imam took the place of the first and spoke with a thick British accent, which always reminded Rez of the professors in the *Harry Potter* boarding schools, full of wisdom and magic. They filmed this imam in close-up and Rez saw that he was young, not much older than Javad, and that his hairline had sweat on it and his throat occasionally trembled when he spoke.

Brothers, the Prophet would implore you. Defend yourself. All around the world our men, women, and children are slaughtered for their devotions. Muslim men. Muslim women. Muslim children. If we sit aside, our sons will become usurers and our daughters prostitutes, our caliphate a lost dream.

The beach outside the windows of Javad's house was empty and clean and Rez knew if he slid open the glass doors, the wind that came in would be warm and salty and he listened to the imam and wanted to make a joke about his marshmallow turban or his unibrow or something to break the spell in the room and get Arash and Fatima to laugh and follow him outside. Before something funny came to mind, the screen split in four, the imam's face in one quadrant and the other three filled with pictures of women in head scarves on their knees, prostrated over a dead body; dead families in rubble; children's toys spread across a blast site; a father carrying a wounded, bloody head. A group of men in fatigues and turbans being barked at and bitten by dogs. The photos from Abu Ghraib. A mosque with the minaret demolished. The images changed every few seconds and the names of the cities beneath changed too. *Grozny. Mosul. West Bank. Kabul.* The imam kept talking. *Everywhere there are Muslims, there is sorrow.* The screen went dark and then filled with a field of sunflowers blowing gently in an invisible breeze. *For an eternity of peace, we must fight this last fight.* Fatima started to cry. Rez stood up.

Comeeeeeoooooonn.

He waited for the room to unbuckle, to open up and agree with him, but they all just looked at him, with near identical expressions, Fatima and Arash and Javad, their sad open faces, on the verge of rage.

Really? You are going to buy into all of this?

No one said anything.

Rez grabbed his backpack and looked at his friends on the couch. Fatima wiped her eyes and Arash stood up. Rez had had enough.

I gotta go.

Whatever you need.

Arash gestured toward the door.

I don't need this bullshit, that's for sure, Rez wanted to say, but kept his mouth shut, afraid the anger would spill out until it turned into what he really felt, which was sorrow. He wanted the old Arash back. The fun life. He didn't want to beg his friend *Why can't you just chill. Like we did? Like it was?* So he kept his mouth closed, but his eyes must have said something because Fatima rose too now and stepped toward him.

I'll walk you out.

She stood behind him and neither of them said anything until they were just outside on the gravel path to the street.

Fatima, what's going on?

You won't understand, you don't get it. I just can't be this way. Not anymore.

What way?

This way. This stupid American way. It has no honor. No kindness. I don't know who I am.

I know who—

Just go. Please.

Fine.

He turned on his heel and kept himself from calling her a name and swallowed a few times, but when the tears came, there was no more blinking, no more wiping them away, and he let his eyes drip and his face stay wet until he was at the bus stop, where he cupped his palms over his eyes and cried.

The bus came and he got on and the driver saw his transfer and Rez went to the back. The only other person was an old lady, elaborate jewels and puffy gold hair and a large black Lab. The dog wore a vest that said SERVICE ANIMAL and the woman wore the dark glasses of the blind. For all of Rez's low whistles and tongue clicks the dog did not move from his curled position and Rez turned his face to the window to stare at the faint outline of his reflection and then through that, to the just dark sea that told him, by its color, that it was early evening. Where to go? There was nothing at home but thinking and television and his computer, and all of that would remind him of Fatima, so fuck it. He checked his phone. A picture of Mavericks during a swell went bright and then dim. He rode the bus until Laguna and the shops and people walking around, and got off, walking the mile between where he was and Matthews's house, where he would go, smoke a bowl, and kick it until it got dark.

He skipped the front house, skipped Matthews's sulking sisters and his nosy mom, and walked around to the pool house, where the same Kanye record he heard at Javad's now pounded out loudly through the glass of the windows and Rez heard the sound of people laughing. He listened to the song and picked up his pace, around the pool and the gazebo, to the closed French doors of the little house, where he saw two heads on the couch in front of the television and Matthews walking up and down reciting the lyrics of the song, a bong in one hand, a lighter in the other, enjoying the music, performing for no one.

Rez thought about turning around, going home. He hadn't been close to Kelly, in a room that wasn't a classroom, since all the shit happened so he stood on the far side of the pool and looked in. They were hotboxing the pool house, playing on the PlayStation, chillin'. The smell of herb seeped out of the house and Rez thought, Fuck it, and stepped toward the house and all its happy sounds and smells. Matthews hooted.

Hey, Rez!

Matthews, happy Matthews, easy, glad, all balloons and smiles Matthews. Rez bumped his fist and took the bong from him and knew his friend was so high he had forgotten that Kelly and Johnson hated Rez and that Kelly could at any moment bring up Paul or the cheating A Rash and no one could argue with him and his loss and Matthews didn't know it but if Kelly wanted to be an asshole right now and throw a punch or spit on Rez's shoes, no one could say it was wrong or bad or rude.

Johnson said, Whatsup, and Kelly gave Rez a cold, focused look and turned back to the game and smiled as he pressed his controls with zeal and shot and slammed heads against stones and moved his avatar, a blond head in a Kevlar jacket behind the bouncing barrel of his gun.

Rez sat on a stool at the bar and lit the small ball of green and black and ash at the bottom of the bong, sucked at the tube until the water bubbled and the cool gray smoke filled his lungs. He listened to the Kanye and bobbed his head. He listened to the sounds of the game, grunts and screams and bullets and yells. No one talked and Rez closed his eyes and waited for the high to come, to make things lose their edge, to make him feel like it was ok to stay. He felt a punch on his shoulder.

Dude. Did you hear about Meegan and Fatima?

Matthews stood in front of Rez with his phone on and the Twitter feed going.

Yeah. I was there.

Crazy right? Girl-fight city.

Yeah.

The haze cleared and the other two apostles sat on the edge of the couch now and pushed the buttons and moved their bodies in twitches and jolts as if they were in the game, as if their own bodies filled the military garb, their own hearts tucked into the Kevlar, behind the sweating skin. Rez watched the split screen where their two soldiers marched through various alleys and marketplaces, knocking down doors and pushing over stalls of spices and rugs as men in long shirts and turbans protested and women cowered over small children whose eyes peered back through the shawls and robes. A man rushed before Johnson's character and said something in broken English and took a few bills from the hand of the soldier and disappeared back into the maze where he'd come from.

Intel!

Nice, dude.

Johnson got his man to run and soon the split screen was one and the two forms were joined in a single setting, a small dusty road with dark houses on each side. A dog picked through piles of trash and then ran away as the soldiers approached. Rez wondered at the reality of it all, the street, the garbage with flies, the huffs of the fast walking, the

123

shifting fabric of their uniforms. To what end, all this reality? He was high now and the television was the biggest thing in the room and he wished it were more fake.

Now? Johnson asked Kelly without looking at him.

Yeah. This house. Here.

They both twisted their bodies to the right and their guys turned right and their boots were in the frame, kicking down the door of a house that was otherwise dark and quiet.

We are soldiers of the defense force. Where is the sheikh?

The avatars shouted now, one and then the other, into dark rooms with faint rugs and small-framed pictures of men and women smiling in the dimness. Ahead of them light shot into the hallway from a doorway and they moved toward it and inside a girl, the oldest sister maybe, sat in front of a few other children, the girls all in head scarves, the boys all with shaved heads.

Where is he? Where is the sheikh?

The girl, almost a woman, attractive and tall, shook her head and said something in Arabic. One of the avatars moved forward and used the butt of his gun to pry the children apart from their pile, to separate them to make sure no one was hiding in the midst of their small bodies. Rez felt his heart beat fast, like he'd just done a line instead of taken a hit, and he took a few deep breaths and cleared his throat and then someone in the television coughed loudly and Johnson and Kelly jumped.

Dude!

He's under the floor! Pull back the rug.

Kelly moved his avatar to do it, and as the floor door opened, the girl yelled and threw herself down at the avatar's feet and then the shooting started and Rez closed his eyes and the shooting was loud and the screams pierced louder but loudest was Kelly yelling.

Sheikh and bake, motherfucker! Sheikh and bake!

When Rez opened his eyes, he looked at the TV and saw the girl outside her house, a boy's head in her lap, his body covered with blood. With his own eyes closed, Rez's mind jumped to the TV at Javad's house and he shook his head to get the memory out, to make it change, but it didn't, the image stayed the same. A Muslim girl in a head scarf, crying. Blood in her lap. The imam's words from Javad's TV slammed Rez's consciousness ... *the Muslim is the persecuted of the world* ...

Rez let himself out. No one noticed. Matthews was on the phone and Johnson and Kelly were shouting *Yeah, man* and *Nice* and *So much for the sheikh* and other shit that Rez couldn't hear because he was out the door and across the yard and around the pool, sweat coming off his palms. He loped down Matthews's driveway and heard the voice of Matthews's mom behind him. She stood in the front door with a glass of wine in her hand.

Hey, Rez! How's it going? You ok?

I'm good, he shouted back with a high wave. And she held her glass of wine in one hand and waved with the other.

Say hi to your mom and dad for me!

Will do!

Then he ran. Down through the neighborhood streets toward the highway and then down the crumbling shoulder. When he got tired, he'd jog but the images came back to him and he had to sprint again. First he thought, The game is not real, just a game, a stupid video game. Then he thought: the imam's pictures were not real, the imam was a known and crazy manipulator. Then he thought that Kelly and Johnson were not real but video-game avatars or that Fatima and Arash were not real but simply brainwashed puppets. After a mile or so he could not run any longer and then he didn't know what to know, he did not, in his high head, know what was and what was not.

When he got to the quiet streets of his neighborhood, confusion and exhaustion churned violently in his gut and he stood in the empty kitchen and threw up into it once and then again. When his mom came through the door, she looked at him and rubbed his back and ran the water from the faucet.

Joonam. I'm sorry. They called from school and said you left early. They didn't say you were sick. Some tea . . .

She put her hand on his forehead to take his temperature, just as she had his whole life.

Let's pray this is just a twenty-four-hour bug.

PART III

To a Good Country

21

THE MORNING OF graduation the fog was so thick Rez stared into the blank white and tried to imagine the house across the street. Home of Mr. and Mrs. Haas. Retirees. Proud keepers of bonsai trees and Japanese moss gardens. A matched pair, same white hair, same white teeth, same white sneakers. Parents of a famous movie star, a comedian who took only serious roles now and spent most of his time in a bluegrass band. Once or twice a year the son came to visit, always in a new-model European sedan, always in sunglasses, always alone and in a rush. When Rez was younger, smaller, cuter, the couple would see them in their driveway and call, *Come over!* Mrs. Haas always had lemonade and Mr. Haas once put his enormous bony hand on Rez's shoulder and asked if he wanted to see his sports car. Rez was four maybe five, and followed the old man into his tidy garage, where a dusty green piece of metal sat without a hood, the trunk where the engine would be. It looked like a piece of junk. *It's nice,* Rez told Mr. Haas, and Mr. Haas agreed, *Yes. Yes, she is. I thought you might like to see it. All young boys dream about the same things.* After 9/11 the Haases stopped waving. Mrs. Haas would look up at him from under her gardening hat, then turn her eyes back at the ground. Rez mentioned it to his mother. *They're mean now.* Rez's mother just shook her head. *They are old. Sometimes when people get older, they become quieter.*

But this morning they were gone, disappeared. Between his house and theirs a mist so thick Rez let himself pretend there was no house, no Mr. and Mrs. Haas in their old worn beds, backs to each other, their saggy white bodies silent and still. The sound of Matthews's truck rumbled through the fog and Rez picked up his backpack and his board and wished for a clearing, for some visibility and blue sky to calm his nerves, but knew there was no hope, not until one or two o'clock, until after the ceremony with the gowns and the photos and the dumb hats, all of it pressed down and dreary under this dark low ceiling of wet.

*

Then he was high, floating in the salt water at Old Man's, not giving a fuck. The surface was glassy and almost no one was out, and if they were, Rez couldn't see them. A pod of dolphins glided nearby, their fins up and out of the mist, then down and gone again. The idea of a sea, an infinity of width and depth, filled with life he would never know, dropped his shoulders and opened his breath and he paddled out farther and saw the set as it was coming in and got caught under a huge wave just as it crested and crashed and the big weight of the water pushed down and pressed his body to the seafloor so completely that all the nerves of the day pushed out of him. He caught the next one he saw and rode it almost to shore and then went back for another and another until his body and mind were as numb and loose as any ocean fish.

Matthews drove him home. They wore the hoods of their hoodies up and ate breakfast burritos from Santo's and listened to the morning show on the rock station. When they got to Rez's house, he put a fist up and Matthews bumped it.

See you on the other side.

Not if I see you first.

Matthews cleared his throat and then smiled wide.

So. Uh. Not to get sentimental, but I have really loved sharing these past four years of high school with you . . . It's been really . . . special.

Very funny, jackass.

No. Really. You've been like a brother to me, a brother from another mother, but you know, still . . . Matthews was trying not to laugh, was trying to keep a serious emotional face, and Rez felt his own face try to do the same and soon they were both cracking up.

No. Seriously. I got you a gift.

Matthews put his hands into his hoodie pocket and tossed out a baggie that landed in Rez's lap. Caps and stems. Hard to get. Harder to share.

Dude! Score.

I thought we could take a few right before the ceremony, get loopy during all the clapping and speeches and shit and then be nice and trippy for the family stuff after. Say eleven o'clock launch?

Perfect.

Sweet.

Rez jumped out of the truck and grabbed his board and wanted to wave and shout *See ya* to Matthews, but the fog swallowed the truck and it was just Rez, next to the sidewalk, up the steps, into his house.

An alphabetical-order event. Just like the SATs, class photos, roll call. Rez took his seat between Melizza Cales and Emily Custer, girls he only knew from these ordered arrangements. Melizza had changed the spelling of her first name in tenth grade and then changed her hair color and kept an anarchist *A* in her locker and didn't talk to anyone at the school. Emily. Plump Emily. Emily of Christ and church and the cross that rested just above her cleavage. Mousy until junior year and then born-again and part of a young Christ group with its own music and movies and dates and still chunky, but confident now, looked pretty good, called herself a good daughter of God. Goth and born-again, with him in the middle. What would he be called? He thought of a few names, some types, but nothing went together, none of them fit, and he had to stop thinking because the queasy feeling started and he had to concentrate on unwrapping the ginger candy he'd jammed in his pocket so he could focus on the words of the headmaster, who was up at the podium now, talking and gesturing and smiling, a man so clean shaven and pleased he looked like a baby. Rez tried to turn the blah-blah-blah sound into words.

The meaning of ceremony, through time, has been to mark, to denote a moment of significance. To bring together family and friends and teachers and support networks and take a moment to mark an achievement, recognize a transformation. You have seen these fine young adults as babies, as eager elementary school students, as moody middle schoolers, and now as men and woman on the verge of their own lives. Such tremendous changes and more changes to come. Every student before you has read the works of the great Roman poet Ovid. In his timeless collection, *Metamorphoses*, he says . . . everything changes, nothing is extinguished. Try and remember this when they come to you as college seniors with impressive internships in foreign countries, or as doctors or as parents, and you can remember that they were once on this stage, once in your lap, once a thought in your heart: Everything changes, but nothing is extinguished.

Rez wanted to cry. He also wanted to throw up. The desire to expel from himself some pent-up substance came and went and he held it together. Clapped. Stood. Sat down. Stood up again when they called his name. Walked to the edge of the stage. Held the diploma, shook the hand, posed for the picture, and then slid back to his seat in the flowing long black robes that made him feel like an eel. When it was done, he tossed his cap like the rest but didn't bother to catch it and stayed back, behind a line of tall hedges, for ten, twenty, twenty-five minutes, while the drugs came up in him and he watched life play out before him, suddenly nude and beautiful and tragic.

As it was in the hallways of high school, it was today, and the families gathered in little clumps, everyone segmented out by color or last name or style. He saw a group of younger brothers and sisters stuff catered cookies in their pockets and then run to hide under the long table-cloths. He saw the old ladies with skinny ankles in saggy hose and men with too-tan faces and guts held back by shiny belt buckles. The fog still covered most things and Rez felt everyone and everything as if it were on the verge of death. A small ray of sun opened a hole through the mist and he concentrated on its glow in a far corner of the quad, knew if there were more, he could do this, he could go into the space of the celebration and celebrate. And then there it was, sun like honey to wash over the scene and make everyone fine looking, make all the eyes glint and the teeth shine. Sun to put gold on the leaves of the trees and warmth on the faces. Rez stepped back from the hedge and took a moment to appreciate the magic of life on earth, just enough water, just enough carbon, just enough oxygen, such a crazy precise formula and yet this one planet had it just right and so there was this: families, trees, soil. He started to cry a little and then a lot, full free sobs of joy, and when that was all done, he took a deep breath and shook himself out from top to bottom and then side to side like a wet dog and walked into the crowd of family and friends and happy teachers. Drugs were so good. The day was so good. All of this was the universe at peace with itself, everything as it should be.

He let the good feeling guide him and he floated from clump to clump, where he hugged kids he'd never said hello to. Their parents shook his hands and he said *Berkeley, Yes, sir,* and *Yes, they are very happy,* and *Thank you, same to you.* And on and on around the quad until he came to Sophia Lim's family, the men in designer shoes, the women in impossible heels, the old ladies seated and snacking with the little kids. He grabbed Sophia from behind and she squealed. Her robed body slipped under his grasp and she turned around, saw his face, laughed, and hugged him back.

Rez! Can you believe it? So cool, right?

Very cool. Graduation day. Just like Kanye said it would be.

Watch out for the college dropout!

She laughed and took a step toward him until they were standing close.

I can't believe we made it. I mean, everyone knew you would always make it, Mr. Chess and chemistry whiz and all that. I'm surprised I got through! I stopped going to class all last term . . .

She kept talking and might have said something about next year or tomorrow or remember when, but Rez heard nothing because her lips, a sharp and shiny pink, flashed in front of his eyes and he could only stare at them, think about them, wonder why they winked at him and then grow embarrassed that such a sex organ should be on a woman's face, right in the front, for everyone to see. Sophia, his first. His virginity and childhood lost to her many holes. Gratitude swallowed him and he reached over and gave her another hug.

Thank you so much. So much.

For what?

She giggled.

For everything. You're the best.

Ooooh k. What parties are you going to tonight?

Um. I don't know . . . all of them?

She gave him a kiss on the cheek and he squeezed her hand. Fifty-two bones in each hand. Sophomore bio. He let the hand go and walked on looking for the next person, the next warm brother-sister feeling.

In a far corner of the quad his mother and father sat on white wooden chairs. His people, and he was their person, their only son, and he walked toward them with tears coming up into his face again. They smiled at him and said things people said all day long and he felt their happiness and wrapped his arms around his mother's small narrow frame and the recognition came to him: I lived inside you once. Once you were my home. But he knew it would be crazy to say it so he said nothing and enjoyed the way mushrooms turned the world into an enormous, pulsing, generous truth. He pulled away and reached for his father, once a monster and now, today, meek, but the strong tall body of straight-up-and-down bones and old skin did not give in to the embrace, and that stiffness, the up-and-down, not-bending body made Rez's thoughts snap toward the dark, the desert, pain, and a million stars. He took a few steps back and felt goodwill leak away.

We are proud of you, Rez. Your mother, myself. You have done well.

Thanks.

Should we go? This is over, isn't it? His father looked across the quad.

We have a reservation at the restaurant at one.

It's only noon, Dad. I need to say hello to a few more people. This might be the last time I see them.

His father sat back down in his chair and looked at his phone. His mother smiled at Rez and pushed him back toward the gathered families.

Go. Go, see your friends. We will meet you at the car in half an hour.

He walked through the groups of families and kids and waited for the good feeling to come back but everything had a stain on it now and all the shadows seemed to fall the wrong way. He heard laughter, clapping, and proud deep voices and he turned in their direction and saw Fatima's entire clan of uncles and aunts and other people he could never name, gathered in the dappled light of a tall Japanese maple, joyous. He walked toward them and they took him in with handshakes and knowing nods and shouts of For you! For you! Our Fatima goes to Stanford. You and your excellent tutoring. The old woman, Fatima's grandmother, approached him and took his hand in hers. Their eyes met and Rez waited for her to say something but she did not and so he stood and felt her vibrations, the coursing out of something sure and strong through the soft parchment of her hands and face. When she seemed satisfied, she let go of his hand and Rez bowed his head to her in some Japanese version of thanks that made a girl nearby laugh.

Getting a little emotional, are we?

For the first time in three weeks he heard Fatima's voice, felt her body close. Three weeks and not a phone call or a text, not even a glance in the hallway or at the year-end assemblies. After the first week Rez wrote her a nasty message about how stupid it was to get so involved with an Internet cause and how Arash was turning into a kook. The second week of silence made Rez sad and he walked around low and angry and tried not to listen to too much Beyoncé or Adele. By the third week Matthews convinced him that the summer was full of girls and Rez started to believe him, wipe his mind of the want of one thing and move into the want of many and let himself flirt, hook up if offered, drift. Now she was near him, it all left him—the anger, the sadness, the want for distraction—and he saw her, beautiful in the black robe and high heels, a colorful bouquet held near her face, and all he felt was gratitude. He took her in with both eyes and felt a calm near numbness take over his frazzled tripping nerves. She seemed like a beacon of all good things, and he stood without speaking like a dumb devotee before his guide. She looked back at him, her face alive and warm and curious.

What are you on?

Rez laughed and Fatima moved a few inches closer and he whispered in her ear.

They made out in Mr. Joseph's room and did as much as they could in fifteen minutes. At some point he had her in his mouth and his eyes opened and looked up to see the posters of Whitman, Brontë, Hemingway, Angelou, that Josephs had stapled above the whiteboard and Rez's heart rushed and he thought, Terrific. Terrifying. Terror.

The mushrooms wore off during lunch with his family, and when Fatima picked him up from the restaurant, she brought tabs of ecstasy and soon he was up again, up and flying. She drove him to the parking lot just above Laguna Cove where every spot had some kind of view of the sea. They laid down the seats in the back, threw a blanket across the flat surface and let themselves go. Three weeks of energy flowed out of one and into the other until they were both empty and full. When Fatima finally sat up she looked out the window and shouted, *Sunset. Holy shit. Sunset. We've been here for six hours!* And they laughed and rolled around against each other's skin until it was dark.

The night was full of parties, each one wilder than the last. Rez enjoyed them like presents, one sweaty dark room of dancing friends, one poolside bonfire, one round of shots after the next. They held hands all night long, entered and exited each party like the couple they never admitted to being. At Haleh Mernissi's house he followed her outside to the pool, where she took off her dress and jumped in and he did the same and underwater they grabbed each other and kissed and slowly sank. They dried off on lawn chairs, her head in his lap.

I miss Arash.

Rez put his hand on her head and tried to keep his thoughts of Arash away. All day long he'd had to do this, turn his thoughts from the empty space where his friend should have been, laughing, making people laugh, giving congrats, getting them, celebrating his next step, to Harvard or Oxford or some other fancy place. Rez tried to guide her away from the empty space of him.

He will find his way. A's a smart guy. And a good guy. He'll figure it out.

Fatima looked up at him, her eyes alive, black planets all their own.

He already has, Rez. He's already figured it out.

He woke in a hotel room, Fatima beside him as a mass of hair and skin, the bedside lamp still on; condom wrappers, Red Bulls, half-smoked joints all over the table and floor. He felt the great freedom of it, waking in a bed with a girl. He stood and walked to the curtains, which he pulled aside just enough to see the sixteenth-floor view down onto the highways of Irvine, the neat business parks and sprawled-out shopping malls with parking structures that ran up against the strawberry fields where men and women crouched, covered mouths and noses, heads and hands, to pick and pick and pick in the cool morning sun. He let go the curtain and went back to bed. The first day of summer. High school done. Childhood done. Life at home nearly done. His skin shivered at the thrill of it and he pulled the sheets up over his shoulders and put his body next to Fatima until he was hard and she was awake and they were fucking, quietly at first and then loudly, in a hotel room, like adults.

They ate lunch at a fancy place in Corona del Mar where they were the only ones under sixty. The old men stared at Fatima in her cocktail dress and heels and washed-clean face. They stared at Rez too and a few of them smiled. The drugs left them hollow and wanting and though it was long past lunch they ate breakfast and drank champagne and orange juice and coffee. They both wore sunglasses and neither spoke between bites and Rez let Fatima's bare foot travel up and down the inside of his leg.

On the ride home he looked out the window at the waves off Highway 1 and hoped for a swell big enough to call Matthews and work off the hangover with a long session in the water but the waves looked mushy and Rez felt so sleepy that when Fatima started switching stations, a habit that drove him crazy, he almost didn't notice until he did because each station she turned to played a version of the same thing: breaking news, breaking news, breaking news. DJs that normally sounded like jocks or beauty queens were serious and scared and some of them already angry, reading off the bits of information as it came in. *South Coast Plaza, at least four gunmen still loose, a suicide vest discovered, undetonated, people held hostage in stores, security footage showing attackers firing at random in the food court, in department stores, at the carousel. One of Southern California's largest high-end malls . . . At this point, untold dead . . . Surrounding areas shut down for two miles in every direction . . . a live situation.* Around them cars slowed and some pulled over. Fatima drove twenty and then ten and then five miles an hour and whispered, Oh my God, Oh my God, under her breath. She turned to the NPR station, the same one Arash listened to, and the announcer, her voice steady, told them, *This just in, we have confirmation of the identity of two of what seem to be six attackers.*

Fatima stopped the car in the middle of the road and there were the names, a son and daughter of Islam. Rez watched her hands drop off the wheel and into her lap.

Pull over. You've got to pull over. You can't park in the middle of the street.

She started to cry. Rez reached for the wheel.

Here. Just press the gas pedal a little bit. Can you do that?

She shook her head no but her knee moved and Rez steered the car to the shoulder, where others had parked and sat head forward, listening to their radios, fingers on their phones. They were less than twenty miles from it. Twenty miles south and Rez looked around for signs of a massacre and saw traffic lights that still turned colors, an ocean that kept churning, and bougainvillea swaying up and down in the breeze. Fatima was crying and there was *untold* death close by, but otherwise everything was ok, it was going to be ok, like all the other shootings, this would be ok. Rez put a hand on Fatima's thigh.

Stop. Don't.

Her voice was caught in the back of her throat and she didn't clear it so when she spoke it sounded like a growl.

Leave me alone.

It's gonna be ok. This shit happens now. It's the way the world is and it will pass just like the other shootings and bombings. This is just the—

No. No. No. This is not going to *just* pass. We are fucked. At a mall?! What if there were children? This is right here. Here! Where we live!

She stopped and heaved in a breath and wiped her nose.

Maybe it will pass for you, since all you do is try to pass as some white surfer dude . . . maybe everything *just passes for Rez.*

Rez felt her jab in the middle of his chest, and shame like a hot liquid swallowed too fast spread through the middle of him and he moved away from her, considered getting out of the car and then thought about the walk home, the long miles to his door.

Whatever. Just take me home.

She wiped her nose again and started the car. They drove and even though he was too angry to look, he did, every few minutes, to see if she was still beautiful, to see if he could stop liking her right now, forget about her face and hair and mouth and damn her in his mind, but there she was, wild hair and smooth skin and shiny black eyes. When he couldn't glance at her anymore, he turned his head and looked out the open window at the world of his home. They stopped at a red light and Rez saw the driver beside them, a middle-aged woman with gray in her black hair, younger than his mom, crying, both hands on the wheel. Rez heard the radio in her car . . . *the death toll continues to rise and one gunman, a woman, has been injured by authorities . . . the situation remains dangerous . . . law enforcement encourages all residents to keep away from Costa Mesa, and immediately report any suspicious activity should this be part of a larger attack . . .* The woman stared back at Rez and Rez held still with a singular thought in his brain: Will she know? Do I look it? Can she tell? The woman, her cheeks streaked with makeup and her eyes wet, peered at him and then past him to Fatima and her face hardened and Rez heard her sobs skip and her breath catch and then the glass of her car window rose between them and severed the air.

Fatima dropped him off in front of his house and Rez pushed himself to forget what she'd said, to lean in and kiss her, to comfort her and say something like *It's going to be ok,* but she did not bend to him, did not take her eyes off the road. He tried a last time.

Call me.

—

Last night was fun. With you. I had fun with you.

—

We can have fun this summer. Things will get better and then we move north. Remember? You said you couldn't wait . . .

—

He got out, closed the door on her silence, and opened the door to the house. No one was home and he moved as quietly as he could, grabbed a towel from the laundry room and took it to the edge of the pool and spread it over the green grass beside the blue water and then took off his shirt and his shoes and pants and lay down to bake his worn body until he felt some calm.

22

FIRST IT NEVER happened and then it happened all the time. Sometimes once a week, sometimes a few times a day, but it didn't matter because he thought about it every time he left the house and so the summer was fucked. For a few days after the massacre Rez stayed home, like most people, and watched the news, cycle after cycle on all the channels, every few hours a new detail, a bad detail, to capture the attention and keep you glued. Eighty-three dead. The Spanish tile fountain filled with blood and the floating bodies of two security guards. Men and women and children hidden in dressing rooms, restrooms, clothes racks, play structures, air-conditioning vents. Eighty-three dead. Twelve children. Six attackers. Two Yemeni men, two Iraqi women, a brother and sister from Saudi Arabia. Three of them asylum seekers. Three American-born. They all left the same statement on their Twitter accounts. The same sentence with no remorse: *And we will strike at the heart of America's most sacred center, where the sins of usury, vanity, devotion to false gods, collide, where the souls are damned long before we destroy them.* And then a prayer. There were images of the food court, the glass atrium blown off, shards piercing the bodies of the dead, dressing room mirrors streaked with blood, mannequins toppled over and beheaded. Only Fox, and the Internet, showed those images, but everyone talked about them and debate ramped up on values and freedoms and the coming clash of civilizations. Rez thought of the practicing-Muslim families he knew, Omid's, Yuri's, Arash's, Fatima's, and he thought about his own, his mother's prayers when they left the house, the no-pork rule, the undercurrent of devotion from something long-ago believed in practice. Every house was different. Some had prayer rooms, some did not. Some of the women covered, most did not. Some fasted for Ramadan, some did not. Every one of them shopped. Most had been to that same mall because America was the great place where you could worship many things at once, until now. After a few days even Rez's dad got tired of the news and one afternoon switched the channels until they found a James Bond marathon and the two of them sat easily and then happily through old ideas of danger and fear and courage.

He didn't feel like calling anyone and no one called him. Matthews was on vacation in Hawaii with his family and Arash hadn't answered his phone in weeks and Rez was still angry with Fatima for what she'd said about his being a poser and how it was and wasn't true.

On the third day he wanted to get outside and left around sunset to go for a walk. Old Mr. Haas stood across the street, his hand in tiny scissors trimming a bonsai tree. Rez raised his arm and waved and shouted, *Good afternoon!* And the old man, who always, at least, waved, put a palm up but did not shake it, left it frozen in the air and then pushed the air back as if to say, stay back. Then he put his scissors in his pocket and moved into the shadows of his garage. Because that was the first time and it hadn't really started happening yet and Mr. Haas was an old kook, Rez shrugged it off and kept walking up the street toward the cul-de-sac that led to the trailhead and then up to the sagebrush and cacti.

Then it happened again. And again. In instances big and small. Sometimes nothing more than extra-long stares, the eyes asking, *Mexican? Middle Eastern? Where from? Should I be scared? Are you the same evil?* And Rez forced himself to look back and say hello or smile. As long as they didn't know his name, that was as far as things went. Only when he showed his name did it get serious, his driver's license to buy rolling papers, his debit cards to get a sandwich after pickup soccer or to buy a brick of surf wax at the store across from the ninety-nine steps, that's when the situation would change. Refusal to sell goods or an error in the transaction, or a hard look and then the question, like a cop would ask, in the same right-to-know tone: *Where is this name from?* To which Rez either answered Iran, or kept silent, grabbed his card and left.

This was not the summer he had planned. No pool parties, no beach fires, no hangouts or trips to Vegas, everybody stuck at home because of the massacre. And the stories like the one about Hassan the day after it happened and how the cops stopped him for a broken taillight and then took him to the INS, where he sat in a refrigerated room with lights that didn't turn off for two days while his parents tried to find him. He posted about it on Twitter but not a lot of people responded. The air was filled with other noises. Everyone on the radio or television or Internet spewed presidential proclamations, acts of Congress, news of local civilian curfews, and then the death count. The death count that kept rising. The mall with the ring of flowers and candles five feet deep outside its modern glass storefronts. A few times Rez thought, How could this be? This is Laguna Beach, where everyone, even the most uptight housewife, learned how to relax, chill, be kind. It was the way. The beach demanded it. The wealth made it possible. He had known nothing else his whole life. But now his whole life included this, and this included going to the car wash with his dad and waiting for the Mexicans and Salvadoreans to hand-dry the car as a man in golf pants walked past and spat down on the ground, casually, on the toe of Rez's father's shoe. His father didn't look down but Rez did and the man walked slowly on, as if blameless. One of the car wash employees brought over a rag and handed it to Rez's dad. *For your shoe.* And walked away. No one said anything after that.

It can't stay this way forever, Rez thought, day in and day out. After the trip he'd come home and find Omid and Hassan at the gazebo in Laguna Beach and they would smoke and watch the tourists from Riverside and Death Valley eat frozen yogurt and buy T-shirts that declared LOVE SAND and CALIFORNIA RIVIERA and everyone would do as before: Relax. Chill. Be kind.

When it was time for the trip, Matthews started the nonstop texts: *Are you ready? Dude are you listo? Can you hear that? It's a Bali girl calling your name* ... Rez wanted to say more than *Yeah man, let's do this!* but he was tired and stressed. For a month he did a hundred sit-ups and a hundred push-ups every morning and before bed to get in shape for waves he had only ever read about, rides he could not even imagine. He was completely packed a week before his flight and tried not to read the guidebook to Bali more than once all the way through. Indonesia. An island chain made of volcanic residue, majority-Muslim population, sophisticated craft culture. Every ten minutes he wanted to go up to his mom or dad and tell them how much this meant to him, the ticket and traveler's checks and the emergency insurance card and the new backpack. When his father gave him the envelope with the tickets and the money, he looked away as Rez opened it.

Your mother wanted to get you a watch. I told her this is what the American parents do. Send their children out for a test run. It is a good practice. Maybe you will come to see your place in the world.

Surprised, Rez couldn't hide his joy.

Dude! This is awesome. Indo?! Thanks, Dad. This is great. Really great. I mean, thanks.

At the airport Rez prepared himself for whatever. He shaved closely. Wore the clothes of a traveling surfer and made Matthews promise to watch his back, tell Rez's parents if he got handcuffed or taken away to some little room. *Just call them and tell them to come here, but try not to freak them out.* But nothing happened. They went to the ticket counter and the pretty Singapore Airlines lady looked at their passports and printed their tickets and gave them neon OVERLARGE tags for their boards and said, Have a nice flight. At security a fit man with a gray mustache looked at Rez's passport and then his ticket and then the computer. He asked the nature of his trip and Rez said leisure and the man nodded his head and let grow a faint smile. Sounds good to me.

Then they crammed into seats and were up in the air, up and gone from the problems of the land, and Rez let his body empty of gravity and roam without limit on any axis. He stared out the window at the open ocean, bright and unbordered, and when he felt the thump of Matthews's sleeping head fall on his shoulder, he left it there and thought, This life.

They landed first in Singapore and sat in a daze at a soccer-themed bar, and then Jakarta, where Rez gave himself over to the jet lag as if to a good dream where the tweaks on reality were a delight, nothing dark or scary, just surprising in a pleasurable way. In all directions the faces were brown, not a white face in the whole city, aside from Matthews and the random backpackers that crossed their path on the busy streets. Open, soft faces smiled at Rez regardless of whether he smiled first. Everywhere young girls and women gathered in groups and laughed, their heads and bodies draped in colorful patterned cloth, unconscious of their beauty. The food was sticky and sweet and salty all together and from suspicion he ate little but craved much more. The two drank beer in small bars where the music was British or French or Jamaican and sometimes local. Rez listened to these new songs and could not find any sounds of anger or confusion in their jaunty notes and he wondered what the words meant but did not ask.

Neither he nor Matthews tried to pretend this wasn't some amazing happier version of the world they had known their whole lives. The women were mostly in head scarves, but for some reason Rez did not recognize them as Muslim, did not hear the muezzin call above the sound of traffic and music and laughter.

Dude. I feel like I'm stoned, or tripping.

Totally.

And that was the extent of it. *Totally.* They spent an entire afternoon in a craft market, sober as donkeys, looking at rugs of woven straw and wooden masks and life-size Buddhas carved out of teak, all of it smooth and fine and with the mark of hands. Rez stared at the masks for hours, their expressions wholly foreign to him, a single face at once conniving and gracious. Another blissed and demonic. Another repulsed and seducing. Eyeballs unique to each mask just as in an actual human face. That night they went to a club the guidebook listed as *hip international* and met a pair of Australian surfers, brothers, headed to West Java, to Cimaja. Matthews was beside himself.

Dude, that's where we are headed!

Rez, thinking of Mexico, kept his mouth shut.

Yeah. Crazy swells. Super-rides. Four, five minutes. No one for miles.

The Australians had done their research, made solid plans. Their skin was orange and their hair near white; when they spoke, their accents made whatever they said sound like a joke.

Heard you have a black prezzie over there in America?

Yup, first one, Matthews said.

Hard to imagine Aussies electing one of our aborigines, toothpick through the nose making laws and all that.

The Aussie brothers laughed and Matthews laughed a little.

Rez heard the top of the comment, and the bottom of it sank through him. He took a step back from the group and the conversation floated to surfing and comparisons of Australia's west coast and America's west coast and after a few more beers and surf talk, Rez liked them too and it was agreed they'd all take off together tomorrow and split the cost of a rental car.

One of the Australians joked, Best avoid the public buses, what with the goats and chickens and all.

And everyone laughed and they drank more cheap Thai beer and danced with a few girls from England. The next day Rez woke up and swallowed fresh juice of a fruit he'd never before seen and went with Matthews and the Australian brothers to rent a jeep with racks and sat in the back as they drove away from the blurred, muted sunrise of the city into the thrumming green countryside. Rez kept the window down and looked out at the scenery for as long as he could; the humid air and lush land quickly sucked up his head and swallowed him into a happy sleep.

Eight days passed as a single day of wet and dry, day and night. The water was warm and the waves perfect, as if designed by a surfer to please surfers. It did not take them long to find weed and a bar and girls from Japan and France and Holland and they had fun and a little sex and epic sessions that started at dawn and went on long after the sun set. Rez walked about with his skin coated in sand and his hair stiff with salt and each day they talked less and less and simply watched as the ocean stretched out its long hollow arms to meet the land, meet the land, meet the land.

On the second-to-last day a jellyfish stung Rez on the outside of his calf and he rode the board in on his stomach and tried to piss on the sting but no matter how he turned or twisted or bent, there was no way to get to the spot. A vendor of drinks and snacks watched him and laughed. The vendor jutted his head in the direction of the town and said, Cream cream, and Rez said thanks and grabbed his board and walked away from the beach and into the rice fields that led to the streets. The man at the store took a quick look at the wound and put the tube on the counter and said the price in English. Rez pulled money from his board shorts and felt his leg sting and then burn and then light itself on fire and then sting again. He stood outside the store and rubbed the ointment in and took some relief and walked back to the bamboo shack he and Matthews shared with the brothers. A woman was cleaning and his presence did not upset her. She wore a pink headscarf and Nike sneakers and cotton pants that looked like they could belong to a nurse. He sat on the thin couch and drank a beer and waited for her to finish and then took his first shower of the week and put on something other than board shorts and went for a walk.

The town was small and, unlike Jakarta, quiet. The streets had no order to them and he walked down one and up another and bought a bowl of rice and sweet chicken and ate standing and then walked on until he was lost. In a small alley the call to prayer came over him and he saw that he was standing in front of a loudspeaker, laid into a building that looked a lot like the bamboo hut he was staying in, just a little bigger, with a wide doorway that showed a single room covered in rugs. Men and woman walked toward the entrance and left their groceries and strollers and shoes outside and then disappeared into the dim room. Rez followed them.

The room was full and men took up the first ten or fifteen rows of bodies and the woman sat farther toward the back. Rez removed his shoes, washed as he remembered washing with Arash, and took a place near the back beside a wall to watch the men rise and bow and rise and bend and felt himself want to know the movements and join in. The imam was a small round man with a shiny brown face. He took his place and smiled as he spoke, smiled as he gestured. Rez found himself smiling in the midst of the happy room, and though he had no idea what was being said, he felt a great and easy joy come from the faces and the hands and the breath in the mouths of the people around him. He sat straighter and tried to find a way to interpret such gentleness among humans, such open love. They stood. They bowed. They opened their palms before their faces and kept a humble gaze.

In the shoe area a few men put out their hands and he shook them and the old imam gave him a jolly grin in passing and a few words that sounded familiar to Rez, but were without meaning. A younger man in a thin hoodie came up to him and gave him a fist bump.

Asalaamalalekiem. English?

Yes. From California.

Nice. I surf too.

He was maybe five or six years older than Rez and his eyes flashed with enthusiasm.

We love visitors here. Not many come to mosque.

Rez said nothing.

It is good you are here, brother.

They guy reached around and gave Rez a hug and then a quick wave and walked out the front entrance. Rez stood frozen for a second and felt eyes on him. At the far end of the room was a young girl, her purple head scarf, inlaid with rhinestones, barely covering the masses of black curls that tried to push out from under it. She caught his eye and dropped her head with a demure expression and Rez felt his breath rise, his body warm, his sex stiffen. For a moment he took her as Fatima, the mouth and cheeks and hair, but without the anger and for a moment he saw what she could be, a person in peace. Rez searched the ground for his flip-flops and walked back into the small streets of a million shops and turned the idea around in his head: *So this is Islam? This is the real Islam. I get it, Arash. I get it.* And with a lifted mood and soothed heart he made his way through the rice paddies and to the beach with such an obvious looseness that Matthews teased him.

Did you get a massage?

No.

Are you sure? There is something very post-blow-jobby about you.

Rez laughed. What can I say? High on life, man. Good surf. Good friends. Beautiful place. A guy can't bliss out?

But Matthews was right, the ease he saw in Rez was real and Rez stood before his friend and smiled. Today was different from days before, now he was different, a door, long closed, had opened in him and his soul stepped through.

23

IT WAS MATTHEWS'S idea to wear skirts, blue and green sarongs with block patterns on them. *Why not? They will be so much more comfortable on the plane.* Finally Rez agreed and they dressed for the airport as if for some sort of costume show-and-tell of their summer vacation. The beaches and good food and days of waves had made Rez silly and happy and he and Matthews spent their last night walking around Jakarta buying gifts and acting like they owned the place. They stood in front of a stall selling fabrics and the owner tried to get them to try on the sarongs and they looked around on the streets and saw men wearing thin cotton skirts like it was nothing. Rez and Matthews tried them on over their shorts and the fabric guy shook his head no and laughed. They took off their shorts but kept their boxers on and walked around the city with warm humid air between their legs and did not hide from each other how great it felt.

Women must have felt like this when they put on pants.

Totally.

They went to a bar and then to dinner and then drinking and then to the club where they met two girl backpackers from New Zealand. Matthews bought them all drinks and they drank way too much and went to a noisy outdoor rave and the girls used the open folds of the sarongs to give the boys hand jobs while they danced close.

Now Rez waited in the passport line in America, waiting to be let into the country that was his but he felt too happy and silly and calm for. All around him the travelers from places that were not Indonesia wore bad-fitting gray or black or blue and seemed pushed down by sleepiness and their dark bland lives. He looked at Matthews beside him tinkering on his phone and laughed at his bleached-out hair, colorful skirt, and neon shirt that said COCA-COLA in Indonesian. Matthews stuck up his middle finger and kept tinkering and Rez knew it would be some time before their souls returned back to their American-born bodies.

Rez whispered to Matthews, Keep it going as long as it lasts.

Totally, dude. There has got to be an Indonesian restaurant somewhere in the OC.

We'll hit it up on the way home.

Right-o.

The line inched forward and Rez opened up his passport out of boredom. The few stamps were mostly European, with one for the family vacation to Canada, but Indo was the wildest place he'd been. He stared at the photo of himself. Ten years old. Pale skin, light brown hair, bangs cut straight across his face. A serious expression. Maybe even scared. Rez knew that kid, knew he wasn't a happy kid, because of his mean dad and his quiet mom. He had a few friends and soccer and his textbooks and video games and those were fun, but the rest was tense. That was the word that came to him as he looked at the picture of the boy. Tense. Rez closed the passport, he couldn't be more different, that kid had no relation to him now and he tried to clear his mind of the ten-year-old's stare and then the passport official gestured to him *come*.

Her nameplate said FENG and she wore exactly no expression on her face. She opened the blue book, ran the first page under the scanner, and stared at her computer. A small beep came from the machine and she pressed a button and looked again at the screen. Then she looked at him. She closed the passport.

Reason for travel?

Leisure.

Length of stay?

Eight days.

How many cities did you travel to?

Umm. Two, I think. Yeah. Two.

Did you travel alone?

No.

Rez gestured over to Matthews, next in line, his sarong and neon-green tank top and dark tan skin and Rez could not help it and laughed.

I traveled with that clown.

Feng did not smile. She did nothing to change her posture or her face. Rez tried to steady himself, to get himself serious, though he could find no good reason for her seriousness.

Sir, I am sorry but I will have to ask you a few more questions. I'd like you to answer as clearly as you can and keep your eyes on me.

As she spoke, a man entered the glass cubicle where she sat. He stood behind her, in the same green outfit the border patrol wore in San Diego, and leaned down toward her computer screen. The two of them had the most stressed faces Rez had seen in days, their whole selves taut and forced and behind all that a little scared.

Ok.

What cities did you visit?

Jakarta. Cimaja.

While you were there, did you visit any schools, religious organizations, nongovernmental organizations? Please list them by name and location.

No. We just surfed.

He did not think of it, the afternoon trip to the mosque, the room of men and woman at prayer. He thought of the waves and the beaches and the soupy rice fields he had to walk through to get there. There were clubs and restaurants and that nice hostel they stayed at in Jakarta. Feng stared at him and then stared at the computer screen. The border patrol guard did the same and then they briefly looked at each other. The guard walked out of the room and came to stand beside Rez. Feng spoke, her face soft now, lenient, even a little kind.

Mr. Courdee, we need to ask a few additional questions.

Rez looked at the guard beside him and the woman behind the glass and felt no panic. His nerves lay somewhere deep below his skin, deep and out of reach. He had done nothing wrong, he was full of the warm sea, and it gave him a luxurious patience from which he could mine no fear. The country he'd left ten days ago was the same as the country he returned to now, but he, Mr. Reza Courdee, was different.

My pleasure.

He and the guard turned their backs to the line and began to walk away.

Behind him Matthews yelled, Hey! Wait! Rez!

And Rez turned around and called back, Chill. Chill. It's all good. Just some questions. Meet me at baggage claim. And don't ding my board!

The guard took him to an elevator, pressed a button without a number next to it, and then inserted a key beside the button, and the big box moved up and then what felt like down and then what Rez was sure was sideways. He looked at the guard and smiled as if to say, *This is cool,* but the guard stared straight ahead with his hands behind his back.

They walked down a long bright hallway where men and a few women sat with clunky large plastic bracelets on their wrists that flashed every few seconds. They looked at him and he looked at them, every last one of their faces a shade of brown all the way from dark tan to near black. There were a few women in hijabs and a few women in tracksuits and a group of men in Mexican soccer jerseys. Santos Laguna. Club León. Cruz Azul. They seemed tired and bored and Rez tried not to look at them too much and kept his mind on the waves and the clouds of Cimaja, the place most opposite this.

They put him in a room with a single chair and a low table. The guard said nothing and left. Rez looked around and eventually sat down in the chair and closed his eyes and when he heard the noise of the door, he opened them again and took a look at the two men who came in. Both tall. Both thin. The asked him if he was who he was and he nodded again, surprised at their formality, their suits, and that there was nowhere for them to sit.

They took turns asking questions from memory and Rez said what he felt to be true. Yes, he was an American citizen. On a surf trip. A graduation present. Berkeley. No political leanings. Not devout. Not his mother or his father. Yes, he knew of the terrorist threat. Yes, he felt it was a threat. Yes, he was worried for the country. No, he had no other plans to leave the United States in the near future. Chemistry.

Then he paused.

Minor in religion if I can find the time.

He didn't know why he said it. The thought had not once crossed his mind, a minor, religion. But something inside of him was roiling, some defiance, some anger that life was going to be hard again, hard and ugly and tense. He thought of the boy in the passport picture, serious from the pressures of the outside world, and wanted to be other than that, wanted to embody the bright spirit of these last eight days. The men stared at him.

Religion?

Yeah. With everything going on now, it would be good to see what it's all about. Don't you think? Figure out why people are killing each other for it.

The one who did all the talking said nothing and the other left the room and returned seconds later with a small black box.

Retina scanner. Please look into the lens.

A tiny red speck stared back at him and Rez blinked and the machine beeped and the man who held it left the room and the man who stayed walked toward Rez and crouched until his face was at the level of Rez's knees beneath the sarong.

We have no reason to keep you.

Great.

We saw your name, your travel destination, your smart-ass attitude, and thought we'd take a minute to tell you what is at stake. Every day someone with malicious intent for the innocent people of this country walks or flies or drives across our borders.

Ok.

The people you come from, your mother, your father, their families, the people you know at your fancy school, the rich Indian and Lebanese and Syrians just like you, are not the pride of this country.

Ok.

The man stared straight at Rez.

We let you in because we couldn't keep you out and you know that, your parents know it. You feel it every time someone wins the prize instead of you, gets the part in the play, gets into the better college. Gets the promotion. All of this adds up. And your people, who think they are worth a great deal, know that even after making all that money, they are worthless. Their children are worthless, and if this violence continues, their children's children will be worthless too. The American dream will never play all the way out for you. Do you understand?

The man was not wrong. And his speech repeated inside Rez, his voice, his clean-shaven face, his long torso, and his narrow head stamped themselves onto Rez's mind. He sat up in his chair and focused his thoughts on the mosque, the kind glances, and the jolly imam.

Yeah. I am just trying to do my part. Be a good guy. Go to school. Make my parents proud.

The man stared at Rez and between them not a single vibration of belief pulsed. The man stood up and walked out.

By the time Rez got outside, it was dark. He found Matthews sitting on his suitcase smoking bummed cigarettes playing Candy Crush on his phone.

Dude. What the fuck?

Exactly.

You ok?

Fine. They had me confused with one point three billion other people.

Matthews didn't laugh.

Your folks texted me. I told them we were getting dinner in L.A.

Cool. I'm beat. Let's hit it.

They found a shuttle that would take them to Laguna and loaded their gear and Matthews tried to talk to him on the drive, but Rez finally put a hand up and leaned his head on the window.

Dude. I gotta take a snooze. Long day.

24

. . . **OK OK OK.** It's not as bad as it was the first week. I mean, I didn't even leave my house. Did you leave?. . . No. No one did. It was just the fam, sitting around, Moms, Dad, Haleh and Darian, watching the news on TV. Not that it changed, but we watched anyway. Dozens killed. Six attackers, one of them Hassan Amajalad. My name is Hassan. That burned for a few days. I thought about having it legally changed, Henry or Harold or Hank, something . . . Go ahead, laugh. I least I am honest about it. You probably thought about it too. Though I don't know, Rez is such a weird name, like *razor* or *reservation* or something, not as easy to fuck with. But Omid, man, with Omid you are fucked. Anyway the first week sucked and now, look, two months later and we are out, sitting at Maryam's Luxe, smoking apple tobacco and talking shit and welcoming home our friend from his fancy surf trip. What's there to complain about? Are you scared? I'm not scared. Things will go back to normal. They always do.

Man, that is bullshit. Who says you are not scared? Your ass drove under the speed limit all the way here. Two months and my sisters still get shit wherever they go. Yesterday Shadi got coffee at Starbucks and some dude yelled at her from his jacked truck, *Scarf head go home!* She just covers her hair. Nothing else, and this asshole didn't even get out of his car. My uncle says the mosque he goes to gets tagged every night and that the FBI and CIA are parked out front, not even hiding . . .

It'll die down. This is America, man. Didn't you listen to anything in civics class? Plurality? Liberty for all? Remember after 9/11, shit was bad, and way more people died and there was a war and still, things got normal again.

This is different. Something about this is different. I mean three miles from here there was a massacre. Not 9/11 bad, but bad. People died because Muslims freaked out. In our hood. All that America and equality and liberty shit goes out the window! I mean, how many checkpoints do you have to go through to get gas? To go to the mall? How many times do they pull your car aside after they see your license and look you up and then stare at you and treat you like criminal shit? It's not going to go back to normal for a long time. At least around here. We might not have done the deed, but the police can't tell us apart and we are going to be suspects as long as this crazy Islam shit keeps going . . . All that rap music you love, the cops and gangs and injustice, well you in it now . . .

Omid the pessimist. Relax, dude. Stop listening to your dad's conspiracy theories. Smoke more weed. Just look around. A month ago no one was here. Smoking hookahs and Middle Eastern vibes were like a curse. And three months ago you couldn't get in, the line out the door was so long. People are slow, but they want the normal, the good life, the shit money can buy. It's gonna be nice again, just wait.

Indo was nice. Nice all day. Nice all night.

That's right, dude, listen to us, we're here to welcome you back and you haven't said a thing, how was it? What is the state of the rest of the non-freaked-out world?

Sweet. Good surf. Cheap beer. Nice people. Very different. Most of the people were Muslim. Muslims walking around going to mosque, everything peaceful.

—

Dude, that's right, Indo's got more Muslims than anywhere else. Pretty brown girls in head scarves. It's supposed to be really chill.

Yeah. Makes this place seem like a pressure cooker.

I hear that. And the surf was good, right?

Epic.

They give you any shit at the airport?

Nothing I couldn't handle.

And the massages in Bali?

I plead the Fifth.

THEN DAYS AND days of nothing to do. A checkup. A trip to the dentist. The occasional session with Matthews, but mostly Rez's phone stayed silent and he spent the days barefoot in the empty house, reading, watching movies, staring at the surface of the blue pool and then swimming in it, the underwater as quiet as his mind.

He thought about college, the month left until he could get on the Amtrak at San Juan Capistrano to sit for fourteen hours until he got to Berkeley, where a welcome van would pick him up and take him to his dorm. New streets. New building. New bed. His parents agreed to let him arrive alone and he imagined the handshaking from his proud father and hugs from his mother and then he'd be on his own, free to live as he liked to live, whatever that meant. He looked up the beaches closest to Berkeley and the surf spots and saw the wild brown waters of Ocean Beach and the mellow tubes in Pacifica and the late-winter monsters at Mavericks and thought, That will be enough. He'd find a friend with a car, go early in the morning before class, smoke a bowl, harmonize with himself as only the ocean allowed, and then go back to school and learn it up.

He spent his days in preparation; went through his clothes, filled garbage bags with T-shirts and old uniforms and pants he didn't like and left them in the laundry room for his mom to take to Goodwill. He took down the posters of surfers and Champions League soccer stars, the prizes from school and the old anime cutouts, and rolled them up and put them in the garage on the shelf beside his artwork from middle and elementary school, pastels of sharks and paintings of spaceships and a papier-mâché mask of his own, much smaller, face. He did not try it on but pushed it aside to make room for the new old stuff and wondered if these objects, years of things, were the all of him, a person defined by what he had touched.

Rez looked up to the top shelf: a long row of photo albums, thick spiral-bound books with fake leather covers and gilded edges Rez had seen the million times his mother or father pulled a car into the garage, though not once had he actually looked at them.

He pulled one down at random. Photos of the trip to the Grand Canyon, his whole family smiling with terror before the sheer expanse of rock; himself at four years old and crying at the sight of a giant mouse head bending down to embrace him; at the beach, in a hat and thick white sunblock. A few birthdays and a few picnics and his face, round with pale hair and green eyes, unfamiliar to him but for the serious stare. Maybe he had always been that way in the center, the serious boy, and he felt bad for a moment that he'd tried to smoke it away, surf it away, somehow erase the gravity that radiated from deep inside.

He skipped a few albums back and saw his father's friend the rug seller, younger, a full head of hair, and a smooth face. There were pictures of his father at a rug store, rolling rugs and writing out receipts and posing with a family, an older woman and three long-haired daughters. Rez's father stood a head taller than everyone else and his clothes and hair and sunglasses were fashionable and showy and Rez could not even bring himself to laugh, the man in the photo so different from the man who ate and slept and shat in this house. Rez turned the pages to see a series of photos without human subjects. Landscapes of the desert, mountains that looked like Tahoe, the Golden Gate Bridge.

Rez flipped to the back and a thick envelope slipped out from between the last page and the end, covered in Arabic script, airmail stickers, and stamps of another country's bridges and dams and turbaned men. The only things written in English were his father's name, Saladin Courdee, and an address in Westwood, the handwriting careful and shaky across the front. Rez opened the envelope and shook out a single sheet of paper no thicker than onionskin, and half a dozen photographs, black-and-white with scalloped edges, fell out. The letter was in Arabic script and Rez stared at it for a few minutes and understood nothing. From the pictures he understood less. He did not recognize a single person, did not understand their poses or the places they gathered. In one, a tall man in a military uniform leaned on an old black car, a ciga-rette in one hand and a half smile across his lips. In another, the same man, same uniform, was on a blanket in what looked like a desert, surrounded by a few men in turbans and a few men in suits. The man again had the lopsided grin and Rez stared at him, his square jaw and light eyes, and saw something familiar. In another photo a woman stood in front of a lake with a few children at the level of her hip and a few at the level of her knees. The woman's hair was uncovered but behind her crouched another woman, surrounded by pots and pans, and her hair was covered and her face sour with some old expression. Rez looked at the children, probably old people now, no one he'd ever met, yet every face familiar. He flipped through to the last photos, the man in the military uniform again, young, younger than Rez thought there were cameras for, his uniform still part of an army's but an older army with tight boots laced up to the knee, stiff wool pants tucked into them. The jacket, the belts, the rifle behind the shoulder, the serious look on his perfect face, and Rez stopped and stared down and saw his own self, the same serious face, neither boy or man, lost to time. The same look, the same concern. He put the photo in his pocket.

He put the rest of the pictures and the letter back into the envelope and the envelope back inside the album and thought about the line of life, from the man in uniform through his bride through to Rez's father and into Rez and then what? And how? He sensed the momentum of it, the whole long unfolding line of fucking and fighting that somehow ended here in this garage, at the Santa Claus with a cotton-ball beard and the badly painted clay balls of the solar system he made in fourth grade, all of it the spinning tail end of something started in a time far before the times of these photographs, in the mountains and rivers of a faraway place where Rez's face already existed in the bones of the faces now long dead, the faces of men and woman who didn't know Reza Courdee, but knew one day he would be.

He heard the garage door open and stepped away from the shelf, and his mom's white SUV pulled in. From inside the sealed car his mom waved. Rez waved back and walked into the house.

How to become a man?

Rez held himself and knew the organ in his hands was not it. He was male but that didn't make him a man. Fatima slept beside him in sheets that tangled around her limbs, black hair flung out around like a dark halo, all woman, no part girl. But how? Because she bled? Because her chest was no longer flat and she didn't giggle? She hadn't had a baby, wasn't married, and yet when the world looked at her, they saw a woman and when it looked at him, they saw a boy.

Fatima rolled from her side to her back and Rez looked at her, the ribs coming into and out of view as she breathed, freckles spread out on her breastbone and shoulders, the neck a strong thin muscular cord, and the head, eyes closed, totally still. He filled his eyes with her as if this were the last time. He looked and looked.

Why did his body jump to her and only her? All the girls before, Sophia and everyone else, never made him feel like this. He wanted their bodies when they were in front of him, offered or teasing his eye, but afterward he forgot about them. It was only Fatima he craved in her absence. When she called him, three weeks after he came back from Bali, nearly two and half months after the massacre, he answered the phone on the first ring and said *Not much* and *Yeah, I can hang* and *Cool.* Then he begged his mom for a ride to Fatima's house. Now the desire had a destination and he focused on that moment with such discipline that when she answered the door in a long loose dress and silk scarf wrapped around her hair, Rez still let out a short sigh of relief, like a man whose plane has landed in a war zone after a turbulent flight. He smiled and said hello and wanted to say thank-you, for asking him over, for letting him back into her, and she took a step away from his attempt at a hug and pulled the door wide, her face a warm open smile.

It is nice to see you, Reza.

You too.

He put his hands in his pockets and took them out again. She stood back from the open door.

Come in.

The house was empty, the whole family gone to a cousin's wedding in Santa Ana, no one back until late. Normally Rez knew what that meant, but now as he watched her move around the kitchen steeping black tea, he tried, with difficulty, to tame himself of any expectation.

They sat outside under an overlarge umbrella and drank the hot tea. Rez took tiny sips of the bitter drink and realized she had never before prepared anything for him, never served him more than a soda tossed from a fridge or a perfectly rolled joint. He drank and kept his eyes on the hummingbirds that came and went from the ornate glass feeder hung from the branch of a nearby Japanese maple. It took some time but they started to talk, and when they did, it was not the talk of adults but also not the conversations they had had as high school kids. Rez did not ask when they were going to smoke, said nothing about how good she looked, and Fatima sat up straight and the drank her tea with patience. She smiled each time she asked him a question and behaved as if the thing that had once banged around her bright pale face had come to land. They sat in the empty garden and Rez felt seriousness between them, becoming them.

How was the trip?

Rez wanted to answer in a few words but talked for a long time and with much excitement about the world he'd found in Indo, a place where Muslims were everywhere and no one, no single life, even the poorest ones, seemed stressed. He told her about his visit to the mosque and how he'd sat there and the way his whole body felt loose with a kind of love.

Sounds nice.

Fatima looked into her teacup. Rez saw the sweat bead around her forehead and lip. He wanted to lick it off. He pushed himself farther back into his seat and adjusted his shorts. He didn't mention what happened at the airport.

Your scarf looks hot. I mean, it looks like it is making you hot. I mean warm. You know what I mean.

She laughed and adjusted the edge of it to cover the stray bits of hair come loose around her face. It wasn't well tied, like the ones the girls in Bali wore, and he wanted to see her hair.

It feels nice. Keeps my hair in one place. Doesn't stick to my neck now.

He knew better than to ask why she was wearing it, what was going on with the outfit and the tea and the invitation.

What have you been up to?

Studying.

Studying? Rez nearly laughed. School is over, Stanford doesn't give summer reading, do they?

No, thank God. I've been studying other things. The Koran, politics.

For what?

For me.

Oh.

Rez tried not to let his mind go back, to the afternoon at Javad's house, the violence on innocent people, the determined imam, the YouTube clips.

And what have you learned?

That there is much much more to learn.

Rez waited.

And I've learned that so much of what we think is important, isn't.

—

It is important to believe in a power bigger than yourself. To pray. To honor your family. To serve. To have a spiritual center. To love.

Love. In six months of sex, long stoned afternoons at the beach, and parties, it was a word she'd never said. Whenever he wanted to say it, he resisted, knowing it was not her language, not even in that way that girls always said, *I love those shoes. I totally love that show. I love that song.* Now here it was, from her lips, *love,* and Rez wanted more of that word, more of her lips, more of more.

She drank the tea and sweat.

I started to cover the day after the attacks. The day after we graduated. My mom wears it and I wanted to do something to show I was with her, with my aunts and cousins and other Muslim women to show that not all Muslims are terrorists. To challenge anyone who came at us. I am young. This country teaches young women not to be afraid, I am not afraid.

A hummingbird buzzed up to the feeder, extended its beak, buzzed away. Stillness and motion.

It took only one day. Some guy threw a full jar of peanut butter at me in the parking lot of Albertsons and called me a terrorist whore. The jar just missed my head. I called the police, and when they came, they acted like it was my fault. They asked if maybe he dropped the jar by accident. If there were any witnesses. Maybe I cut him off with my cart. Without witnesses there was nothing they could do. Then they told me to be more careful.

She stopped talking and took another sip.

One of the officers said I should be brought in, just to make sure I had no affiliations. The other cop, a Mexican guy, told him to drop it. Then they left. There have been other incidents since. Mostly harassment. But that was the worst.

She put the teacup down and sat back and stared at Rez, her posture still straight, her gaze harder now. Rez waited and she said nothing. He waited a little longer.

Tomorrow I'm going to a new mosque, to begin my studies, to see what I can contribute.

Rez waited for the invitation to join her, waited to see what his heart felt at the thought of it, but she did not ask. Fatima stood and tucked the new loose hairs under her scarf and then put out her hand to him, not with the palm sideways like a handshake, but with the palm up, as an invitation. He placed his hand on hers and they closed fingers and for a minute the garden, the table, the three-tiered fountain, and the million-dollar house swirled as his head went light and his balance gave.

But first I needed to see you. The way we used to. One last time.

He followed her to the bedroom they'd spent countless afternoons in, smoking and fucking and not even pretending to do the chemistry they were supposed to be doing. At first their bodies met in silence, with intensity; the second time slowly; and the third time with a violence she did not protest. She fell asleep nearly immediately afterward and he sat up beside the smell and sight of her, the woman of her, and thought the thought that wouldn't leave him: how to become a man?

Choices. To make them yourself and then live by them. To know what to do with your own body and mind. A man made choices. A child did not make choices. He thought of the man in the military uniform from the black-and-white photographs. His pleased gaze, in command of his fate. He saw his father, just arrived in America, the man in him beginning to make the decisions that would take him into manhood and now old age. Rez stared at Fatima, who directed the course of her life, regardless of what people thought. He considered himself, and the way he moved in reaction, like a pinball, from one thing to the next, as he was told, as was expected, as made the least friction, and he knew this was the lazy behavior of a scared boy.

He watched her sleep. He watched her sleep and stretch and sleep again and told himself this would not be the last time to see it, her naked body full of him, this body that made him awake to life. No, this would not be the last time. He let this feeling form in him like a strong sense of direction and slowly it became a determination and a decision. To be a man was to be with Fatima, to have the woman of his choice, to make a union with her, see this body without cover, available to him at any time. To be a man he must enter into love.

27

THE PACKET CAME with the rest of the mail and Rez grabbed it off the floor. It was heavy and stamped with the words WELCOME, FRESHMAN across the front and the back. He went to his room, threw it on his bed, and closed the blinds against the heat.

Afternoon today was hotter than yesterday and the day before and probably not as hot as tomorrow and this was late July in SoCal. He should have been at the beach but he liked the cool empty vibe of his house and stayed home, in board shorts, in and out of the pool, reading the old copies of *National Geographic* his father collected before the Internet showed the world at a glance whenever they wanted. Rez fanned out the pieces: magazines and leaflets and flyers and a decal of the university bear. The pictures showed students and teachers and classrooms, lots of grass and lots of backpacks. Rez saw a photo of a clock tower with a great bay behind it and the Golden Gate Bridge in the distance. The water looked steely and flat and Rez wondered where exactly the waves were.

Consent forms. Class offerings. A letter from the head of the chemistry program. Orientation schedule. Social mixers for freshmen. Dorm assignments. Sports clubs. Academic clubs. Student health clubs. *10 Tips for Surviving Your First Month.* Rez wondered, what would kill him the first month? All the images in the pamphlet showed students all around campus, smiling in various versions of the school logo, sweatshirts, shorts, T-shirts, soccer socks. There were no heads in any of the photographs, just artfully shot body parts. The pages were numbered like a *Letterman* countdown: *10. Don't overpack. 9. Attend welcome events. 7. Don't forget where you come from. It is ok to feel a little homesick at first, or to even feel like you've outgrown your home . . . 3. Ask an upperclassman for help. 2. Call home. 1. Keep an open mind.*

Rez gathered the materials and shoved them back into the envelope and threw the whole packet into the bottom drawer of his desk. In three weeks he could look at it again, maybe then it would mean something.

28

WHO DOESN'T LIKE surprises?

Fatima asked again and again until he finally said, Ok, and when she came to pick him up, he had to talk himself down from horny expectations and just be happy to see her and sit in the closed space of the car with her skin and scent.

Salaam.

Hello to you too.

The last time they hung out she'd brought a picnic and they went to a park and sat in the shade not far from a playground full of blond kids and OC moms. She sat across from him and snacked on grapes and read passages from the Koran out loud to practice her Arabic, to *try out the thoughts.* Rez resisted the sound of them, their order and severity, but after a while he opened his ears and his brain switched to student mode and listened to her slow and faulty Arabic and the translation she did immediately afterward. He wondered about the passages, their odd directives and complete certainty, and considered the feelings they left him with—at once gentle and determined—his mind turned toward them now, curious. Fatima read on.

And forget not your portion of legal enjoyment in this world and do good as Allah has been good to you and seek not mischief in the land.

Rez noticed her scarf, nicely tied, was cleaner around the face now, neater over the head. He'd complimented her on it when she picked him up.

YouTube, Arab girls in the projects in France have their own channel. The girls in France don't mess around.

He saw how much care she put into it, how it was ironed and smooth, and when the wind blew, it fluttered a little but nothing was exposed. She continued to read as if in a kind of musical meditation.

Stand firmly against injustice as witness to Allah even if it be against yourselves or your parents and relatives. It feels like it was written for me, maybe for all of us. Here we are, in this country suspicious of us, in a world that is trying to make life miserable for Muslims who want to be peaceful and devout. Stand firm. Stand firmly.

On and on it went until the grapes and the chips and the lemonade were gone. Rez absorbed each passage like the solution to a long problem he tried to solve every morning. How to be good. How to trust. How to be a person. The words from the Koran were clues, and when an ant crawled slowly up his flip-flop and his foot, he let it alone and thought of grace. Fatima read and he listened and watched the children play their games on the playground, their souls unconcerned with God, and the words of the old text came through him and he understood them as a call to a devotion complete and without error.

When she dropped him off at his house, Rez said thank-you and wanted to touch her but instead just let his eyes settle into hers for a moment longer and the heat built between them. Rez felt himself light up from the center out to the fingers and toes and Fatima blushed.

Ok. Bye.

Bye.

When he sat for dinner with his parents, he stared at the food, eggplant stew and rice, fresh radishes and mint and green onions, and thought of the perfect symmetry, the crisp and soft, fresh and cooked, and opened himself up to it and to the gratitude he had to his mother and father for providing it. Another kind of heat began to spread, evenly and throughout his form.

This is so good.

His mother looked at him and tilted her head.

Same as it has been all these years.

From the head of the table his father gave a loud, solid laugh.

Yes, but he is just starting to realize how much he will miss it in two weeks! Don't worry, we will visit. I am sure she will bring a cooler full of food.

Rez did not know what he had done to deserve the mother before him, the father, and it broke his heart to imagine himself far from them, detached. He stared at the flat blue water of the pool outside and focused on the single yellow ginkgo leaf in a slow float across the surface, the water's easy way.

She drove down Highway 1 until they turned into an anonymous strip mall where Rez assumed she was going to run some errand. Nail shop. Dry cleaner. Designer consignment. Walgreens. Sushi restaurant. FedEx. Kinko's.

The surprise is dry cleaning?

Hop out.

He followed her into the Kinko's and waited before the counter as she paid the cashier in cash for an hour on a computer.

What's wrong with your computer? Why the cash? What happened to your card?

Don't worry about it.

The cashier, in his late thirties with soft thin blond hair and crooked shoulders, pointed at the computer farthest away from him and said, Use the headphones if you are going to chat and don't talk too loud. He seemed to have an idea of who they were and what they wanted, which was more than Rez could say.

Fatima woke the screen and logged on to her Skype account with a name he didn't recognize. She scrolled through a list of contacts Rez had never heard of. She clicked on one before he had a chance to read it and the screen went blue and they sat and stared at the reflection of themselves: two people, a pretty girl in a scarf, big cat eyes and pale skin, and a handsome guy, younger than a man but older than a boy, square jaw and close-cut hair. For that instant Rez did not recognize himself or Fatima and saw two strangers, a boy and a girl, waiting. Then the call connected and a guy in a funny hat, with a spotty thin beard, spoke to them and Rez nearly jumped out of his seat.

Dude. A! What's up?!

Light filled Arash's eyes.

Reza, my man! Long time!

And it was him. Arash. The same voice, same happy face, thinner and smaller under the hat. Different costume, but everything else like it was. A sharp sensation went through Rez and he wanted his friend here right now, to hang with, to fill the hot, empty days with thinking and talking and smoke. Rez remembered the night they went to the Hollywood Bowl show, how fun it was to have a friend like that, how much better college would be with someone he didn't have to explain anything to. Fatima spoke to Arash in Arabic and he spoke back and Rez tried to give them a moment but he was too excited.

Dude, where are you? Where have you been? What's with the beard? It's a little . . . fluffy . . . and not total coverage exactly, but the hat's dope . . .

From wherever he was, Arash laughed and then Rez laughed.

It is good to see you, brother. Looking well. Looking ready.

Where are you, dude?

Arash went quiet for a moment and Rez was about to repeat himself when his friend's face got serious and the voice that responded was deeper.

Brother, I am in the good land. The land of right and wrong. A place I cannot even describe.

Rez looked at his friend and started to see it, in bits and pieces, the truth as it was before him. The clean white shirt, the try at the beard, the Muslim beard, the fundamentalist beard. The beard that proves you believe Islam in all its force as the imam in one of the YouTube videos had said.

Yeah, but, are you, like, ok?

I am well, Rez. Better than well. Don't even think otherwise. You?

Good. College in a few weeks. Gonna be better since Fatima is coming with. Stanford. Her family is really proud. I don't want to brag, but I think my tutoring in AP is really what did it . . .

Arash said nothing, made no gesture with his face or head, and Fatima looked down at her hands, clasped tight in her lap. She did not share in the joke that had always been a joke. On the screen Arash leaned forward, the smile still pasted across his face. The screen unfroze and then he was talking again.

No one can tell the future, my brother. Only Allah knows the way.

Yeah. Well. I know my own way.

There was the defiance again, the defiance Rez had felt the day at Javad's when they watched the imam's talk about Muslims as the victims and the need to rise up, to fight. Rez wanted nothing to do with it. Fatima placed her hand on his knee.

Remember? The suras I read you? Patience? An open heart?

Rez felt her fingers not as if they were on the outside of his pant leg but as if they were stroking him, keeping him calm and safe and pleased.

He looked at Arash and saw his old friend in new form and took a breath and pulled his roller chair closer to the screen and took another breath.

So then where are you?

In the good land. Building a new country.

Building? Building what?

A country. A community. A homeland where there is no punishment for believing in Allah. Only rewards. I am happy for you and your life, Reza, my brother. I hope that you can be happy for my life as well. Like I said, we are all on the paths set out for us.

Yeah. Well, I wish you were here too. There were good times this summer. Rez lied.

That's good, man. I wish you were here. There is so much to show you. We are going to build beautiful new hospitals, smooth streets without beggars, all the children in schools. I've even got enough engineering under my belt to work on a water-treatment plant. Can you believe it! Work my father wasn't allowed to do until he was thirty-three! I am only eighteen!

Rez smiled at his friend's giddy brags. There he was, just a million pixels in a weird costume, still Arash.

My time is up soon. What a great day to see both of your faces. We need people like you here. But I guess the world needs good people like you everywhere. Rez, stay true. You know how we do.

Arash put his fist up to the camera and in simple reaction Rez did the same and hit the screen with a bump and felt dumb as soon as his knuckles hit the screen. Fatima said a few words in Arabic and Arash listened and said a few words back and Rez looked around at the empty Kinko's and caught the eye of the cashier, who stared at them, his look impatient and suspicious and Rez saw them as they seemed. Two kids, Middle Eastern–looking, talking to a guy on the screen with a beard. That is all he needed to make a call. Rez took off his head-phones and tapped Fatima on the shoulder and tilted his head toward the door. He heard Fatima keep talking, saying good-bye the way they always did at her house or Arash's house with long phrases such as Alhamdulillah and Bismillah again and again until there was the silence and the frozen image of Arash, the cement wall and smiling face.

29

IT WAS HOT in the car and it was hot outside. Rez sat in the driver's seat with the windows down and watched men and women come and go to the Jummah prayers and to the small grocery store next to the mosque. Then it was sweltering and he got out and stood beside the car, on the sidewalk, and paced the few feet between parking meters and wondered how it could be so hot in Anaheim. It was only twenty minutes from his house, thirty with traffic, and yet the air, the plants, the dirt, was all desert. He got back in the car, rolled up the windows, and turned on the AC and the radio, and when the car was an icebox and he was still burning up, he knew the heat was inside him, and had been all morning since the beach.

He went because Matthews said it was the best swell of the year and there would be nothing like it at the mushy beaches up north and so why not? Matthews had time for a super quickie, two or three waves before the doctor's appointment he'd already flaked on twice, but he could take Rez and then Rez could stay and bum a ride home. Rez texted. *Fatima can pick me up.* There was a pause and then a ding and Matthews's jokey reply: *Oh I bet she can . . .*

Rez texted her and she told him he'd have to come to mosque with her afterward and wait in the car and he said fine and he and Matthews went into the August ocean with just board shorts and spent an hour so blissed out that he thanked Matthews for the heads-up and thanked the tectonic plates for the way they made the shelf off the coast of California and thanked the ocean herself for the fast, elegant heaves. After he surfed along for what felt like a lifetime, Rez rode a shallow wave in and walked onto the shore and up to his small pile of things.

Next to him a group of guys, still wet, sat together and looked out over the water and he gave a what's-up nod in their direction and a few of them looked back and a few of them looked away. He took off his leash and his rash guard and heard laughter. First quick and quiet and then big and loud. He stared in the direction of the group of guys and the sounds stopped and Rez grabbed for his towel and wrapped it around him and took off his board shorts and looked around for his jeans, naked and searching, he heard the word *monkey* and then *hairy* and then *Arab*, and then *I didn't know Muslims could swim. All that desert and shit.*

Rez first looked down at his body. Were they talking to him? He had hair on his chest, a thin patch between his nipples, and his shoulders and back were smooth, like a kid's. He looked like most guys his age, and certainly not as hairy as some, or as dark. What were they talking about? He wasn't an Arab. His parents were from Iran. Rez was born here, as American as they were. They didn't know shit. What the fuck?

I hear those guys are hung like camels. Should we check?

The laughs were snickers now, fast and furtive. A few stood up and walked toward him.

Rez grabbed the towel around his waist, clenched it to him, and straightened his body and faced in their direction.

Fuck off.

It's cool, man. It's cool. Just doing a little research. Gotta know your enemy.

They put their palms up in a fake innocence but kept moving toward him.

I mean, you are a population under suspicion here, it's not like we don't have a right to take a look. For national security.

The other two also stood up and Rez did not want to take the chance. There were four of them, enough to do whatever they wanted, and he couldn't stop them. He felt them, behind him, next to him, around him, their thoughts thinking, and their bodies on the verge, and just like the times with his father, he felt his own body, already loose with fear and pain. He held the towel with one hand and grabbed his jeans and board with the other and walked down the beach, and when he was far enough, he turned back to them.

Rez shouted. You deserve what's coming. Fuckers.

He had no idea what he meant, but it got them quiet. The four stood back and didn't move and Rez stomped through the sand, each step sinking a little deeper than the last, until he was at the parking lot, fire in his belly, through his chest, up his neck and into his head. He put his pants on and checked for his wallet and his phone and pulled his shirt over his head and waited.

Fatima asked him what was wrong and he said nothing. She asked again and he said, Nothing, just a wipeout. I wiped out, that's all. And he knew she didn't buy it, and she patted down her white silk scarf and drove with her eyes straight ahead.

On the ride inland Rez said nothing, his body hot and his mind flashing. He thought about himself, his face and body and his features and how they said something that he never said. A few other guys with hair on their shoulders and hair on their backs didn't swim at the pool parties and didn't take off their shirts in front of girls. He wasn't like that. Was it his face? What the fuck did those guys know about faces? He knew he had a strong nose, strong eyebrows, features that did not belong to the pale kids. Sophia looked at him after sex once and said, *You're no Ken doll, thank God.* And didn't understand what it meant.

Can we turn the AC up?

Fatima moved the buttons without saying anything and he knew that soon his silence would piss her off. He tried to calm down, to think of nothing, to breathe and watch the highway and then the streets and the strip malls and whatever else passed by.

After an hour he was crazy with heat and got out and locked the car and went into the grocery store attached to the mosque. It was the middle of prayers and the store was empty; the only action came from the television screen hoisted onto the back wall that was playing the English league soccer play-offs, tiny specks running on an impossibly green pitch. Beneath the flatscreen four or five young men stood with their arms crossed and their necks craned upward in fixed ardor. They were a few years older than him and he liked that they chose English league finals over Friday prayers. One of them turned around and walked behind the glass deli cases.

Welcome, my brother. What can I get for you today?

My brother. The sound of it landed softly in Rez's ear and he thought, Am I? How so? I can be your brother. Why not? This same face and body that marked him as unbrother at the beach, at the grocery store, with the assholes at the airport meant brother here. His face cooled first, and then his neck and shoulders and chest, and within seconds he was hungry and thirsty.

What's good?

Our combo—kebab, lavash, hummus—can't be beat. Lunch special includes a Coke. Or whatever soda you want.

I'll take it.

A cheer came from the guys gathered at the television and Rez and the server both got distracted by the game.

Unbelievable. We thought for sure they had no chance. Hot sauce?

Sure.

The server was tall and lean with cropped hair and a pencil-thin beard that lined his jaw and reminded Rez of the character from *Aladdin.* The server got to work with the plate as the guys at the end gave each other fist bumps and moved a little to get the blood flowing in their legs again.

You a fan?

Yeah. They're good this year. It's hard not to get behind them.

Exactly.

The server held the plate up and looked at Rez. Rez reached for his wallet and the guy shook his head.

Not today, it's on me. Come sit back here, you can see the TV better.

No. Thanks, but I got it . . . Let me . . .

You are our guest, next time you can pay.

Rez followed him to the back and the circle of guys looked at Rez for a second and nodded quickly and went back to the game. They wore Adidas tracksuits and Ecko hoodies and flat-brimmed caps and Rez sat at the table off to the side and watched and ate the delicious food and felt his body relax for the first time since the sea. After a little while he started to cheer when they cheered and groan when they groaned and it seemed like he was back with Omid and Arash and everything was fine. When his plate was clean of kebab the server looked over and smiled.

Good, right?

Yeah. Good.

Best in the OC.

The game ended with Arsenal one, Birmingham zero and the guys seemed pleased and checked their phones and lingered around before disappearing through a doorway in the back of the grocery store. Rez checked his phone too. There was a message from Matthews: *How'd it flow this morning. Incredible right? Don't tell me, it was probably ridiculous . . . ok tell me. No don't tell me . . . aaaaaaah.* Matthews was a good guy, it was almost chemically impossible for him not to be a good guy.

Rez walked around the clean well-stocked store and recognized a lot of the products from his mother's kitchen and from Fatima's kitchen. In the pastry section he saw the sweet chickpea cookies in the shape of clovers Fatima served him when she gave him tea. They were good cookies. Weird and crumbly and nutty, but just sweet enough, and he grabbed two boxes to surprise her with. The server was not behind the register and Rez looked to the back of the store at the doorway where the guys had disappeared and he walked toward the sound of their voices laughing and teasing and mixed with a new voice, a British voice young and digital as if from computer speakers.

All right, lads, all right. I knew Birmingham wouldn't take it. I knew tonight was not our night. But still, a lucky win by your dear Arsenal. Lucky is all I'll say.

The guys had gathered around a laptop that showed a young man in a white prayer cap as he grinned and shook his head.

Now isn't it a good thing we are not betting men? Thanks be to Allah for that.

The guys in the grocery laughed and Rez took a step back from the doorway but kept his eyes on the screen. The face of the kid was not familiar to Rez's world—dark skin, thick brows, handsome—but it was recognizable to Rez as likable, as a good guy.

If you keep cheering Birmingham it's always gonna be like this. And we will brag hard, bro. We will brag so hard, one of the guys told the screen, and the rest nodded their heads and snickered.

Ok, ok, now, I didn't call to let you gloat. Ok, sure, gloat, especially since you all look ridiculous, five grown men squeezed around Farouk's dad's laptop in that back room. I called because I feel bad for you blokes. It is hard over there right now, I know it. The massacre at the mall was bad business, but got me thinking.

Don't do that man. You could hurt yourself. The server joked.

No seriously. If it's anything like after the subway bombings here then you are in for it. Bad times to come. The other day I was talking to my imam, just chitchatting about this and that, and I am telling him how hard it is to be a good man in this country. To find a good home, a good wife, a good job. As a black Muslim, you know? Here is my father, in this country thirty years, still on the night shift for the school's cleaning crew. Boss of the cleaning crew, yes, but still on the night shift. My mum same thing, at home, can't get a job, and doesn't complain, says this country has been good to us. Took us in when no one else would. And I am thinking, this is no good country. At best we're third-class citizens. Every day I ride the Tube, people look at me scared, with fear leaking right out of their eyeballs, and I want to shout, *What?!? What do you think I am going to do?* So I tell the imam all this, and I tell him I am falling for this girl, good Muslim girl, also from Nigeria, good family. But I don't want to have a child here, who is going to grow up and be kept down at the same time. The imam is listening and nodding and then he just says this one word to me and my mind starts spinning.

The guys in the grocery store lean forward and wait, and when the guy on-screen doesn't say anything, the server eggs him on.

Ok then, what was it? The word?

Raqqah.

What?

That's just what I said. But I think I said, Excuse me?—because you've got to be polite you know—but I was thinking, What is Raqqah? I thought it was some new kind of prayer, and the imam knows I have no idea and is looking at me like I am an idiot. Then I say ok and he tells me it is a city in Syria, and a civil war is coming and that Raqqah is going to be the new capital, of a new kind of state, a Muslim caliphate. And I am nodding because I kind of understand him and there are these words between us, like *Muslim* and *capital* and *caliphate* but I have no idea what he is talking about. And then the imam looks at me straight on. Yes, brother, Raqqah, the capital of a country with no borders, a country for the believers, for the devout, for the citizens of Allah. And they need men. Men to move there and start their lives. Men and their wives. There is an open invitation to join in. Simply pack your belief in Allah and show up. There will be jobs, a house for you and your family. Schools for your children, hospitals, Islamic law, a good life. And then he leans forward and his bushy eyebrows lift and he goes, You will know always where you stand because you will always stand in the eyes of God. He went on and on and, man, I thought I was gonna fall asleep but I kept listening, to be polite, you know, and then he gave me some sites to check out and some numbers to Skype if I wanted to know more and I did, so I called them and talked to one bloke in Raqqah and then that's it. He showed me around his apartment, I met his baby, but mostly we talked. He came from Peckham and knew the same life I know and told me, Right away, man, right away you must come here. We are ready for you. The city is not ours yet, we need your help, so come. Come fight and live and thrive in a place where you can be a real man. This caliphate will be a good country, the best country. He was so relaxed. I can't even explain it.

A tall guy in an Adidas jacket spoke up.

Let me get this straight. Syria is on the edge of civil war and you are going to move to a city you've never heard of to join an army that was just invented, to make a country that doesn't exist?

The face on the screen smiled.

Tell me Hussein, what else is there? Night shift on team janitor?

The guys in the room moved listlessly and the server spoke.

There's always a lifetime of watching your team have its ass handed to it on a plate.

The laughs came slowly but with relief and good-byes and the connection was cut. Rez knocked on the door frame and held up the box of cookies and the server jumped quick and walked him up to the register, his movements nervous for the first time, his talk fast, his eyes down.

Sorry, man, an old friend from London, Khalil. Came here for an exchange year at UCI, prayed here. Incredible footballer. Good guy. That's going to be eight fifty.

He sat in the car with windows down, radio off, the cookies on his lap, and listened to the noise of the street and thought about Khalil and Raqqah. Rez had heard the name of the city, and of the mess in Syria, some ugly civil war that no one in America paid attention to, but didn't absorb it. If Arash were here, he'd know all about it. Rez wondered if Arash was over there, *building*. What if there really was such a place? A new place, where you could be a child of Muslims, in love with a Muslim girl, a place where he himself could become Muslim and so be accepted, taken in, left alone to live a life, among brothers, every day, every year. A place where he didn't have to repeat his dad's shuffle and silence and quiet anger.

The possibility turned slowly in Rez's brain. To be Muslim. Why not be Muslim? He already was, sort of. Even before the thoughts formed themselves completely, the idea of it came with a sudden relaxation. He slumped back in the seat and closed his eyes and felt the calm of the decision made ease into his blood. To pray. To believe. To be silent in the audience of an imam. To have rules and guidelines. To know God. He never had, and just the hint of it opened doors and windows in him such that he was no longer hot. To know God. He opened his eyes and watched the streets of Anaheim, the SUVs and nail shops and mothers pushing strollers with two or three kids inside. To know God. He saw the men cross the street, hands in pockets, eyes on the ground. To know God. The sky above blue with wisps of white clouds, an airplane, a faint moon. To know God. Rez felt his muscles let go their clench as he recognized everything before him as part of a larger picture in which he was inconsequential, as meek as the rest. To know God. He felt the power of the change in his limbs before he'd even given it a full thought in his mind. Conversion, the base of chemical sciences, the transformation from one state to another.

When Fatima came back, her face flush from the devotions, Rez handed her the cookies and she squealed and opened the box and whispered, My favorite, and then took a bite of the crumbly clover-shaped chickpea treat and he watched the powdered sugar cover her lips and her tongue lick the same lips and he thought of other gifts he wanted to give her that might make her squeal and bite and lick her lips.

30

FATIMA DROPPED HIM off. He told his mom he was tired and needed to skip dinner and tried to be tired and slow getting to his room when in truth excitement burned through him like a clean fuel and he wanted to explode through this life and these days with great velocity and get to what came next.

He set up his computer and typed in the word Raqqah and in one instant images of a dusty city with traffic circles and spindly palm trees appeared. More photos: old yellow-white ruins, families picnicking beside a slow brown river, intersections full of motorcycles. He looked at a few maps and couldn't decipher much beyond the river and the city center. The aerial shot reminded him of Sacramento or Stockton, brown land with buildings and a course of water running through it surrounded by a bit of green. Nothing new about it.

He clicked on. The newer images came from news sites, photographs of war, buildings with huge holes through the side of them, ambulances surrounding the scene. There were men in green fatigues, men in street clothes with bandannas over their mouths and then a third kind of man, in black, with the longest beards and the heaviest guns. *Islamist groups vie for the city. Assad and his forces fight on.* He clicked and clicked, to find some definition, some explanation of who fought who and why, but all he saw were headlines that announced the growing strength of an Islamist movement, a residual or amalgam of various Al Qaeda affiliates, their men in black, marching in sparse parades with no crowds, moving down the streets of cities that didn't seem to welcome them or turn them away, life carrying on as usual around them. Most of the rest of the images showed guys, young and masked, at dusty camps, training.

Rez read articles in UK papers from just a few months ago—Raqqah was now a city under a more specific siege: harassment for smoking, a women stoned in public for adultery, the imposition of taxes on non-Shia families, impossible to pay. In one news clip a body swung from a lamppost. *A city in chaos as state forces, rebel forces, and a new force calling themselves New Country scramble to take advantage of the instability.*

Fuck.

He stared at the uniforms of the Islamist army, new fatigues with old boots, scarves for their faces and foreheads, only their eyeballs available to the camera. *The ambitions of the New Country as outlined on their website are to spread a caliphate to the east and west and south and north . . .*

Fuck.

This was not what he wanted. It was not the peaceful faces at the mosque in Indonesia, or the brotherhood inside the mosque in Anaheim, or Fatima's sweet thoughts about right and wrong. It looked like a gang, no different from the gang at the beach, only more desperate, more violent: men in search of power. He thought of Khalil on Skype and of the guys at the grocery store, pictured them in the black fatigues, soldiers for this new army, and Rez stared at the silver square of his laptop and kept himself from crying but could not keep himself from feeling like an idiot, a fool's fool.

His parents slept, the whole neighborhood slept, and in the quiet after midnight Rez sat at the edge of the pool. The moon was new and sharp and its ivory reflection sliced across the flat navy water. He dipped a foot in to disturb it and watched the white light dance across the ruptured surface and flatten again. He must have typed in the wrong word. Done the wrong search. This could not be it, the land of the good Muslims, the city for the center of Islam, the religion Arash loved, Fatima adored, this could not be the religion of murders and massacres that the Americans said it was. He moved his foot around in the water and thought of earlier that day, at the gas station with Fatima and pumping her gas and feeling the stare of a grandmother outside her SUV, the stare that said *Fuck you* and *Don't kill me* all at the same time.

*

He went inside and opened his computer and sat before the empty search box and waited. He thought of nothing, and then when something came, he just typed it, *How to be a Muslim*. And there they were, instructions. Five steps, ten steps, twelve steps. Fourteen steps with pictures. *Learn about the Five Pillars of Islam—Shahada, Salat, Sawm, Zakat, Hajj. Study the Quran. Align yourself with the one God and the path of your life will never be lonely and will never be dark. Brothers and sisters all over the world will welcome you when you arrive on their doorsteps.*

No corpses, no blades, and no guns. He read through a few quoted passages about generosity, about abstinence, about humility and virtue, and he felt Arash near, heard his voice the night they spent at the party in the Hollywood Hills, on the pool chairs after everyone else had passed out. *It feels good to be good.* He felt Fatima close too, her new calm and confidence, and he read on and followed the thread of sites until he got to YouTube videos where men and woman of all ages sat before cameras and told of their journey to Islam, to the caliphate, to be a part of the new country.

Most spoke Arabic, and many more spoke French. A few spoke German and a few spoke British English. Rez listened to the English testimonials and he got stuck on one, a tall skinny teenager with a faint mustache and patchy beard, who explained that he *answered the call.* He said his years in England had taught him to question himself, the smell of his mother's cooking, his name, and his family's customs until the questions turned into disgust, and he couldn't stand the sight of himself.

So I started doing drugs, you know, marijuana and some coke to fit in, to get by, and this took me further and further from the call. Alhamdulillah, my sister brought me to it, sat me in front of the computer, and told me which imams to watch, showed me what was happening in Raqqah, what was possible for us, if we wanted it. If you are watching this, you are lonely. Like I was, confused. Let me tell you what my life is like now. I have never felt so much respect. Now I have a purpose, first and above all to Allah and to my community and to a future of peace for all followers. I live in a city where I can make a good living and love a woman who honors me. Before my life was not my own. I lived under so much suspicion I was sure I had done all the evil they suspected me of. Now I am myself.

He went on about the propaganda about the New Country in the media, the violence, the news of radicals and gangs of Muslims. *Rumors. Don't believe them. The western media is full of these rumors to distract us, to stop the rush of believers. This is the only place of peace I have ever known. God willing we will be victorious over the forces of Assad and begin our work to build new roads, new hospitals, new schools, and centers for the elderly. For this we need more brothers, more sisters, more devout hearts.*

Rez watched it again and was about to watch it a third time but his computer chimed and he saw a dialogue box open at the bottom of the screen.

Hello brother. Hello sister. Are you interested in joining the Caliphate? My name is Daoud and I am here to answer your questions and provide you with any guidance you might need.

Rez pulled back. It was like on porn sites or when he hacked into a movie site or got illegal downloads of music: pop-ups, text messages, Gchat sessions with people he'd never met. Those were easy enough to ignore, but this put Rez on edge. He stared at the question mark at the end of the sentence *Are you interested in joining the Caliphate?* Another line popped up beneath it.

As-salaam alaikum. Don't worry brother, I'm not a bot, just checking to see if I can help you out.

Rez paused the video and looked out at the night. The moon dropped to another part of the sky and the pool was still and navy now. He closed the computer and went to sleep.

He had rich dreams. First he was in the ocean, surfing a big day at Old Man's, which was a medium day anywhere else. Other people were in the water but he didn't know any of them and he surfed without competition or aggression. He had the good feeling in him, the dropped-shoulder, slack-jaw sensation of acceptance, of a life at the mercy of the enormous ocean, much greater, much truer, than his small self. In the warm water he let himself be swallowed, taken in. He paddled around the afternoon sea and watched the sun glint off the water and looked back at the hazy shore, in the dream as it had been so many times in waking life.

He woke clearheaded and hard and ignored his desire and jumped from the bed into the shower and knew the time of thinking, of listening and waiting, was over. He dried his body and took a long look at himself in the mirror. The face they called a monkey yesterday. A face they called brother. A solid face. A face inherited from his father and from the father of his father and maybe even further back. The nose, the eyebrows, the eyes themselves, all part of long look through time, across lands and wars and bodies and oceans and love, and he dressed and put on shoes and left the empty house without knowing the time and walked in the direction of Fatima's house, an hour walk at the least, his body light and ready, quick almost, in these first steps on the path of his own choice.

31

MAYBE THEY ENJOYED college. What they learned allowed them a good life.

His father talked and drove, drove and talked, and Rez sat in the back, daydreamed, and ignored him while his mother sat in the front and did the same. They drove the windy roads up the highest hills of Laguna and the voice in the car told them where to turn in a patient and calm voice. His mother had dressed up and his father had put on a tie and Rez wore a clean polo and pants and school shoes but didn't look in the mirror to make sure it all worked.

The house, small and modern and expensive and made entirely of glass, was vaulted high up above the sea. When they stepped into the entryway, the ocean was everywhere beneath and ahead of them, like a new kind of ground. For all his years going to parties at the homes of rich friends, Rez had never felt this high, this much like flying. He waited in the line with his parents to meet the hosts, unable to take his eyes off the living room windows, the ocean huge, the line of the horizon closer somehow, the beams of the sun, long set, aimed up, dim and yellow into the dusky sky, just like a child's drawing. All the surfaces of the house were stone and gray and angular and so were the hosts, architects, in their fifties, clean cashmere and linen, glasses without rims, white white smiles. They welcomed the incoming freshmen and their families with kind handshakes and sincere pauses over the foreign names, which they listened to and repeated before they pointed everyone in the direction of the drinks table, where a man in a crisp black shirt listened and poured and listened and poured.

Rez's father went first, made the introductions, Saladin, but you can call me Sal.

And this is Rez then?

The man looked at Rez with his hand outstretched, his soft eyes buried in the soft face. Rez put out his own hand.

Reza actually.

Please excuse me. Reza. Nice to meet you. Welcome, you and your family should make yourself at home. There are drinks there and a table of hors d'oeuvres in the dining room. Please.

Thanks.

Rez felt his father look at him for a long second and then move toward the drinks table, taking Rez's mother by the elbow.

The families, eight or nine of them, walked around and spoke to each other politely and Rez saw nothing hot about the girls and nothing interesting about the guys, who seemed preppy and a little straitlaced. He walked around behind his parents and overheard conversations and tried to open his eyes wide and friendly or lift his eyebrows or even smile when someone looked at him. The host and hostess, both class of '78, gathered them in the living room, welcomed them, and explained why they were such devoted UC Berkeley alumni: it was responsible for their marriage, for their successful careers, their community of friends. Even though they had no children, their association with the school had given them such fulfilling lives. They were happy to answer any questions about campus life, freshman year, parent involvement, and participation in the Orange County alumni chapter, *when the time comes.* The room laughed politely and a few hands went up. Rez let his eyes wander to the ocean, let his mind drift. The sea was dark now, the sky a little less so above it, and in the far distance a few boats, an oil rig, the outline of Catalina. God's view, he thought, this is how God must see things. But these people aren't God, just rich. He felt himself grow frustrated that money could buy such magnificence, money and not devotion or commitment or a generous heart. His mother coughed gently next to him and he looked at her with the small paper plate neatly on her lap, her few hors d'oeuvres arranged in a line. Why was he thinking about God?

Everyone asked questions, parents and freshmen, about the dorms and the commons and visitors and the Cal Bears and drugs on campus, and Rez grew impatient. Who cares? College was just like high school, except you didn't have to go home every day and your mom didn't cook for you. It was another controlled environment with expectations, rules, and achievements. His job was the same. Do well. Don't embarrass his family and don't strike out in any way that would draw attention. This exercise in college seemed like a pause, a trick. Rez raised his hand. The old man called on him.

Yes, Reza?

About student life, specifically services for Muslim students on campus. Is there a mosque? Are there halal foods offered? What sort of support is there in case of discrimination, harassment, you know, because of recent events?

It felt good to bring it up, to make the room uncomfortable, and Rez kept his gaze and posture steady as students and parents shifted and throats cleared. Without looking Rez knew his father was staring at him, the heat of the look burning Rez's cheeks and forehead, and he tried to keep from withering. The host admitted he did not know the exact details but was certain all religions were equally supported on campus. His wife spoke up.

As you might know, Cal has one of the most progressive and accepting student bodies in the nation. It is a point of pride.

Yes, Rez replied. Now they all stared at him. His parents, other parents, the students-to-be.

Let me be in touch with student life and I will make sure to e-mail you more information. Does that work for you, Rez?

Reza.

Oh, I'm sorry, yes. Reza.

Rez made sure to draw his lips tight in a face of dissatisfaction and responded in a cheery voice, Thanks. And I'm sure I'll find out more when I get there.

Hell to pay. Rez always liked that phrase, though no one he knew used it. For the rest of the evening he prepared himself: once they were in the car, there would be *hell to pay*. His father would probably drop his mom off and then drive Rez back to that abandoned dirt road in the desert and punish him one last time, for this one last fuck-up. But now they were still stuck at the polite party and Rez's mom was talking to a tall woman about sculpture classes and she looked as lively and engaged as Rez had ever seen her, and in an instant he knew that if he left, if he went to Raqqah and became a man and started a new life from which he could never return, from which he would forgo the attachment to his mother, it would be all right, she would be sad, but she left her own family too, a long time ago.

They drove home with the classical radio station on and nothing else. When the garage door opened, Rez's father kept the engine on and told Meena to get out. Rez felt the little boy bloom in him and slumped in the backseat with the old fear and reminded himself only ten days more and this would be the last of these times.

They drove south on Highway 1 until they got to an upscale supermarket. His father parked and they went into the store together and Rez watched him buy a six-pack of beer and some pistachios. Then they drove to the parking lot of a construction site, a future luxury hotel with views of the harbor and ocean, and Rez wanted to relax; the beer, the parking lot under bright lights, the proximity to home, read like signs that everything was going to be all right, no great violence would take hold of his father tonight. But his father was not a drinker, and Rez watched him grab the beers and step out of the car and he followed him with suspicion until they both leaned up against the hood with bottles in their hands.

I always wanted to do this.

Do what?

Drink beer with my father. Do something with my father as a man, two men together, instead of a father and his son.

Rez looked at his beer but didn't take a sip. It had been weeks since he'd drunk or smoked.

My father was strict. All the fathers of that world were. In this country you and I are allowed to see each other as people, not just who is in charge and who isn't.

Rez wanted to reject him, reject these words—for the whole of Rez's life this man had been in charge, held the power of the fist, of the word, over the quivering soul of himself as a boy, as a teenager—but he could not, as his father then and his father now were two different people. Since the night in the desert, his father's anger and violence had recoiled, pulled themselves back like a tongue, and Rez lived with a much meeker man who took the massacre in step, took the demotion at his lab in step, said nothing about Rez's SAT scores or final grades and spent most evenings by himself in front of the classic movie channel, a dreamy look on his long thin face.

You feel good about this next week? College? Moving out?

Yeah. Great.

You feel like yourself?

Sure.

Why did you ask the alumni to call you Reza?

It's my name, isn't it? The one you gave me?

His father looked out over the dark sea and then down into the hole of his beer bottle.

You know that to be a Muslim in this country right now is not something to joke about?

I wasn't joking. A lot of my friends are Muslim.

And they will have a hard time. They are having a hard time.

And it's not fair.

No, it's not. When I came to this country, I saw religion separate people. So many different beliefs, all against each other, and I thought, Why put my kid through this? This is going to make their life harder, not easier. We have Islam in our background, yes, in the way we eat or think sometimes, but it is not who we are. We are people first, then a family, and then Americans. That has served us very well.

Rez kept quiet but his mind moved angry and fast. Has it? Has it served us well? Let you be a man who is spit on at the carwash? In public?

He watched his dad take a long sip. It looked awkward, the way he held the bottle to his mouth, tilted his head far back instead of the bottle. Rez considered his father—maybe he'd never ever seen his true self, through the stress of his American self. Maybe at the rug seller's house where he sat on the floor, comfortable in his skin, tongue, and thoughts, were the only times he let himself relax. Rez felt the anger seep away and his throat and mouth filled with a sudden sadness. For a second he wanted to tell his dad about this other country, where Rez and Arash and Fatima could live among brothers and sisters and make a state in their image, not at the mercy of money or the laws of people who dismissed them. To be in their own skin.

It's cool, Dad. It's just something I've been thinking about. That's all.

Of course. This is a big change for you. Give it a week, once the classes and assignments start coming and you start soccer and meeting girls and friends, you won't even remember this feeling now, you will be as solid as a rock. We are here and very proud of you. I am very very proud.

Rez imagined himself not in one week but in two, or even three or four, not in college at all, but maybe in a distant desert, arrived in the New Country, welcome citizen with rights and responsibilities, no longer boy, no longer teen, but a good man with Fatima beside him, a good family to come. Rez looked at his father, and his father looked back, eyes warm and generous with love, and Rez had no armor, no argument against, and forced himself to swallow and straighten up and talk.

Yeah, you're right. In a few weeks I'll be fine.

I know it. Beginnings are bumpy. Look at me. I landed in this country and slept on the beach for a week! I took a chance, a single huge chance, and everything turned out fine.

Rez blinked back the liquid in his eyes. For a moment, he was proud of himself too, many years the obedient son, not knowing who he was or where to go until told, now stepping into a new world, a foreign world, the chance at a bravery all his own. Rez took a sip of his beer and stared out at the open lightless sea.

Yeah, you're right.

32

THE MORNING OF the mosque visit he showered and dressed in a clean oxford shirt and ironed slacks and his mom asked, What's the occasion? He told her lunch with Fatima's parents and she said, That's nice, and left him alone. Fatima laughed a little when she saw him.

Fancy.

Well. You know . . .

They were both nervous and rode in silence down the 5 past small beach towns and the enormous military base, where Rez saw a line of tanks in the distance, rolling, on a military exercise. They drove through the San Diego suburbs and near the In-N-Out he'd stopped at with the apostles on the way to Mexico all those days ago. Rez felt a shake of embarrassment go through him and tried to change his thoughts and was glad when they pulled up to a clean white building with a blue-tiled roof and a thin spire minaret. The Abu Bakr Masjid. The parking lot was lined with tidy tall palm trees and Fatima circled a few times before she found a spot.

Busy.

Friday prayer.

She adjusted her scarf in the mirror and touched up the little bit of makeup she still wore, mascara, some blush.

Remember, we are cousins. You grew up secular but your parents were born Muslim, they just don't practice. And now you are curious about your religion, about Islam.

That is true.

It is?

Yup.

Her stare was long and flat and without any emotion Rez could easily read.

*

He followed her down clean long hallways and watched as she greeted other women with Salaams and eager smiles. Rez did not recognize this happy public person. In all the years at school he'd never seen her smile in the halls, in class, at the assemblies, and now she glowed openly. All around him men and women did some variation of the same: saw one another, clasped hands, kissed cheeks, greeted each other with love. He stood a few steps away and she did not once introduce him.

At the end of the hallway bright light shone through two separate doorways. Cubbies for shoes lined the walls and the sinks and towels were set up further beyond that. Fatima went to the door on the left and greeted an old black man whose prayer cap covered a bald head.

This is my cousin. He is here to pray with us.

Welcome, my brother. It is a good day. We ask that visitors sit in the back rows.

Ok.

The old man gestured for Rez to enter and he did but when he looked back Fatima was gone. He stretched his neck but there was nothing of her scarf or her shoulders. For a second he panicked, alone in the unknown world of belief, and stood in the entrance to the enormous room and watched men and boys sit down cross-legged and barefoot and quiet. And like the times before, Rez felt their powerful goodwill toward each other, toward him—the stranger—and he found a space against the wall and sat down and let his mind wander.

The imam was young, in a navy suit and green tie, and he spoke like Omid did, as if maybe once all his friends were from Compton. Rez tuned in and out of the lecture about the nature of love and the story of Abraham and where the allegiances of the heart lie when you pledge your life and soul to Allah and thought of Fatima in the room next door, watching the same lecture on the large screen, surrounded by women she liked and maybe even loved.

He found her afterward looking for her shoes. He tapped her shoulder and she beamed at him, clean and energized as if she had just come out of the shower.

So good, right?

Yeah. It was cool.

Something had happened to her during the prayer. The nerves and suspicions were shaken off and now she looked up at him with a ready face and he wanted to hold her cheeks in his hands, bring her fresh lips to his, and take her and take her and take her until the beams shone through him as well. He stepped away from her.

Lunch?

Let's do it.

They ate at a deli next to the mosque. Tables were set up off to one side, girls at some, boys at others. Men and women shopped and ordered kebabs and tabbouleh and drinks and watched Al Jazeera. Fatima and Rez took their food to a table of guys their age and Fatima introduced Rez as her cousin *just visiting* and they made space for him and said *What's up?* and kept on with their conversations about the Lakers or the new *Fast & Furious* movie. The person next to Rez, a little older, with a nice watch and a clean beard, turned to him.

Where are you coming from?

The Bay, Rez lied.

Nice. Mom's side or Dad?

Dad.

Cool. Fatima's awesome. So glad she joined this mosque. Not a lot of new young woman come on their own. Good to see a fresh face. And fresh other things, if you . . . you know . . .

The guy looked up from his food as he spoke and Rez followed his stare to the table of women where Fatima sat and laughed and covered her mouth as she practiced some Arabic phrases. Rez looked back at the guy, who turned to him and winked.

She's so lovely. Such a lovely presence.

Rez spoke quickly, I am not sure she wants to stay at this mosque forever. Just trying it out, you know, like me.

That's interesting. See that girl she's talking to? That's my sister. Fatima told her she really likes it here. Wants to settle down in this community. I am hoping my sister will invite her over sometime, meet the rest of the family.

He turned to Rez and smiled, part shyness, part something else. Rez stood up and left his tray of food on the table.

Nice to meet you. I just remembered . . . a phone call . . .

You don't like the food?

No. I just remembered my mom is expecting me to call.

Ok. Well, um, have a good visit.

Yeah. Thanks.

Rez walked to Fatima's table and leaned down toward the place her ear would be inside her headscarf.

I want to talk to the imam.

Why?

I have some questions.

Now?

Yes. I mean, if it's ok?

I am still eating.

I can wait outside.

The women at the table grew quiet and Fatima nodded at him. Ok, just a minute.

Outside she was fast with her words. Dude. What's your problem? Are you fucking with me, with this, for some reason? How I appear matters. You can't just show up because you are curious about my religion . . .

It might be my religion too.

She stopped midword and dropped her head and took a few breaths.

Fine. Let's go.

The imam sat in a small room just off the main prayer room. Up close he looked older than on the podium, and when he took Rez's hand, the grip was stronger than he expected. He was very clean, his skin, his teeth, his hair and clothes. To calm himself Rez imagined him as just another of the guys from lunch and thought about him on the basketball court, throwing bricks at the net. Fatima left them and Rez wiped his wet palms over his slacks and waited for the questions.

Welcome.

Thank you.

The imam smiled and let the room, its single potted palm and dusty burgundy rug and leather-bound books, sit in stillness and silence. Unnerved, Rez waited and the imam waited.

I am interested in Islam. I think I am. I mean, I might want to start practicing.

Yes.

So . . . I thought, what I wanted to know . . .

Your parents? Are they devout?

No. I don't think so. My mom a little, maybe.

A little?

The room got still again and Rez waited.

The imam righted himself and Rez saw that the back of the chair rose high above the height of the imam's head. He reached for a few pamphlets and pushed them across the table.

You must begin at the beginning. Talk to your parents. Read these and then, when you are ready, go be by yourself, turn off your phone, and think about your need for faith. Think with your heart and with your head. The strictures, the lifestyle, the bond with Allah. It's a long road from curiosity to belief.

The kindness never left the imam's face or his voice and yet Rez hated him. As he spoke, all Rez heard was *You're not serious, you are young and foolish and in search of something else.*

The imam stood and offered his hand. Rez stood and shook it. Fuck this guy, he thought. He tried to pull his hand out but the imam held on to it.

If you don't mind me asking, what got you thinking? About Islam, about our *masjid*?

Rez stared at him directly.

Love.

The imam's face did not change but his grip tightened.

That is a good start. The love of Allah is like no other.

33

HE TYPED IN the same search, *How to be a Muslim*, and went to the same sites as before and watched all the testimonials he could find. An Australian doctor, the child of Chechen refugees, told of his sense of obligation to join the New Country when it most needed his skill, when the future of the *khalifa* depended on it. *To be Muslim in Australia is to be a second- or third-class citizen. Why should I settle for that? To be a lesser man among men?*

Rez watched two English girls, young from the sound of their voices, who spoke off camera while a still image of a dove showed on-screen. *We were lucky to get out when we did. So many of our girl-friends at school were giving us a hard time for covering, for going to mosque, for not listening to music anymore, and we had to explain: our beliefs are what make us feel respected and useful in the world. We don't have to worry what our bodies look like, our hair, our makeup. A woman is more than her skin here. Here we are the pillars of our households. Our husbands work every day to build the* khalifa *and we work every day to make our homes beautiful, raise our children, make Raqqah a city for the new times.*

A teenager from Germany spoke only in German but his words were translated into English and French subtitles. *This is my apartment, three bedrooms, though I only have two wives. Well, right now I only have two. Let's see what happens in the future. God willing. Here is my kitchen, very modern, my cooler full of food. Here is the room where I keep my guns, a rifle and a pistol, ready when the call comes. Raqqah is a beautiful city and it is the work of every man to defend it.* Rez looked into the teenager's face for some madness, some hint of a craziness for violence, but saw only a young man proud and not at all interested in his own past.

Rez watched and listened and watched and waited for the dialogue box to pop up. Finally it did. The same message and the same name flashed on the screen.

Hello brother. Hello sister. Are you interested in joining the Caliphate? My name is Daoud and I am here to answer your questions and provide you with any guidance you might need.

Rez laid his fingers on the letters.

Hi.

Salaam alaikum.

Salaam.

Who is here?

Reza.

Nice to *meet* you Reza. Where are you?

California.

Great! Northern or Southern?

Southern.

Sweet. I visited L.A. once. Wanted to learn to surf.

Yeah. I surf.

☺

Rez punched in the hang-loose emoticon.

Are you interested in Islam? In our work in Syria?

My parents are Muslim but don't practice, and I've got a Muslim friend, Fatima, and she's very devout now and I wanted to . . .

The box interrupted with a line.

Just a friend? ☺ ♥

Rez left it and waited to see what would come next.

Listen, my brother, I don't know everything but I'll answer as much as I can. Let me just say, first off, your curiosity is a sign that Allah is present within you and that you are trying to return to your original perfect state of being. Step toward your belief and you will step toward perfection, and probably toward Fatima too. ♥ ⌀ 🕋 🕋

Rez stared at the screen.

34

ALL OF IT the same, yet nothing the same. In the days since the assholes at the beach, since the video of Khalil, his chats with Daoud, the nature of time had changed. Rez felt as if he were astride some great wild wave of time that heaved and swelled fast into a tube and then slow until he saw everything in raw epic detail. Whole mornings passed in quick minutes while dinnertimes at the awkward family table stretched out so long he saw neither beginning nor end of them. At night he could only lay his body down for four or five hours before waking up so fueled he had to do fifty push-ups and a hundred sit-ups just to shower without agitation.

He spent the new time differently. He no longer stayed at home in the mornings, watching TV and floating in the pool. Now he ate breakfast with his parents and caught a ride with his father to the main library in Huntington *to get back in the swing of things, you know, get used to staring at books again.* He waved his dad off and then walked around the cool, silent building with his backpack and plugged himself into the most private computer in the public computer lab and did all the things he wanted and needed to do. By the time he let himself be distracted by a piss or a snack, the clock said two thirty or three. His work was never done, but every day he made inroads, read more history, found new sites, connected to better contacts, came up with quicker, cheaper logistics and paved the path out a little farther from where he stood.

He began each day where Daoud told him to, with the Koran. Rez fell into the calm cadence of its calls for generosity, humility, the quiet decorum required to properly follow Allah. He recognized stories from the Old Testament, and new stories for how to be a man, how to be a woman, how to have a family, livestock, money, and honor. Some sites helped him to think about his conversion, step by step, from the *shahada* to the hadiths, from the best ways to offer prayers to the correct attitudes toward women, food, clothing. Sometimes he read out the phonetic words of the shahada in practice for the day there would be a witness and these words would seal his commitment. He always did so in a whisper, Daoud having reminded him that simply speaking Arabic in public had got people pulled off planes, taken to detention centers.

Then he read history, tried to understand why things were the way they were, why a new country was necessary, vital. He went as far back as the early 1900s, when there were no countries, only dry lands covered in tribes with some loose association to kings and empires, all in service to the one God. What a time that must have been. He remembered the photographs in the garage, his grandfather as a young man among the men of his area, men in turbans with scythes in their loosely bound robes, lives lived on the thick skin of the desert beneath the thin enormous sky.

Then what happened?

He read on. Into the history, the hunger for oil, Europe's keen eyes on the region and the carving that followed, random and haphazard, of tribes into nations, nations into influenced states. He looked at maps that showed random shapes and sizes with their own names and presidents and prime ministers and read of mandatory reeducation programs, tribal language eradication, a tilt toward European customs, the chair, the fork, the necktie.

But then what happened?

The great corruptions, the great rapes of gold and oil and gas and minerals and whatever could be mined or drilled and taken away. Some tried to resist—Mossadegh, Sadat—and came to a quick end. He read on: American support of Israel, American support of the Saudi royal family, and the slow noose of greed threading the neck of the region. And now the modern punishments, just as the imam on YouTube laid them out in Arash's living room: Bosnia, Palestine, Kosovo, places where to be Muslim meant to be a target, to believe in Allah meant a separation, then a discrimination, then a mass slaughter. Rez came to resent his teachers, his life, for not telling him these truths and he read on, hurt head, hurt heart, to find the center chord of information, a truth he could find and pluck and so feel it resonate in the bones of his new self.

In the encrypted chat rooms Daoud told him what to read, what sites to check out, and who to talk to and Rez would enter and start up conversations with men he'd never meet, kind men with useful information who said the faith had ways for him to turn the anger into action, and explained how they themselves had done it just six months, ten months, one year ago.

And then it was too much. His head was full, he knew what he needed to know, about right and wrong, good and bad, like he knew calculus equations and chemical formulas. His heart, not empty, was not as full as his head and he cast about trying to find passions to lead him. Finally, when he could think of nothing else, when the same idea came to him again and again, he e-mailed Arash.

It took two days but then the name popped up in his in-box next to *hello brother!* In the e-mail there was a quick what's up and instructions on how to get into a video chat room on a site Rez had never heard of, a date and a time. *See you soon! A.*

Rez did as he was told and the next morning, he waited for the library to open and was first inside, first in the computer lab. He logged on with his new fake names and sneaky passwords and soon sat in front of a black screen with a tiny black and white flag waving in the center of it. In his headphones a phone rang and rang and rang. When four or five minutes passed Rez looked around the room and saw the same senior citizens he saw every day and thought about hanging up, then the ringing stopped and Arash popped up. His head was closer to the camera this time and Rez saw his face was thinner, the beard more full. There was a greenish bruise just under his eye and his lips spread beneath it in a large smile.

Rez, dude. Salaam! I was so glad to see your name in my in-box. Thanks be to God. I had a feeling you were going to get in touch.

He sounded different. Rushed. Arash never said things like *I had a feeling.* He didn't say much, usually his manner was so chill it did all the talking for him.

I'm good. Glad you called back. I thought maybe you, well . . . hey. How's it going?

I am not on Mars, dude. Of course I'd get back to you. Was thinking of dropping you a line soon.

Arash didn't move far from the camera and Rez couldn't see what was behind him, what world he was in.

Where you at, dude?

Arash shook his head.

In the good place, the great place, doing the good work. Setting up.

What happened to your face?

A soccer ball. Right to the eye. You know my defense was always crap.

Rez wanted to say what defense? Arash didn't really play soccer. Whenever he went out with Omid or Yuri for a pickup game, Arash sat on the sidelines and read the news on his phone.

Soccer huh? What else are you up to over there? You staying with friends? Family? Beard looks good.

Thanks. I've been combing it.

Arash stroked the hairs under his chin and the grin got even more lopsided.

Yeah. Friends, good friend, I'm staying with some brothers, it's pretty dope. A compound with a pool and gardens and the whole thing.

Yeah?

Yeah. You should come.

And do what?

Build the new country. It's better than I can even describe. Real people. Real respect. Skip college, give yourself an education in truth. Bring Fatima with you.

You sound like an infomercial.

Listen, Rez. It's for real, this place. If you are calling me to check 'cause you are kinda interested that means you are already halfway here. Better than life in the OC by a million. Come, bro, come.

How can I find you?

Get to Raqqah and then just ask around. I am not sure where I will be by then, in terms of digs, but everyone knows everyone here. Come. I am not going anywhere.

Rez could not imagine it. This place. It sounded like camp. His friend's face seemed so present. So ready, skinnier and a little pale, but full of joy, almost too full. Rez leaned forward to speak directly to the speaker in the computer, hoping no one else would hear.

Yeah. I was think . . .

A sharp noise filled the headphones and scratched through Rez's ears. The screen went sideways, cut Arash into a thousand shards, and then went black.

Hello? Arash? Hello?

Nothing. Rez took off his headphones and put them in his backpack and logged out of the computer. It wasn't everything he needed, but it was enough.

By the time he got outside it was early afternoon and Rez went to wait at the bus stop with the Latina maids and nannies and the leather-skinned white guys who made homes out of the caves and park benches up and down the coast, regardless of the season. Rez stood among them and thought about what he had read and seen and about Arash and wondered how different his life would be if he had been born into the skin of a woman in servitude or a man without a way.

35

SHE LET HIM sit close again. Close enough they touched at the thigh and hip and shoulder, and if Rez wanted to reach for her hand, she let it be held. He wanted to make a joke about how this was the first time they'd held hands but decided against it, so they just sat, side by side, in the gazebo above Laguna Beach and watched the waves and kids and dogs dash in and out of the water's reach.

The new learning rang in his head like loud bells and he wanted to tell her about all he knew, about Islam and the New Country and Arash, but Rez stopped himself, he'd already said so much to her today, now it was better to sit and squeeze her hand.

This ocean is amazing.

She looked at him and smiled. And then laughed a little. And then she laughed a lot.

What?

Nothing.

She laughed more.

He had never heard her laugh like this. Or do anything bubbly and girlish. He'd known Fatima since seventh grade; she'd always been serious about everything—grades, her opinions, even getting high—and now she was relaxed, almost silly.

I just can't believe it. That's all. I mean, this morning I had no idea you were going to show up at my door and tell me you wanted to embrace Islam. Like, what?! . . . It makes me happy, but, come on, it's a little wild, admit it, Rez, a little crazy.

Reza, he corrected her.

Reza, she repeated, and tried not to laugh but started giggling anyway. I mean, Rez Courdee. All-American. Never said a nice thing to a Muslim kid, never recognized his parents were Iranians. Nothing. And now. *Now?!* Wants to become a Muslim and marry me? If I say it out loud, even if I think about it too much, it sounds crazy. I am not going to think about it.

She took a dramatic breath and got very still, stared out at the sea and got even more still. Rez watched her, worried she would get serious again, get serious and change her mind. Nothing happened for a long time; five and then more minutes went by and he was about to say something and saw she was crying.

Hey. Don't do that. This is all good, right? I want to change my life to be a good Muslim man, a good man in the world and a good husband to you.

I know. It's just weird. Really fast.

It was hard already and Rez hadn't even gotten to the hard part.

What if we left?

And go where?

I dunno. Away. Would that make it easier?

In her stillness he felt her listening.

There is a place for us, in Raqqah, if we want it. An apartment. Jobs. A good life. You are Syrian. It will be like a homecoming. I have already started talking to people.

Raqqah? Syria? In the middle of a war? That's not funny. You *are* crazy! All my family is trying to leave Syria and you want to go there?

I think some good things are going to happen when the fighting stops. I've been talking to people who say a new country is being built there. A fair place for Muslims to live . . .

And I've heard about that group in Raqqah. It's not the Islam I know . . . it is an interpretation, an old Islam and it can be very violent. Very bloody. Why are you even talking about it? This is stupid. You're nervous about college and this is your freak-out.

Rez looked toward the beach. Beyond the first spread of families and picnics, a group of boys took turns with a dragon kite. The tails were many and the nose kept diving down toward the sand until the last minute, when some wind or fast maneuver lifted it back into the sky. He couldn't tell if it was an accident or a trick of skill that got the kite up and flying again.

You know all this is bloody and violent too?

She looked up at the beach.

All what?

These kids, all these families, having fun, driving cars, living in big houses, watching stupid sports games, voting for war in the Middle East every chance they get? How much violence do you think it takes to keep this all so pretty?

He stared at the ocean because he didn't want her face to fuck with his thoughts, with his anger and determination and need.

At least in Raqqah the violence is on the surface. And temporary. At least there we can have a life devoted to something other than lies.

The afternoon light glowed more golden, the laughter of children braided in with the hush and hush of waves. Rez forced himself to see through the beauty of this paradise he'd believed in his whole life. He forced himself to think of pictures of Afghanistan, Abu Ghraib. The bombed-out apartments of Baghdad. Kelly and his maimed brother and their constant threats. The assholes who tried to fight him at the beach.

Arash is there. I talked to him. He invited us. Wants us to join him.

She stayed quiet.

Arash would never do anything on the wrong side, would never match himself with people involved in bad shit. You know that. You've known him your whole life, he's too good for that.

They heard the sound of footsteps on the wooden planks of the gazebo and they turned to find an elderly couple, hands clasped, walking toward the railing. They both wore pressed collared shirts and slacks and white rubber-soled shoes and when they got to the view spot the man took the woman by her shoulders, drew her body close, and kissed her lips. It looked dry and chaste but the woman blushed, her skin flush with color, and the man smiled at her and kissed the top of her forehead and then turned to Rez and Fatima.

Our sixtieth wedding anniversary today! Can you believe it? Sixty years ago I married this woman after proposing to her on that exact same bench. We were probably even your age. Eighteen, nineteen. Made the decision before we knew too much, before we became different people. Best decision of my life. Good times. Good time. Don't you waste this time.

The man smiled as he spoke and joy shone from the pockets of his old face.

36

THERE WAS NO fast *Yes*. No easy *I do*. She asked to see what he saw. Read what he read. Go to the websites that made him think goodness lay at the bottom of the evil.

With some pride Rez introduced her to Daoud in the chat room, quick to mention their engagement and plans to marry.

In Raqqah, God willing. Where the young married couples are blessed. Please direct her to a site run by our sisters. They will give her guidance as to our interpretations and organize the details of her preparation. I will e-mail the address and encryption code.

Rez looked at Fatima to see if she agreed, if it was going to work. She stared at the screen and then at her lap and then at the screen again. A message popped up from Daoud.

The truest unions are under Allah's gaze.

Fatima went down another hole. Even though they went to the library together and sat side-by-side at the public computers, they drifted away into separate worlds, typing, reading, thinking, typing. After a few hours they'd leave and go to the halal deli in Newport to eat and talk and think.

They told me to stop wearing the hijab.

They told me not to grow a beard. To keep my hair short. Not to convert until I was there.

If I take off the hijab, my parents will think it's strange. They'll know something's up.

A few days she skipped the library to stay home, with her mom and grandmother, or to go to the mosque by herself. Rez tried not to worry when this happened, tried not to text her every five minutes and ask if she was ok; if she was against the idea of the trip; if she still loved him. On these empty afternoons he rode the bus down Highway 1, getting on and off whenever he felt like it or at the beach if it looked nice. He sat on the sand and stared at the sea, the bodies of the people, the sand itself, and when he felt better, he'd get back on the bus and ride a ways until he had to do it again. By the time he got home he felt almost ok with the idea that bothered him most: that she might bail and he might have to go it alone.

Two days before they were supposed to leave to take the train north she texted: *walk?* And he said *sure* and they went down to the San Clemente pier. She wore a bright yellow head scarf and held his hand.

Ok. I am good to go.

Really?

Yes. Really.

Rez tried to pretend he wasn't as happy as he was and kept his eyes ahead of him.

You are sure? What did it?

Positive. Last night my mom and I got our nails done and I asked her about getting married, in passing, you know, casual, like when I should do it and if I had someone in mind did I bring it up now or wait. And she looked at me and laughed like I was crazy and told me I had no choice and when the time came they were going to pick a husband for me. They thought it would be later, after college, maybe after grad school, but ever since I got interested in Islam my dad's been asking around.

Rez felt his brain swim around in his skull, banging against the possibilities. His breath caught and he wanted to stay cool. He looked away from her, out to sea.

What did you say?

I said *Ok, mom.* And now I am saying *Ok, Reza.* Let's go.

Daoud helped him out. They kept in touch nearly all the time, through one of many accounts, Facebook, WhatsApp, Twitter, Instagram. Rez wondered if Daoud ever slept. Rez could reach him at any hour and never asked where he lived, but now and again Daoud offered stories and still seemed amazed at the turns his own life had taken to get to Allah.

Most of the time they hung out in the virtual space and talked about Rez's travel plans, how he and Fatima were to move about, whom they were to meet and how best to cross the border into Syria. Daoud asked him repeatedly about money, and Rez explained that his parents were to fill his checking account every semester to cover the costs of living at college. *And they won't notice if you withdraw it all at once?* Rez said no, though he wasn't completely sure.

Daoud gave precise instructions on how Rez was to act. *On your flight from LAX to Istanbul, order drinks, sit next to Fatima, be happy. When you get into the city, stay in Taksim, go to clubs, go to bars, don't drink, but be there. Act like a young American tourist. Make sure Fatima does not wear the hijab. On the second day I will arrange for you to meet the smuggler in charge of taking you over the border. He will speak English and look Western. You will follow his instructions from there. Whatever you do in your few days, don't act suspicious and, inshallah, doors will open all the way to Raqqah.*

Like a movie. When he thought about it that way, the coming days terrified him. In the movies guys like Rez always died. When he thought about it as his life, as answering the call of a higher power, as making a choice, he relaxed enough to catch the thrill of it, the covert steps, the disguise of his old self, the company of Fatima as his girlfriend, the secret of her as his wife. The adventure and love and belief and deception mixed into a heady potion and Rez spent hours, alone, drunk on the possibilities and always came back to Daoud's words: *Act normal, act regular, don't let your parents, your friends, suspect anything. All deceptions will be forgiven.*

Rez considered himself from the outside. Rich kid. Freshman at Berkeley. A girlfriend at Stanford. Good little immigrant. Off on a nice start to the American dream: behave and you will earn, earn and you will have a place. He imagined the final scene, the good-bye at the San Juan Capistrano train station, two kids going to college. Proud parents.

Maybe some crying. Hugs. They had behaved and now the next door opened to them. He remembered the words of the agent who interrogated him at LAX: *And your people, who think they are worth a great deal, know that even after making all that money, they are worthless. Their children are worthless, and if this violence continues, their children's children will be worthless too. Does that sound familiar?*

This is how the mind comes to understand the future, by imagination. Rez let his thoughts linger and speed depending on his mood but he could not control the way he felt, brave, renegade, righteous. A single man in control of his fate against the forces that would forever keep him low and scared. And of course the fantasies: Fatima in the hostel room, in the one bed, her body and hair and mouth available to him. He had not mentioned it, not brought it up even as a joke, and practiced his new prayers through these grips of desire. He had only a few Arabic phrases to string together and the rest he had to say in English. Either way, after a while, it always worked.

FROM OUTSIDE HE was the same old Rez. He ate dinner with his parents every night, spent the afternoons packing the small shipment to his dorm room and convincing his mother again and again it was a good idea he go up alone.

I just want to have the experience.

You don't want your parents to embarrass you in front of your new friends. You want to pretend you don't have parents.

Even as she tried to joke, sadness leaked through her voice. Rez tried to be annoyed that his mom was worried when in truth he worked hard not to let her quivers shake him too. They organized stacks of sweatshirts and books and toiletries and a few framed photos of them as a family. From his desk drawer she pulled out the black-and-white photo of the uniformed man.

Where did you find this?

In the garage.

Do you know who it is?

Family? Dad's family?

Your grandfather, your dad's dad.

She looked at the picture and then put it back in the desk.

A complicated man. A lot of conflict in his soul. Not happy. Not well.

STAY THE SAME.

Daoud's words scrolled through Rez's head when Matthews texted him.

Rager at my house tonight. One last blast.

Rez responded without thought.

Act normal. Daoud reminded Rez and Fatima it might be hard to keep up their old selves as the departure day came close. *But it is more than important. Any suspicion at this point and you will not be able to leave the country, you will be seen as a suspect and arrested.*

They went together and Rez had to stop himself from saying something about Fatima's loose hair, some compliment or evidence of his arousal. They spent most of their time on the dance floor. Matthews had cleared out all of the furniture from the pool house, and the small room with the bar and kitchen was perfect for crowding with bodies. The lights were off and the windows looking out onto the pool had steamed up and Rez lost himself to the music, old hip-hop, new hip-hop, by Drake and a million different remixes. Some old-school Madonna and Beyoncé and everyone in the room went from being eighteen-year-olds to being twelve-year-olds to seven-year-olds and back again, each song belonging to an age they had all shared.

Rez danced around and next to Fatima and each time he thought, I am dancing with my wife, he felt himself get stiff. She sensed it and teased him, moving her hips and hands against the hard-on and laughing. Eventually he left her alone to go get some water and cool down.

When he found her again, she was outside talking to Matthews. They both had their shoes off and shins in the pool. Matthews had on an

OBEY T-shirt with a block print of André the Giant on it. On his head he wore an extra-large baseball hat that said WORLD'S GREATEST DAD and held beer cans, one over each ear. Rez laughed to himself and then took off all his clothes and did a cannonball just in front of where the two were sitting. When he popped his head up, his friend and his future wife laughed and yelled at him and he swam to the edge and kissed Fatima's foot. She gave him a look he couldn't read.

Nice party, man.

Yeah. That pool house dance party is going to go down in the books. Can you at least agree with me about that, Fatima?

She tried to smile. She and Matthews had been in the middle of something, maybe an argument. Rez saw a serious look in her eyes and the way Matthews was quick with the jokes.

Just a little friendly religious discussion in the middle of a huge party. You know how I roll.

Rez wished he hadn't jumped in the pool. He wanted to be dry and ready to leave.

About what?

Matthews took a long sip from one of the straws that came down from the beer can and hung beside his face.

All I am trying to tell her is that I can't choose one God. Why do I have to? So my parents are Catholics, sort of, doesn't mean I have to be Catholic. I'm too young to be anything. I'm just a guy figuring stuff out, and when I've lived enough, I can decide what I believe.

Yes, but how do you know who you are? How to behave? Fatima asked, the calm in her voice bordering on sadness.

I follow the Golden Rule. I am a nice guy. I don't do shitty things to people. I keep it chill. And I am not in a rush to pick a God for the rest of my life. Who knows how long we will live? Just think about it. When we were born, there was no Internet. Now we can't do anything without it. Maybe tomorrow or twenty years from now, half of us will be living on Mars, and then what is God? All I am saying is no one knows about tomorrow's gods. Not me. Not you. None of us. And I choose not to go backwards, forget the old gods, let's wait and see what comes next.

Matthews looked at Rez with his eyebrows up and an unlit joint he'd just pulled out of his pocket, like a man who'd just won an inconsequential debate, like a joker, like a good soul in love with life. Rez gave his friend one last fist bump and was glad he had to pick up his clothes; he had a reason to look at the ground and keep his eyes to himself as his heart tore and tore and tore.

39

BRICKS. THAT'S RARE. No one builds with bricks in California because of the earthquakes. Maybe this station was built before the earthquakes, or before they knew that bricks didn't stand up in shakes. Yet this still stands. Maybe there is a sign. Yeah, over there, a historical plaque. *Plaque* is such a great word. Smack lack quack tack. Yup. I was right. Built in 1915 under the watch of the U.S. Western Railway expansion. Mentions nothing about the Chinese slaves that built the railways. That's the way. And then there is the mud-and-straw stucco of the mission. Mission of San Juan Capistrano. Who was Capistrano anyway? Maybe there is another plaque. Yup. Named for Giovanni da Capestrano, a warrior priest from the fifteenth century. Maybe that's who will be in Raqqah, warrior priests . . . Oldest building in California. No mention of all the dead Indians. All the Native people who lived here before the Spanish. Might as well not have existed. Ok. Something else, something else. That family waiting for a train. What else? Weather is nice. Sunny, not too hot, though it is early. I wonder what the surf is doing? We're so close to Doheny . . . not enough time . . . could text Matthews and ask . . .

And this is what Rez did with his mind while he and his mom and dad waited for Fatima and her family to arrive at the train station. He did all he could not to think about the good-byes. Real good-byes for a fake trip. Or maybe the good-byes were fake and the trip was real. Or maybe they were both fake. Or both real. Either way. Either way. Rez tried to make his head fall down the rabbit hole of these digressions, loop endlessly from one unstructured thought to the next, but he was unable. The light of the sun was warm and the day bright and his father gestured to him to come inside the train station.

The stood in front of the counter and read the fares.

Do you have your new ATM card?

Right here.

Ok. Let's see if it works.

They got to the woman in the Amtrak uniform and Rez felt bad that she had to wear something so silly and so he smiled broadly at her and she, with her fifty or so years of life, smiled back.

One-way to Berkeley please.

No. No. Get a round-trip. Just schedule the other half for Thanksgiving. You'll probably save money.

The idea of spending extra money, $120 that could be used in Istanbul, in an emergency, crossing the border, aggravated Rez but saying something was not worth the argument. *Act normal.*

Round-trip please. I just have to make sure I don't lose it.

Well, your name is in the computer, just in case.

Rez looked at his card. Plastic. Where did plastic come from? Petroleum. The chemical makeup of petroleum he remembered from AP chemistry. But why did everything have to be made of plastic? Because it was cheap to manufacture, durable . . . he almost turned to ask his dad but then stopped himself, not wanting to engage in conversation, just wanting to fall away from the reality around him into the spirals of his mind until this last bit of theater was over and he and Fatima were riding north, holding hands, staring at the sea.

Her parents had dressed up. They wore nicer versions of things he saw them in at their home. Her mother's head scarf, a thin lavender sheath, only covered half her hair and draped elegantly down her back. Rez had only met Fatima's father once. Ahmed. His pressed shirt and slacks and shoes looked fresh from a business meeting and Rez shook his fleshy hand and spoke to him for a few minutes. Rez did his best to smile at Fatima's mother when she mentioned she was sure Rez would take good care of her daughter.

Of course.

His own mother was crying now.

I know they will do great.

She'd kept herself from it for as long as she could, until the last possible moment.

We have good children.

That is true. They are good children.

The mothers agreed and used tissue to dab at their eyes. Rez watched Fatima hug her mother and listened to the enormous sobs that shook out of their embrace, tired and long and without shame. Near them on the platform the family of four stared and then tried not to stare, and the fathers cleared their throats and tried to end the show but the women kept on as Rez's own mother stood alone with her face pressed in and down and no one put an arm on her shoulder.

The lights on the platform lit up and bells began to chime and Rez shook his father's hand and then felt the long arms wrap around him and pull him in toward the heart.

We will see you in October. At parents' weekend.

I will be there.

Don't do anything I wouldn't do.

Rez's father's stern face had gone slack and he handed Rez his duffel bag full of Islamic texts and cash and clothes for the desert.

Best of luck.

Thanks, Dad.

Then the train stopped in front of them and Rez and Fatima walked up to the entrance and turned around for a last good-bye to the four faces that had made their faces, to the bodies full with emotion and hope and history and love, before they walked to the opposite side of the train so Fatima could lay her head against the glass of the window and cry.

By the time they were in Newport she had adjusted her head scarf and reapplied her makeup and he had done his best to convince her their decision was right and they sat quietly beside each other with nothing to say. Rez stared out at the dry riverbeds and fenced-in yards with sleeping Rottweilers and sun-bleached swing sets and let the chaos of emotions drain out of them. The conductor came by to check tickets and Rez watched him walk down the aisle, punching a hole in the small cards that signified *paid*, all the way to Berkeley. He stopped at their seats and looked at their tickets and asked them to please stand up and pull their luggage down from the overhead racks. He slipped on blue plastic gloves and asked again when neither of them moved.

Without your permission I will have to call the U.S. marshal that rides with us. He is legally allowed to search bags. It is easier if I do it.

Fine.

Act normal, Rez remembered.

Under her breath Fatima whispered, *This is bullshit,* and looked away from the conductor. The man, in his late fifties, white hair, pocked and rosy nose, a Californian of many generations probably. Rez watched him unzip Fatima's roller bag and look through the few belongings, jeans, sweatshirts, a hair removal device, bras, lots of bras, scarves, shoes, a few books, a stack of photographs, and a large Koran. He picked up the Koran and leafed through the thin pages.

This your book?

Yes.

The book of your religion?

Yes.

The man stared at Fatima and she stared back, arms across her chest, her breath nearly audible. Rez thought of the books in his bag, not the Koran, but about the Koran, about Islam, and he knew that he would throw them away at the train station in L.A., if they made it that far. The conductor put the objects back and zipped the bag. The train began to slow to the next stop, Orange, and the conductor looked at Rez's duffel, picked it up and moved it up and down to gauge its contents. Then he put it at Rez's feet and hole-punched their tickets.

See that you change trains in L.A for the northbound Coast Starline.

Rez felt Fatima reach for and hold his hand and her hand was cool and soft and ready.

40

THEY HAD SEX on the plane. The bathroom was small, but big enough
for two if he stood behind her, her hair in his mouth and their two
faces in the mirror changing and changing. There was nowhere to go
so he went in, deeper and deeper, in small movements and watched her
watch herself and then watch him and then close her eyes. For a while
he stared at her face in pleasure, all the tension of the day, the good-byes,
the train ride, LAX, the passport lines, the terminal, the takeoff, sucked
down and away and the space between her brows, her lips, opened
and her face was a full moon of beauty. He didn't want to come so he
looked at himself and when his eyes locked with his reflection—the
liar, the escaped son, the convert, the reclaimed—in the mirror his head
started to spin with violence. Not the side-to-side spinning of being
drunk or getting barreled for too long, but a fast up-and-down dizziness
like swallowing his feet or doing a back dive and he blinked and saw
himself again in the mirror, a kind of monster covering his face, green
and grimacing. His hard-on left him and Fatima opened her eyes.

What's up?

Flying made her nervous; the sex was her idea. They'd held hands
during takeoff and the clasped hands became a gentle arm up and
down her thigh and then in between her thighs and after the meal and
the passengers around them either passed out or were catatonic in
front of their televisions, she mentioned it and he agreed and they took
turns walking to the bathroom in the middle of the plane, far from the
stewardess station. They did not discuss it and Rez wanted to say that
it was probably ok, because they were not actually on the ground, on
earth, and he wasn't officially Muslim yet, hadn't taken the oath, and
this was an exception, a distraction, not an offense. He had this all
ready but when he opened the bathroom door, she stood in the small
aluminum box completely naked, her pale flesh perked with goose
bumps, and he thought, Fuck it.

Reza, you ok?

Rez looked at her face, turned back to him in worry.

Yeah, just got a little light-headed. Give me a second. He took a few deep breaths and ran his hands over his face and then ran them over her back and ass and up and down her legs. Nothing. *Reza. Reza.* The new name. He tried to forget about it or pretend it was no big deal but he kept thinking, Reza had never had sex. Only Rez had. Rez had lived all this life so far, and Reza had done nothing more than buy this plane ticket and lie to his parents. She turned around and sat on the closed toilet and looked at him and he put it in her mouth and the sensation of limpness and arousal and fear, the combination new to him, made him panic and he pulled out and pulled up his pants.

Don't worry about it. We should go back to our seats.

She stood up and hugged him with her naked body.

You're right. That's the right thing to do.

They flew through the night, two or three hundred people in rows, each a universe of histories and desires and fears and futures. Fatima slept, her head resting on a pillow propped up on his shoulder. He looked around at the passengers and their sleep or electronic distraction and tried not to think about what was coming or what had been and let himself be up and aloft in these last hours, unbound.

41

THE ICE CREAM here tastes different.

It really does. Sweeter. Or something.

Or. Or. Or.

She teased him and he kept licking trying to find the source of the richness. Eggs? More cream? All he knew about ice cream he'd learned in fourth grade when the class made it as a science experiment about freezing points. He remembered that day in Ms. Motsen's class, the explanation of molecules and how, under cold conditions, they slowed and that slowing was freezing. That night he went home and stared at the contents of his freezer, the mist flowing out toward his face, and tried to understand. Because of the cold the molecules moved slower; time too must then move slower; the freezer is a time machine. Rez explained all of this to his father, who smiled at his son and took the conversation further: *If so, is the oven also a time machine?* They talked science like that until he was in eighth grade, the what-if and how come and this is how, and it was the only time Rez saw his father as a person, a thinker, a curious boy like himself, and not just father of the dinner table, father of the car, hard father of the house.

Hot and cold. Fast and slow. Old and young. The two days in Istanbul split themselves apart like this. When they landed, the two of them still in the center of sleep, they stood in silence in the passport line and they stood alone before the Turkish official who looked once at Rez and once at his passport and then stamped it and called to the next person in line. Rez used printed instructions to get them from the airport to the bus and from the bus to the hostel and everything they passed along the way blurred and creased and failed to catch his eye because it was not real, but some reality buried under the deep confusion of time and space, old and new, Rez and Reza.

*

The hostel was nicer than they expected. Cool in a hot city, tucked into an old stone fortress of some kind, modern rugs and Turkish art. The receptionist was Australian, twenty-five or twenty-six years old and hot with shiny blonde hair and sharp blue eyes and just as with every girl that caught his eyes these last weeks, Rez thought his way into feeling sorry for her and the way she prostituted herself in the short jean skirt and off-shoulder T-shirt and didn't even know her sin.

She took them up to a private room with a double bed and they put down their bags and stared at each other and lay down fully dressed and slept, chaste bodies, chaste minds. Between them the heat had gone and Rez relaxed and gave himself to exhaustion and blank dreams.

They had thirty-six hours before they met the smuggler. They spent their time wandering the tourist neighborhoods of Istanbul, running into people their age, in the same sneakers and T-shirts and trucker caps. Everyone attractive and western and mobile. They e-mailed their parents from a café. Rez typed, *Berkeley is awesome. Foggy in the morning and afternoon, but nice. My room is small but has a good desk and my roommate is from Korea. He seems nice.*

They walked down the Bosporus and bought a deck of cards from a newspaper kiosk and played gin rummy on a park bench. Everywhere they walked, the Hagia Sofia mosque was visible and yet neither of them mentioned it. They joked and laughed and held hands and were happy and then, for no reason, he pulled away, or she did, and they walked apart and kept their thoughts to themselves and complained about the city and the travel and the unknown. On and off. As the day went. She wanted to pray and he reminded her what Daoud had said: *Act regular. Act Western.* And they walked past mosque after mosque and she stared in but said nothing.

At dusk they ate a meal of fried fish and potatoes and green salad ordered from a menu in four languages. They played a game of guessing where people came from by their shoes. They walked down the tourist-filled streets, past clubs blasting electronic dance music and cafés that spilled out into the streets and bars that played soccer matches on huge flatscreens and Rez wished for a faster way back to their hostel. The city disappointed him, it was neither this nor that, not Muslim and not Western, some nowhere in between.

They lay down in the bed, but did not sleep. Fatima sat up beside him in the dark and together they stared at the little line of light at the edge of the curtain, the night outside loud and bright. He said nothing to her but put his hand on her lower back.

What do you think it will be like?

Rez waited until he felt the answer come to him.

I don't know. Weird, at first, then good. Daoud said they will give us an apartment and then give me a job. They said there are labs, and chemists are needed. And we will be married right after I convert.

What do you think it will be like, to be married?

No answer came to Rez for a long time. He waited and his desire grew, harnessed him, and he sat up and wrapped his body around hers until their breath was the same, in and out, in and out, in and out.

Like this.

They fell asleep in this tangle, and when they woke, the day was already well on its way.

Their meeting was at eleven in a part of the city far from Taksim and Rez showed his Google Maps printout to one cabdriver after another and they all shook their heads and said, No no no, and pointed to the water and the water taxis and then drove away. Rez looked at his maps and saw that the meeting spot, a restaurant named Torkoy, was across the Bosporus, on the Asian side, and he asked the Australian receptionist the best way to get there.

Water taxi and then walking, I suppose. Careful your pockets.

The air and wind and sun on the water taxi ride buoyed Rez and for a moment his worries—about being late, meeting the smuggler, getting over the border, the new life—left him and he simply sat in the yellow light and soft late-summer wind. The water soothed him most and Fatima put on her sunglasses and tied her hair up and they looked together, in the back of the forty-seat water taxi, like a happy couple on their way.

They arrived on a street busy with stores and stalls and traffic and Rez took Fatima's hand and carried their bags as they started to wind up through the curvy residential streets where nearly all the women wore head scarves and every one stared at the couple as they passed. Fatima took her hand out from his and walked at a distance from him.

The restaurant was a hole in the wall, as was everything else in this neighborhood. Locksmiths and cobblers and butchers and fabric stores all as small as they could be lined the streets, broken up by doorways that looked as if they had not been opened in many years. Above the narrow streets people threaded their laundry lines from building to building, sheets and men's shirts and children's clothes, and at Rez's and Fatima's feet dogs sniffed little bags of trash left on the curb. They stood outside for a moment and stared at the entryway.

You ready?

I am.

Ok. Let's go check it out.

Fatima, I don't think this is for checking out. I think as soon as we walk in and meet this guy, it's done. We go.

Rez stopped himself. In her eyes and voice he saw Fatima pull up the courage to do it. To take these steps into the restaurant. At the back of his mind Rez thought about return, about *in case it doesn't work out* and the ways they would leave. He'd kept a little money in his savings account, in case they needed to get out, get back, but he did not mention it.

Without a smile or a change of voice, Fatima responded, Yes. Ok. Yes.

The smuggler was thin, not much older than Rez, but already bald. He wore a European-league football jersey, sweatpants, and Nikes. He sat at a table with a cup of tea, punching into a cell phone. When he saw them walk in, he did not stand up and Rez introduced himself and Fatima nodded but said nothing.

Yes. Yes. Sit. You are the Americans?

Yes. For a little bit longer.

There were no laughs and Rez and Fatima pulled out chairs at the table and the smuggler raised his eyebrows at the waiter and soon there were two more glass cups of tea.

Good. I am the man you are looking for. Who is your contact?

Daoud.

Ok. He typed the name into his phone. Rez wondered how far his English went. From the accent and the attitude Rez couldn't tell if he cared about Islam, was concerned with the caliphate.

You have paid him already?

Yes.

But what I see is you have only paid for one.

He kept typing into his phone and Rez waited for him to see that he had paid for two, one price for Fatima to cross and another price for Rez. The man typed more and then looked up.

It says one. One fee.

No. I am sure . . . Can I? Rez gestured to borrow the phone.

You cannot.

I paid for two. I can pay you for two now if you want. Does that help?

If you want to cross.

Rez opened the pocket of his backpack that held his passport, his cash, the pictures his mom had given him to hang in his dorm room. He pulled out four hundred dollars and handed it to the smuggler.

Very good. I am Erdrich. Now my instructions are to take you to the border at Ras al-Ayn. Is that what you are expecting?

Yes.

When we are there, I will not drive you into Syria, but to a safe house where you will find the people who will help you cross.

Yes.

She will have to cover at the safe house.

Yes. We know.

But not until then.

Ok.

The excitement grew through Rez and he found himself trusting the guy more for his abrasiveness.

You have bags?

Just these.

Good. Wait here for an hour. I will come and pick you up. Don't talk to anyone.

The roads that led out of the city were congested and Rez and Fatima sat in the back of the Nissan sedan and sweated and looked out the window at the pulsing city. They said nothing, and when they were finally out and away from the traffic, driving past wheat fields and industrial parks, they fell asleep and woke up in much of the same at a different time of day. The driver did not speak. He drove with one hand and texted with the other and smoked as much as he could. They stopped at a gas station with a restaurant attached and Rez and Fatima went in and stared at a fountain of bubbly milk until the server came by and handed them both cups and poured a ladleful of salty, carbonated yogurt in each. The taste was phenomenal and disgusting at the same time and they drank it and laughed and looked for snacks and the bathroom and Rez felt himself on a road trip like any other he had ever loved being on.

They drove into the evening and at dusk the land around them changed. What was yellow and green turned into the orange of the desert and emptied of plant life. Rocks were everywhere and in the distance jagged dark mountain ranges spread beneath the sky and Rez remembered the pictures of Raqqah, the dusty town center, the one beautiful river, and all the parks alongside. Neither of them asked any questions and the sky turned dark, shade by shade, one degree at a time, as they drove east and Rez thought of them heading into night, into the purple dusk and the navy beyond.

*

The safe house was empty and the driver walked through turning on lights, opening windows, and checking the fridge. There was no furniture but there were rugs and cushions and some flat bread and blocks of feta in the fridge. Each room had a few rugs on the floor and near the electrical outlets tangles of chargers left behind. Rez could not tell how long it had been since someone was here. Two days? Two weeks?

The toilets work. Ok?

Rez didn't know what to say. It was ok. They were four miles from the border and all they had to do was wait.

Yes. Thank you.

The driver took a long inhale from his just-lit cigarette.

For the Islam, yes?

What?

Islam? In Raqqah, yes?

Yes, yes. We are going to Raqqah. For the new country.

The driver looked at Rez and then looked at Fatima.

Ok.

He looked at them again and nodded and let himself out the thick wooden door that he didn't shut behind him and they watched him drive away. Fatima closed the door and took her bag upstairs, and when she came down, her hair was covered and her eyes and cheeks puffy from crying.

Again the night grew dark around them and they could not sleep. They sat up and read the books Fatima had brought and Rez wished he hadn't thrown out his books on Islam at the train station in L.A. Fatima prayed and they pulled out the cards and played and waited for sleep but nothing came. Not too long after midnight the door opened and two men walked in and said, As-salaam alaikum, and Rez and Fatima stood up and greeted them in return.

The two men insisted that they make tea, and they all sat on the floor in the empty living room and drank. One of them wore a long beard and the other looked like a young guy from Istanbul. They were both good-looking, clean, with bright eyes.

We are glad Daoud and our sisters led you here. It is our honor to help you along on your journey.

Their faces stayed jovial and calm and they spoke with precise words. The English was accented, but not terribly so, and they had many compliments for Rez and Fatima about their decision, about their devotion, about their coming marriage.

No one checked his or her phone and no one left the conversation for anything more than another cup of tea or the bathroom. They asked if Rez or Fatima had any questions and then answered them patiently, saying all the things Rez and Fatima wanted to hear—a nice house, probably in a lab if chemistry is still your expertise, there will be other young families nearby, no, no one from California, and, yes, it is marvelous to be in a place where Islam is prized, you will be among the first families to establish a haven for our beliefs, our type of living, it is a brave thing you do, one that will not be forgotten by the generations after you.

Fatima smiled at Rez and he could tell the fear and sadness had left her. She moved her hand closer to his so that their fingers barely touched and the smugglers talked on and on. By dawn Rez himself relaxed enough that all he wanted was sleep and stood to excuse himself and Fatima stood with him and the men, cross-legged on the ground, told Fatima to sit and she looked at them and Rez. He kept her stare, wondered if she would do it.

Fatima, please. There are a few details we need to discuss with you. Moving a woman across the border is much more difficult than moving a man. There are details, please, we will keep you only a half hour, no more . . .

Fatima sat back down and Rez sat down beside her.

The bearded man smiled broadly.

We are brothers here, please do not worry about her, she is in company as secure as yours.

The man from Istanbul nodded.

Yes, my friend, tomorrow your day will be long, it will be hot and there are difficult portions. It is better you rest. But it is your choice.

Rez looked at them through a head thick with sleep. He took in one face and then the other. The two of them appeared without malice. Strangers in this strange life. He had no energy left for nerves, for suspicion or fear, and wanted more than anything else to erase this world for a time, to draw down into darkness and forget his commitments, his pledges, and his changes and changes of heart. Want of sleep was all of him.

Fatima gave him a gentle nod. I'm good.

Rez looked at her face, its beautiful round moon glow tired and dim. The exhaustion made her soft and willing and the man next to her tilted his head at Rez to gesture up toward the bedrooms.

You sure?

Yes.

Go, my brother. Get your strength. Take a stretch. We will wake you when it is time to go.

The room had a few mattresses strewn across a dusty tile floor. Rez found the one closest to the door so he could hear the talk downstairs. At first he sat up to listen but then he quickly felt himself slump over and then fall onto the bed and into a sleep, heavy and syrupy, over which he had no control.

When he woke, his body was in the same position and covered entirely in sweat. The house made no noises and his limbs did not lift as he ordered them and his thoughts stayed irretrievable somewhere at the bottom of his head. He closed his eyes and fell asleep again. The second time he woke, the sun had moved across the walls and he was alert and afraid. Next to him the bearded man sat and read.

Ok, brother. It is time. Time to go.

Fatima. His first thoughts panicked. Where was she? In all this strangeness he needed to see her, to lock eyes on something familiar. He jolted up and walked out of the room and down to the living room where the tea glasses sat washed and set aside and he knew the house was otherwise empty.

Where did they go?

They left a few hours ago. Hamid took her across first. We never cross with more than one at a time. Especially a woman.

Daoud said we would go together, the whole way. Together.

He is not a smuggler. He is not on the ground in Syria. This is our way.

Daoud told me specifically—

Please. Remember your faith in Allah.

Rez stared at the man with the scraggly beard. He saw now how short he was, how there was a weapon, a small pistol, tucked into the back of his pants. Rez edged into anger. Daoud had mentioned nothing about a separation; assured him they would cross the border together; that she would be beside him the whole way. *As it is with husbands and wives, it will be with you.*

Where is she?

I don't know.

Where will we meet her?

I don't know. That is not up to us. My job is to take you to Raqqah, to deliver you to my commander.

But I am going to Raqqah to get married . . . to become a Muslim and get married . . . and my friend Arash . . . This is what I have arranged.

The man smiled with half his mouth.

Yes, my brother! Well done. And now let us go!

Rez carried his bag and walked alongside the man on small streets and then on the side of a big street and then through the dry land with no streets at all. The man walked ahead a few steps and every now and again sang something in Arabic or whistled. Rez left heavy prints with each step and asked about Fatima again and again. Can you explain, please, why did she have to go ahead? How can I be in touch with her? Who is she with right now?

The man with the beard sometimes answered and sometimes shook his head no. When he did respond it was with a surplus of good cheer that aggravated Rez. Have faith, my brother! Things are not as bad as they seem! You must trust that Allah will do what is right for you! This is the faith you want, isn't it?

Rez no longer wanted faith. He wanted Fatima beside him and another earth under his feet. They seemed to walk into nowhere, nothing visible ahead of them, and the small town with the safe house was a dot on the horizon behind. Soon exhaustion and thirst took the place of his anger and Rez thought about Allah, about the all-merciful, all-knowing, and with concentration he told himself to believe in it, to believe what he felt among the men in the mosque, among the faces in Bali; the great truth, the great rightness, the great faith. His steps grew lighter and Rez felt that each move forward was a move toward Fatima, toward a life of peace in his soul and body, and a move away from the harsh hatreds and sad empty lives of a world that lived on the surface of itself. He thought of her soft lips, of the soft skin of her hands, of her breasts when she was asleep, and he craved. Allah will provide for me. He remembered Daoud's saying that to him again and again: *Allah will provide.*

It was dark when they reached the fence and Rez, thirsty, his feet sore, looked around for lights of some sort but nothing shone. The man with the beard kicked the bottom of the metal fence with his foot, and when he came to a section that gave to his kick, he crawled down on his hands and knees and motioned for Rez to follow. There was no hurry, no rush, and the man seemed without agitation at all. Rez looked around at the land again, rocks, dry hard earth, this fence, and nothing else. The stars were abundant in the sky, maybe more than he'd ever before seen in his life, and he took this as a sign. He stopped and gazed, let his neck stretch back as far as he could to see the uninterrupted scape, the infinity of depth, and this unknown put Rez in mind of the sea, the great ocean that had breathed beside him his whole life that was now nowhere to be found.

Now, brother. Now is the time. She waits for you on this side, not over there.

Rez dropped to his hands and knees, threw his duffel bag in, and crawled through. When he stood, he looked up and saw this side was no different, the sky just as infinite, the land as dry. He looked back up to find a constellation, to center himself on something, anything, to remind him he was still on earth, and as he did, the want for the ocean swelled and he desired it now more than anything, more than Fatima, or belief or belonging, a night of surf, the feeling of his board under him, his body lifted and dropped, swaying and swayed, the great unfathomable beneath, rocking him to and fro.

EPILOGUE

Ras al-Ayn, Syria, March 2014

EVERYTHING IN THE right way.

In training they learned how a thing was done. How to stand, the proper way to sit with attention, the way to approach a target in clear daylight, and the best way to attack at night. They learned how to load and aim automatic rifles, took lessons on how to fire, what verses to recite as the bullets flew, and what verses for the moment after they hit their marks. Instructors told them which way to wear their backpacks, their face masks, how best to lace their boots. They studied the knife, how to cut across an earlobe, a thieving hand, a neck. They learned how to lie during an interrogation, deny any previous identity, and look directly at photos of their sisters and say *That is not my sister* and pictures of their fathers and claim *I do not know that man.* They were given cyanide capsules and, as backup, instructions on how to hang themselves with a sheet and what kind of knot to make around their necks when the opportunity presented itself. There were long afternoons of recitation, prayers for the night before the battle, leading up to battle, and just before the capture of women and children. Instructors regularly blindfolded them and then said calmly, Run, before firing live ammunition at their feet and legs while the recruits wet their pants and cried for the mothers they had forsaken. Then the blinders were taken off, and the instructors handed them guns and told them to shoot and run from each other, with points given for accuracy without kill, escape without injury. They ran and fought until their fear reached its zenith and crossed over into a numb courage and only then did the instructors shout, *Stop!* And take the guns from them with assurances: *Don't worry. It will be some time before you are trusted with the work of executioner. For now you are soldiers. Allah will test you first. Everything in the right way.*

*

Months of training and study and prayer and practice, and on this, the morning of his first battle, Reza forgets all he has dutifully learned. He closes his eyes and begins to put himself together, piece by piece.

His name as it is now: Reza al-Alawah.

His age as it is today, the day of his first battle, his first pledge: nineteen.

His God as he believes him: all-powerful, all merciful.

Whoever puts his trust in Allah, He will be enough for him.

There it is. The faith.

Allah does not burden a soul beyond what it can bear.

He tries to do as he has trained, but cannot conjure the dozen faceless virgins in heaven or the lavish feasts of paradise, and thinks only of Fatima; of the skin of her cheeks and the curved dip of her back and her soft mouth. That is what waits for him after this trial. That is what the commanders have promised: first he must prove himself, then he can marry.

The recruits repeat it and beat their chests with a closed fist.

A line of open-bed trucks waits and as many men as can fit are packed in and then four or five more. The bodies touch and everything spreads—fear, smell, sweat—from man to man like electricity. They wait, nervous, in the dark of some hour closer to midnight than morning. Commanders appear, each with a flashlight and a map, and spread out to talk to two groups of trucks at a time.

The city is K.

They point to a dot on the map and then at the mountains around it, the streets into it, and the city center. The commanders identify the seven targets that begin the siege and Reza sees the logic in it, generators, hospitals, the television station, a government building, bridges across the river, and nods with the rest even though his Arabic is not good enough to understand and his thoughts wander and run and sprint to the memories of the graduation party at Matthews's pool house and Fatima's hips locked to his. The reminiscence is an agony, a kind of torture that makes Reza shift from foot to foot, changing his weight, trying to change the contents of his mind. The commander looks at them one by one and speaks slowly.

Your trucks are the first line. You will enter the target destination. Fire to kill—all civilians, all police, and military—until the site is secure.

Reza looks around the truck. There are no British guys, no Norwegians or French. Not even a German who can speak enough English to translate for him. There have never been any Americans in his camp and he has spent most of these last weeks with a fighter from Pakistan playing game after game of silent, difficult chess. Reza stands now beside a man who won't look at him, a man he has seen in the showers, in the barracks, in the food tent, always quiet except to tell the same story over and over: that he is from Iraq, that his mother and brothers, aunts and two uncles, the dog, and all the pigeons in the coop were killed in a drone strike that missed its mark. Reza does not try to catch his eye. In the truck beside them he spots Fariq, the DJ from Morocco, and tries to get his attention and ask, *What is he saying?* But Fariq's head is bowed, his long beard touches his chest, so Reza pretends to listen to the commander and stares at his feet and tries to pray. The trucks start their engines and a few recruits lean over the edge to throw up and a few, like Reza, stare away from the faces of the other men and either look down to their boots or up at the purple sky and the million stars that slowly fade.

Before the town is too close the trucks veer off onto a gravel grade that takes them down to a dusty low flatland with a thin creek. The drivers follow one another until the trucks form a large circle, and when the engines stop, they shout back to the recruits to stay where they are. An older man and a commander appear from a small mud-and-grass structure and walk to the center of the circle. The commander is familiar; his presence at the training camp, regular and still celebrated. A fighter of the best credentials—Afghanistan, Bosnia, Kosovo, Baghdad, Mosul— he has a megaphone and hands it to the cleric, who begins with a prayer that Reza knows, can recite by heart to readily pledge himself, his heart, body, life, to a God that is great.

The cleric announces, Deal with them in a way that strikes fear in those behind them.

The cleric opens his palms and asks that God find and honor their cause of a state, so a state may thrive, through time and the hearts of mortal men and woman who can worship Him without persecution, in the proper way. The cleric is old, calm, and his voice is easy to listen to, sonorous with conviction and a kind of love. Reza's head goes quiet and now he can focus, can commit himself, and brings to mind the image that will not fail him, that has served him every time. Fatima in her head scarf, reading the Koran; the look up, her lashes and black eyes and the golden sun of a California afternoon, the sound of kids playing on the playground in Laguna Niguel, the taste of grapes in his mouth, the dream of their children, one day, laughing nearby. Richness and love. A better family. That is all he wanted. A life made of family and God and love. A life of a joy his own life had never known.

And now this. A mistake.

The cleric sings his joyless song and the sky grows bright and the men around Reza sweat their fear and the order of the day is battle and possibly death and if he can only tie himself to the memory of her, at the other end of this, Reza can pull himself through. But his mind fails him and he can't conjure her in a scarf or on that afternoon and instead has an odd, vivid memory, out of time, out of place: his mother making his bed. His room bright and clean, the familiar small woman straightens the sheets, rights the pillow, flattens down the comforter, and hums to herself, *Good Morning America* on the TV in the background, and the sound of the traffic of Highway 1 streams in the open kitchen windows. The cleric sings and Reza stares down at his black boots and knows that here, at the edge of battle, possibly at the edge of his life, belief has abandoned him and he is undone and, so, damned.

Do not fear death. What is offered in God's paradise is far greater than anything on this dry earth.

The commander speaks now and Reza catches every other word, every odd phrase.

237

The prophet says, I have been given victory by means of terror. We spread our message by the sword. To build this state for our sons and for the sons of our sons.

Reza looks around at the other men in the truck and sees that most of them twitch a hand or a knee. Some keep their eyes closed and nod their heads and a few keep nobly still. He thinks of the sons he wanted and he thinks of the sons these men desire or have left behind and Reza remembers a comment by a recruit from Lebanon, that the Hezbollah fighters are given pills, an aggressive kind of ecstasy, that turns the mind red and the body into a fast, efficient machine, and Reza wonders why the commanders don't just give them all pills. He would take a pill now in the place of all this talk.

God is great!

Think, brothers, of the wars waged on you. Your fathers taken into slavery by the enemies of Islam, your mothers turned into whores, you yourselves kept in prisons, kept powerless, kept from the glory of our caliphate!

God is great!

This morning K is ours!

God is great!

The recruits scatter slowly through the valley and Reza walks away from them as quickly as possible to walk the cold ground and leave boot prints in the thin frost. He wonders how long they will stay here, tucked away, worrying before battle. Thoughts of Fatima prance nimbly at the far corners of his mind and he finds himself staring at his boot prints pressed through the frost and knows the sun will come up and erase them and day will finally begin. He tries not to let his mind fail him, to loop back to the life he has quietly and slowly cursed these last weeks and months, but pushes toward the dream of her, the sense and smell and sight of her ahead of him like a mirage. A small sparrow hops toward him, its eyes and neck and chest flit and flit with ceaseless tiny energies. Reza stares at the bird and the bird, a silly serious thing, a creation of God, stares back. He tries to remember a simple prayer, to say a blessing for himself. Nothing. He tries to remember Fatima.

Nothing. He closes his eyes against the day and finally it is quiet. The valley. The morning. His mind. Reza looks around and feels it, the passing over and passing through of all fear and all courage until he is left alone, not a convert and not a coward, no hero or martyr, simply the flesh of a man who walks the earth in search of his woman, and maybe his god and maybe a home on the other side of this battle, if it is to be.

The sparrow hops and then jumps up and flies away and behind him as the trucks start their engines and turn their steering wheels in the direction of town. Reza rises, all the fight drained from him now, and jogs to his truck and hops in next to the others, some with green faces, some with darkened eyes, and sits among them and joins them as empty a man as he can be, a man ready to fire the bullets or receive the bullets, a man ready to give himself away and be received by love.

ACKNOWLEDGMENTS

To the people who make books come into the world. As ever, Ellen Levine and Alexa Stark and the stellar team at Trident Media. Anton Mueller and Alexandra Pringle for your support of this trilogy from word one, remarkable editors with lovely long-distance vision. To all at Bloomsbury who put these words before the readers' eyes, managing editor Laura Phillips, and copyeditor Steven Henry Boldt. Many thanks to Payam Nahid for his help with issues of English futbol and to Karl Mendoca for his assistance in finding that last reader.

Motherhood and writing novels are not, by their nature, compatible endeavors and for this story to come to life I relied (heavily at times) on the gracious hearts of family and friends who must be named and celebrated. David Deniger for his support when the book was just a notion and would have stayed such if not for his help sending a then two-year-old to day care. Andre Julien, who received said two-year-old in his warm and nourishing home. Mary Sue and Patrick Kelly for their availability and kindness week after week, year after year. Antara Medina and Diana Montes Ortiz, whose generosity of heart allowed me to exit reality and enter into the world of fiction.

And most urgently my gratitude goes out to the people to whom I return, season after season, for inspiration, support, and love, who mix art and life such that they are one: Muthoni Kiare, Keenan Norris, Joel Tomfohr, Saneta deVouno Powell, Ramona Ausubel, Micheline Marcom, Cristina Garcia—thank you. To Kamran and Fereshteh and Kamyar, who have supported my adventures in fiction year after year.

Timothy: there is no language for my gratitude, without you this book would not be. To Keon and little (for now) Kassra: you keep me dialed to the station of love, thank you.

A NOTE ON THE AUTHOR

LALEH KHADIVI is the author of *The Age of Orphans*, a Barnes & Noble Discover Great New Writers pick, and *The Walking*. She has been awarded a Whiting Award, a Pushcart Prize, and an NEA Literature Fellowship. Khadivi lives in Northern California.